CW00662707

Eileen Kane

HOPE AND GLORY, OHIO

WEDNESDAY, MAY 26

NORWAY UNDER SAND: MILLIONS SHOVELING

#1

BOOK ONE: LELAND

Copyrighted Material

Hope And Glory, OH

Copyright © 2020 by Eileen Kane. All Rights Reserved.

No part of this publication may be reproduced, stored in a retrieval system or transmitted, in any form or by any means—electronic, mechanical, photocopying, recording or otherwise—without prior written permission from the publisher, except for the inclusion of brief quotations in a review.

For information about this title or to order other books and/or electronic media, contact the publisher:

Kane, Eileen
hopeandglory.ie

ISBNs:
978-1-7360550-0-7 (softcover)
978-1-7360550-1-4 (eBook)

Printed in the United States of America

Interior design: 1106 Design

Publisher:
The Hope And Glory Vindicator, hopeandglory.ie
The Pier, Killeen Arann, Kilcolgan, Galway IRELAND

*To my family—the beloved models
for most of my characters*

*and
to Jake —
my hero!?* oo

Eileen

Contents

The Incident at Winkle's Party-Pak and Live Bait
xi

1. Leland   1

2. Randy   15

3. Laurinda   25

4. Bert   35

5. Zeke   45

6. Leland   53

7. Laurinda   57

8. Leland   61

9. Laurinda   69

10. Laurinda   75

11. Leland   83

12. Laurinda   97

13. Leland   111

Winkle's Party-Pak and Live Bait
127

14. Leland   131

15. Randy   143

16. Leland   151

17. Leland   175

Winkle's Party-Pak and Live Bait
183

18. Leland   185

19. Leland   199

20. Laurinda   207

Winkle's Party-Pak and Live Bait
213

21. Leland   217

22. Leland   227

23. Randy   231

24. Leland   245

Winkle's Party-Pak and Live Bait
251

25. Laurinda and Friends   253

Winkle's Party-Pak and Live Bait
259

26. Randy, Juanetta   263

27. Juanetta and Idora   273

28. Laurinda!   281

29. Laurinda   287

Winkle's Party-Pak and Live Bait
293

30. Leland   295

31. Bert and Leland and Randy   305

Acknowledgments   329

About the Author   331

A glimpse at the end of our story . . .

2005

The bullet shattered the live bait tank next to the donuts and zinged through the back of Mrs. Herman "Bob" Matthews' lunch booth at the Party-Pak. It plopped out again into her lima bean casserole.

"It was my worst nightmare come true down to the last detail," she said later when she called her sister Twyla in Ashtabula. "Beans and worm parts everywhere. I said to myself, 'How'm I gonna get this out of my new aqua pants suit?'"

"Well! And what did the police have to say?" Twyla asked.

"The police? The police down here don't know nothin' about dry cleaning." But as she'd flicked the only live worm away, she'd noticed the police chief, or rather the ex-police chief, making his way toward an angry mob outside the window.

Odd, because only ten minutes ago, most of the group had been eating right there in the Party-Pak, nice and peaceful. Some of the fellows even wore those little whatever they're called now, beard brassieres? Those sure had caught on. But around quarter to one most of them finished up and wandered out to their cars.

"Then the bang," she told Twyla. "I rubbed away some of the slop off the window and what did I see but old Juanetta Wilcox, you remember Juanetta, with her rifle, the one she carries on Wednesdays for her Rifle Tots classes. She was firing at the new mayor."

"The new mayor? The ex-police chief?" Twyla asked. "I was only down there a few months ago. What happened to . . ."

"Forget all that," Mrs. Herman "Bob" snapped. Twyla was always one to be diverted by the least little thing.

And at Juanetta's feet were what looked like the makings of a cat: fur, head, the whole works, all strewn around. The ex-chief held Juanetta's grocery bags plus the rubber ring she had to sit on since that mix-up over in the church toilet. The former mayor, that idiot Randy Anderson, was shaking the daylights out of the ex-chief's daughter, that sweet girl Sylene. Bad blood between those two families; she'd always said it.

"And," Mrs. Herman "Bob" said to her sister, "you know Laurinda McCardle always has to be in the middle of everything. Those beard brassieres were all her idea, and there she was, screaming and pointing at her belly. It was big enough but one thing for sure, she couldn't be pregnant. She's been through The Change and back by now."

"I got through The Change, no trouble," Twyla said.

That wasn't the way Mrs. Herman "Bob" remembered it, but she wasn't going to say anything, this call was on her nickel and she didn't want to run up her phone.

Mrs. Herman "Bob" scraped at her pants and thought back over all that had led up to this mess. Shutting down the boiler factory; it flared up around then. Still, thank God, it was quieter here than in Ashtabula; she couldn't understand how Twyla's nerves took all the hubbub up there.

Twyla was delighted to be anywhere that Herman "Bob" Matthews wasn't. Those TV car dealer ads of his, Herman pointing his finger at you and saying, "You can call me 'Bob.'" He put "Bob" Matthews on his business cards. She didn't like to swear, even in her mind, but he was what others call a horse's ass.

But "I think salt might take out the worm blood," is all she said to Mrs. Herman "Bob." "I don't know about the lima beans. Was there ham in them or was it just the beans?"

And now, how it all happened . . .
2004–2005

HOPE AND GLORY
BEFORE OUR STORY STARTS

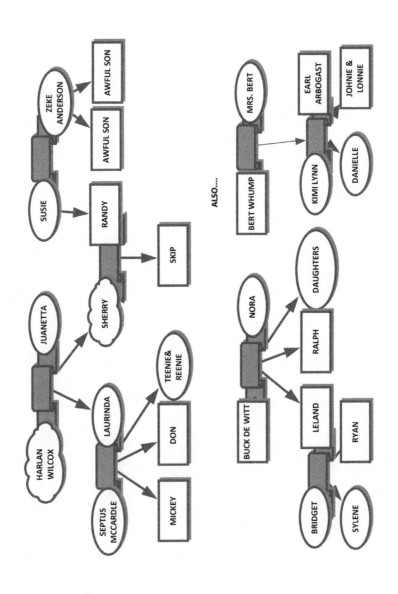

THE HOPE AND GLORY VINDICATOR

Volume 232 Issue 24   Hope And Glory, Ohio

Yeggs Plunder Party-Pak

In a worrying development last night, thugs broke into the ice machine in Winkle's Party-Pak and Live Bait, the beating heart of our town. They stole about 25 dollars in nickels, dimes, and quarters. Mrs. Bert Whump was the only witness. She was in her kitchen, straightening up after a pork chop supper, when she saw two figures in the parking lot. She says she knows who one of the fellows is but wouldn't like to say. "I know his Ma. I want to see the look on her face."

The linoleum in Winkle's prize-winning fine dining section was ripped up when the ice machine was moved.

Mayor Randy Anderson said it was embarrassing that Hope And Glory no longer had its own police force. The police in North Vienna were not qualified to handle this kind of sensitive crime. He was prepared to give Mrs. Whump immunity and even a new identity if she would come forward.

Rev. Wayman Sentenced

The Rev. Dwight Wayman, pastor of the Right Word Church on Muddy Branch Road, received sixty days' house arrest for reckless endangerment of life at his Summer Bible School. The Rev. developed a miniature electric chair that delivered shocks to children aged 3-6 who answered Bible questions incorrectly. Rev. Wayman told Judge Dick Quinn that his Summer Empowerment Program was simply an attempt to spark the children's interest.

The judge ordered the Rev. Wayman to wear an electronic ankle tag, saying that he had been wanting to try one of these for a while now.

Court Notes

Mrs. Laurinda McCardle, who went by her maiden name before her marriage, has petitioned the court to change her name to "s" or "Apostrophe s". According to Mrs. McCardle, women are frequently lumped in with their husbands when being referred to, as in "The John Browns" or "the Dave Jones's".

"I am always receiving invitations addressed to "The Septus McCardles," she said. "I might as well make it legal."

Big Losses at the Boiler Factory

"Dismal" was how manager Mike Casey described this year's figures at the boiler factory.

Meetings will be held this week to decide what steps to take. A four-day week, early retirement for older workers, single shifts, and possibly even (cont'd. p. 3)

New Feature!!

So many of our young folks today are bored, moping, breaking into fine dining establishments, doing drugs, and Lord knows what, that The Vindicator is creating a few new features:

Algebra Antics!, Word Wrestling! Brain Teasers! to test your skills in numbers, words and logic. Each week *The Vindicator* will print a new problem. The first correct contestant will be presented with a gift of an engraved handsome gold-plated jumbo-sized (cont'd p. 3)

Happy Wanderer Found Dead of Bullets in Cell

A hitchhiker, Norland Pinckney, was found dead in a cell in the North Vienna police station this morning. Mr. Pinckney had been arrested for moll-muzzling. "He was a flim-flam man," the North Vienna police chief said, when quizzed.

Septus McCardle, present at the arrest in the Party-Pak's men's room, said Mr. Pinkney had merely dropped a candy wrapper. The term "moll-muzzling" was doubly inappropriate, he said, since it referred to robbing women.

Mayor Randy Anderson called for the FBI to investigate. He decried the use of fancy terms that your ordinary person couldn't understand.

INSIDE THIS ISSUE

2 What's for supper? Easy Toast!

3 Drywalling your dog house

5 Mongolia under sea water again

===

Chapter 1

Leland

If I die right now, Bridget might not find me until she takes the garbage out after supper. I'll be up against the windshield, all googly-eyed. Better shut them while I'm still able.

Leland DeWitt had been thumping along home in the red '95 Ford pickup, ply and radials mis-matched the way mechanics do, when he tuned into WHAG and heard the news.

"Lyle? Am I on yet? Lyle, I jest hadda tell ya, I have a tip for all your listeners. Want to know what to do with those old socks of your husband's? Just cut off the . . ."

"Ma'am . . ." Lyle said.

". . . and they make the cutest . . ."

"Way mint, ma'am," said Lyle. "This is 'Swap Shop.' Do you have something you want to get rid of, or are you looking for an item? Folks, this is Dubbya H-A-G, Hope And Glory, Ohio, and I'm Lyle Stivanski, looking for those gewgaws and appurtenances you don't need anymore. Give us a call here at WHAG between now and the five-thirty news."

Nearly five-fifteen on a golden mid-summer evening in Hope And Glory, Pop. 3870, motto "You'll Wish You Lived Here!" Leland loved this moment, the cool, inviting lawns beneath the huge sugar maples, the memory of soft grass under little bare feet. A few of the older women sat on their old-fashioned porches, all cleaned up, the potatoes peeled for supper, everything ready for the men when they'd come home from the boiler factory. A group of naked toddlers pranced under a whispery lawn sprinkler, some naked, the most impudent ones in their underpants because that was far more wicked.

"Hi, Bear, Hi, Bear!" a tiny strawberry blonde shouted at Leland. Leland waved a meaty paw. She squeaked, delighted at her own brazenness. Kids liked Leland's friendly, open face: big eyes, bristly brown hair that sprang up, some days as bear ears, others as a hedgehog helmet or palms in a hurricane, depending on some principle that escaped him. Adults liked him, too: "Look, he's talkin' to hisself again," one of the mothers said, smiling.

"*Ineluctable*," Leland mumbled in the cab, practicing his Word For the Day. He didn't much care for the sound of it, or indeed the sound of his own solitary voice, and he kept forgetting what it meant, got it mixed up with "*inchoate*." Neither one worth a lot in his current line of work, heavy equipment mechanic at the boiler factory. You don't finish high school, that's what you get.

But he had plans. He was in line for foreman; he knew he could do foreman, easy, so he signed up for a correspondence course for his next step after that, up into management. Forty-eight; it wasn't too late to make something of himself. Most of your U.S. presidents started out a lot later than that. The guy in there now, he was no prodigy. *Protégé?* No, prodigy. Mr. Casey, the factory manager, said a couple months ago that he could even see Leland as a department manager. Now *The Hope And Glory Vindicator* is saying the factory might have to go to a four-day week, maybe single shifts, but he'd believe it when he saw it; that *Vindicator* was always printing stuff about Norway being covered in lizards and such.

Leland passed the village square, a triangle, really, with the old Civil War church on one side. Beautiful. This was first road into the Western Reserve Territory at the end of the 1700's, and some of these houses were over two hundred years old. Leland's was newer, 1910, and if you could be in love with a man-made object, well he was. "Man-made" didn't really do it justice; to him, it had grown there, on his little patch of the planet, his and the bank's, but soon, his.

The woman on the radio program broke in again. "Me, I don't waste nothin', so I take the rest and . . . Lyle?"

"Go ahead, ma'am." Lyle sounded resigned. Folks thought Lyle pined to get back to New York City; he felt nothing much ever happened here. That was the real beauty of the place, Leland thought. The American Dream, nothing happening, and he was living it.

Now that he'd got to the Language Skills part of his management course, he was really hooked. The course booklet said that he should listen to public radio, and sure enough, it paid off. William F. Buckley had become Leland's word hero when he came on one day, speaking like his cheeks were all sucked in, and so wordy. *Recondite.* Leland nearly burned the clutch out the day Wm. F. said that. The radio announcers said his vocabulary was "luxuriously rococo;" he had a "reptilian languor," one guy said. The vistas that opened when Leland heard words like that! It was like getting all new furniture in your house; you felt like maybe you could be a different, better, person, that the old furniture had been what was holding you back.

Of course, he was disappointed that Wm. F. was a Republican. And did educated people like him even know that the kind of people here in Hope And Glory existed? This woman talking on the radio, for instance? Nope. In his starry world, they probably said *"ineluctable"* even in the middle of taking a crap.

"Folks, we got to break in here to bring you some live breaking news happening right now this minute! Mike Casey, the manager of the Hope And Glory boiler factory, has just announced that the boiler factory will be closing down for good at the end of this week. And here we were, thinking we escaped the recession, thinking the new owners, BriarHill Associates, would give that old factory a real boost. Well, lotta people around here gonna be real affected by that. Especially your older workers. Over forty and you're finished these days, that's what the experts say, anyhow. We'll keep you updated soon's we hear . . ." Lyle Stivanski sounded delighted.

Leland pulled into his driveway. He felt a tight pain shooting across his chest and down his left arm. It was a heart attack. No, wait, it was the seat belt; he'd tried to get out with it still on. He sat back again, winded. Forty-eight, no education to speak of, a mortgage, a wife and two kids, his dad down with cancer. Not much work anywhere else, from what he'd been reading in *The Vindicator*. Who were these new owners, anyhow?

Through the windshield he saw his two-storey house glowing white in the late sun. Funny this morning, all he'd noticed were the little imperfections: he maybe ought to get the driveway resealed, get fresh awning for the porch. Had he been crazy, with all these puffed-up ideas of promotion? Now all he could see was paradise: the grass like Sears's best living room carpet, the maples and beeches shading the wide front porch with its white wicker furniture. Geraniums glowed in the boxes he'd just made. Now all his husbandry seemed like tempting fate: the neatly rolled hose; the kennel for Arthur Leroy, solid cedar; the whitewashed stones edging the driveway. *Husbandry*: last Thursday's word.

Well, it *could* be a heart attack. He had put on some in the last couple years, and between work and the house and his correspondence course, he didn't get enough exercise. Poor Bridget, she'd find him here after supper, stone dead. He shut his eyes again.

"Am I on? Am I on now? GeeZUSS, Lyle, I thought that old bat'd never get off," the next speaker wheezed in a thin high wail. "Okay, here's what I think. The factory closin', well whoever those BriarHill people are, never heard of them, but anyhow, what's that fathead Randy Anderson doin' about it? He's the mayor; is he the best the Republicans can do? How come he din't see this recession comin'? That's all you hear on TV: *reecession*. And isn't he the guy that lost us our jail and our police chief? A jail is the heart and soul of a town. So now I gotta phone Chief Arbogast all the way over in North Vienna just to report some dog poop on my grass?" The man gave a high-pitched plaintiff wheeze. "And listen, while I got you, what about that picture a Randy in *The Vindicator*, drivin' the city snowplow in a diaper?"

You could hear Lyle blowing the air out of his cheeks.

Well, Leland thought, all that's true about Randy. Leland had gone to school with him, he *was* stupid. Not evil, like that stepdad of his, Zeke, just dumb. And snobby; he was in the men's room of the Party-Pak one day and and Randy came in and said, "You know, Leland, maybe it's better if my Skip and your Sylene both found somebody else, I know you understand." Leland was stunned: what kind of guy talks to another guy while they're peeing?

And furious; did Randy think his boy Skip was too good
for Sylene? Well, matterafact, nobody was good enough
for his Sylene.

But, to be fair, that diaper story in *The Vindicator*, that
was ridiculous. It was the other guy wearing the diaper,
not Randy. And Randy didn't exactly lose the jail; he just
didn't stop it. Too busy writing fan letters to the Lone
Ranger, people said.

Leland's head pounded; a tumor, maybe, and he cracked
the sidepiece off his glasses trying to rub his eyes, they
were burning out of his head. Never sick a day in his life
and now lookit, all in ten minutes.

The next voice on the radio was a young woman's,
soft, breathy, with a little catch. "Why are men so incon-
siderate, Lyle? They're all insensitive, except maybe my
daddy." She'd finally gone to bed with her boyfriend but
he still went fishing every chance he got. "What should I
do, Lyle? Oh, yeah, I also have a old electrolysis kit I want
to swap for four-five yards of peach chiffon."

Leland resented this attack on men. *Gratuitous*. Look
at his old dad. Hell, he was the most considerate person
he knew. He'd like to meet the bastard that was more
considerate than his dad.

But hold on here a minute. Did he know that voice?
Was that Sylene? He pictured her, yellowy-brown fluffy
hair, big dark blue eyes, sweet little face, her baby hand
in his, that same baby hand on somebody's . . . oh God,
oh God, he was getting kinda nauseous. And what did she
want the peach chiffon for? She wasn't getting married

without telling him, was she? No, couldn't be. Girls wear white at their wedding, for purity. Oh God, maybe she couldn't wear white. That was why the peach. He'd kill that Skip Anderson. Randy, too. He felt a sour wave rising in his stomach.

Leland shut off the engine and stepped out. Now what? His legs! Three? Was that the thing he'd read about once, phantom limb? Nah, get a grip. But how was he ever going to tell Bridget about this? Fuming, he picked up his correspondence course book full of notes and pages all turned down and flung it in the garbage can behind the back porch. He gave the can a little shove and damn near broke his toe. He needed new work boots. No, he didn't, he thought bitterly. House slippers was all he'd need now.

Inside, Bridget DeWitt was fixing lime Jell-O with shredded carrots, and Chicken Divan, Leland's favorites. That shiny cap of hair, still black, the black eyebrows, the blue eyes, most people said "Irish" the minute they saw her. She wore her faded red and white apron over a faded pink and green dress, and Leland's eyes misted a little. He realized he loved that apron. Well, he was going to fight for that apron, like the knights of old, wearing a lady's favor into battle. He would save his family.

"What's new?" she asked.

"Nothin' much," Leland said. "What's new with you?"

"Nothin' much. Your Ma's gutters need cleaned out." Obviously, she hadn't heard. She poured him some coffee, added a little condensed milk, and sat down in the breakfast nook with him.

"You know," she said after they'd pushed the salt and pepper shakers around a bit, "I worry about Sylene sometimes."

Leland groaned. He *would* kill that Skip Anderson. His tumor started up again.

"Some days I wonder if she's all there. Take today, fr'instance. Little boy comes to the back door with a basket fulla puppies. His red setter was the mother. But they were black and white cocker spaniels, exact same as Arthur Leroy. Sylene was sitting here at the table, working on her horse problem."

Sylene had her horse problem for four years now. It was a math question she got wrong in freshman year and the teacher just carried it forward each year. About four times a year he assigned it again to Sylene, and she'd sit with Leland and figure and cry and not get one step further. Now she was in junior year, and the teacher was hell bent she would do the problem right once before she graduated.

A farmer ties a horse to the corner of a barn. The rope is 30 feet long.

How much area can the horse cover?

"Look," Leland would say each time, "you just . . ."

"I *know* all that," Sylene would cry. "But what if he only wants to use part of the rope? Or what if he just wants to lay down? Anyhow, how big is the barn? It don't tell us that." Sylene also had a terrible time with negative numbers. "Once you're down to zero, it don't make any difference whether it's nothing three or nothing four. You got nothing, either way."

"Anyhow," Bridget said, "She was cussing this horse out like nobody's business and this little boy yells through the screen, says to her, 'Our dog just had puppies and your Arthur Leroy is the father.'"

"'Can't be,' Sylene says. 'Arthur Leroy's been home all day.' Well, I tell you, the look on that little boy's face. He must've decided not to say anything, I think he thought maybe Sylene didn't know, you know, about stuff."

Well, Leland thought, if he was listening to Swap Shop, he knew better now. But maybe Sylene didn't make the connection between . . . oh Suffering Jesus. "Did Sylene say anything about any peach chiffon or anything?" Leland asked Bridget.

"No, it was mostly about that horse." Bridget wiped her hands and hung her apron inside the broom closet. "I don't know, though. She ain't right. Maybe she's in love, or something. They say the parents are always the last to know."

Yeah, thought Leland. Everybody out in radio land knows first. The whole metropolitan Hope And Glory area.

Everyone but Bridget. And the factory, how on earth could he work his way around to telling her the factory would close down? He couldn't.

"Bridget," he said. "The factory's closing down."

"I know," she said. "Your ma told me. I was waiting till after supper to tell you."

Later that night Leland woke up from a terrible nightmare about being in a polka contest. You gotta get a grip, he told himself as he lay in the dark, listening to the soft

breeze in the maples. All these people depend on you. His
dad was real bad now and his ma needed a lotta help these
days. His boy Ryan needed a decent piano, his teacher
said. Sylene needed . . . God knows what. And I need a job.

He could see them all ending up in one of your trailer
parks, beer bottles all over, babies running around in dirty
rags, not shaving from one day to the next. His kids were
teenagers, and beer made Leland gassy, but still.

He knew he had a lot to be grateful for: Ryan and Sylene
were good kids, mostly, and this woman was a saint, his
life's partner lying here next to him. He reached his hand
over just to touch her, and it moved down a little, brushed
across her backside, accidental. She was awake, too. Now,
this was more like it. He ran his hand across the soft skin,
caressing the smooth sphere. And then . . . "Jesus," he
said to himself. "Is this only half of it?" She musta put
on some in the last while. Well, he thought, look at me.
I'm not exactly William F. Buckley. Of course, he'd never
actually seen William F. Buckley. Only heard him on the
radio in the pickup, going to and from the boiler factory.
Could be he was like the side of a barn. Corpulent.

THE HOPE AND GLORY VINDICATOR

Volume 232 Issue 25   Hope And Glory, Ohio

Boiler Factory Closes

In a shocking development last night, Mike Casey of the Hope And Glory Boiler Factory, announced that its new owners, BriarHill Associates, were closing it, after 86 years of operation. "We've been left behind in the technology revolution," he said. "Other companies are getting the orders we used to get." An additional factor was the cost of bringing in steel, since the Hope And Glory mill shut down in 1977.

Casey said there was no reversing the owners' decision, "whoever they are."

Today stunned workers talked about how they were going to get by. Most had not been looking for other jobs because news of the closure had been kept secret until yesterday. "Anyhow," said Septus McCardle, a lathe operator, "there aren't any other jobs."

The Hope And Glory factory is a fixture in the town. Many of the current workers' fathers and grandfathers worked there. A few eyes were damp as older men recalled starting at 15 or 16, getting married, buying their own homes and putting their children through college. "I never thought it would end like this," said one elderly man. "No notice after 40 years."

Council Issues Statement

In a special meeting this morning, City Council members voiced their fears for the future of Hope And Glory. Voiced also was their concern about the lack of communication between boiler factory officials and the Council. Cllr. Ronnie Zweig said now was the time for leadership if ever there was one, and what did the Mayor intend to do? Where was the Mayor, in fact? Had anyone mentioned the meeting to him?

Cllr. Mrs. Laurinda McCardle said she had called him to say hi earlier, but forgot to mention it, she didn't know where her head was these days.

She was sure he would think of something or other. He'd said something about a pedicure.

Various ideas were bandied, including buying the factory, reopening the jail, which had really been the heartbeat of Hope And Glory; and/or inviting a tribe to set up a casino. Chief Grey Wolf was the new music director at the Precious Lambs Day Care and Rifle Range. Maybe he could get some more Indians. Grey Wolf and a few of his tribal mates live on a small reservation behind the Precious Lambs and have been invaluable in familiarizing us with Native American ways.

(cont'd page 4)

INSIDE THIS ISSUE

Mrs. Bert Whump's Cute Coleslaw Tips

Sad scenes at the boiler factory

Making a lamp from compost!

Paris France under sand. Millions shoveling

MAKE YOUR FORTUNE SELLING MAGAZINES. PO BOX 308 NORTH VIENNA

FIN 'N FUR KENNELS AND BIBLE SCHOOL. SALE 15% OFF EVERYTHING

DRIVEWAYS RE-SURFACED. CALL SEPTUS, 330-5785

OLD LONE RANGER COMICS WANTED. GENUINE BUYER. R. ANDERSON 330-9192

IRONING. MRS. REV. WAYMAN. MUDDY BRANCH CHURCH.

SEPTIC TANKS CLEANED. ASK FOR "AL" AT 330-7987

ANCIENT INDIAN MEDICINE. BETTER THAN MODERN PILLS. CHIEF GREY WOLF.

KNIFE SHARPENING. GOOD PRICES. CHIEF GREY WOLF. ALL WELCOME.

TELEMARKETING!! GREAT MONEY & OPPORTUNITIES FOR SMART PEOPLE

GOOD WEEDER. SYLENE 330-1358

Chapter 2

Randy

"Scaring moose?" Lyle Stivanski asked. "That's your plan for saving Hope And Glory, Mayor? You're kidding me, right?"

Randy Anderson had been out back tying his garbage can lid on tighter to keep the raccoons out when Lyle called up to do a live radio phone-in. "The President has asked us all, Republican and Democrat, to work together to save our economy, our homes, our environment. Now Hope And Glory has taken a direct hit, losing the boiler factory. Today on the program we have Randy Anderson, mayor, snowplow driver, motel owner, erstwhile realtor."

Erstwhile? Randy wrote that down on a pad. He'd been planning for a long time to make a list to look up if he ever had a minute.

"Of course you're at Mission Control, Mayor. You can fill us in on this new BriarHill group, right? You must have been marshalling your plans for weeks now, ever since you first heard about the recession."

Matterafact, Randy hadn't heard all that much about it. He had to get cable, no two ways about it, especially since he cancelled the newspaper over that diaper picture. But to be honest, he was a little hurt about the boiler factory and these BriarHill people, whoever they were. He bet Mayor Gilbert T. Arbogast, Chief Earl's brother over in North Vienna, would sure be told if someone took over the firecracker works there and shut it down.

Of course North Vienna belonged to the Arbogasts. They'd always had the mayor's office, and now they'd expanded their jail and moved Hope And Glory's to the new premises. Randy could slap himself for taking a day off to get his get his back waxed; the Hope And Glory Democratic City Council voted to close the local police station as a cost measure, and not replace Chief Bert Whump when he retired. Spend, spend, spend was what Democrats usually did, but not here.

"Mayor?"

"Acourse I have," Randy said. "I been marshalling for months." He always had ideas for developing Hope And Glory, but he didn't think he wanted to announce them right now all over the radio where anyone could pinch them.

"Folks, we're interrupting this edition of 'Cute Country Crafts' to share with you the plans of the man who holds the future of Hope And Glory in the palm of his hand."

Put it that way, maybe he'd share just a couple. Save the visionary stuff for *Sixty Minutes*, maybe then they'd ask him to do a little cameo on *Another World*, the brave mayor saving the little . . .

"Mayor?"

"Yo?" Randy asked, startled.

"Your plans."

"Matterafact, I got *two* plans." He paused for effect. "I got this first one watching a TV program on Britain. Prince Charles was talking. He seems a real nice fella. Them ears, though; that's what you get when cousins marry . . ."

"Mayor . . ."

"Okay, so I was learning about how your British Parliament works. The members, they don't all go to Parliament every time they need to vote. No sirree. You find yourself another fella says he's gonna vote the other way and you pair up with him and you *both* don't go." He let this sink in. Lyle was silent.

"So," Randy continued, "I was thinking, some guy in Fairbanks, Alaska, he gotta fly here to put his aunt in a home, I gotta take a bus to Chicago to attend a convention, so I thought whoa, here's a market niche. What we do is we each pair up with some other fella, somebody in Chicago goes to my convention, I put that old lady in a home here, lookit the wear and tear, the travel, the motel bills you save. Even in a recession, people got to tend to their aunts and such. We'd charge a little for the service, that's the beauty of the plan. We pair people up and then . . ."

"Then?" Lyle sounded dazed.

"We franchise! But wait, that ain't all. I gotta whole nother plan. What's the plural for moose?"

"Moose?"

"Yeah, that's cause of my second plan. I read somewheres that moose, mooses are getting too tame for their own good. You make friends with a moose, you ain't doin' it any favors. So these experts, they're thinking they should teach these moose to be ascared of people, right? And I thought, 'Hey, we can do that.' We set up a pilot program first, get a government grant or such, ship a few in here . . . you don't need a big fancy factory for that."

"Moose? You gotta be kidding, Mayor."

"Well, somebody's gotta do it." Randy hated pessimism. That's one good thing his stepdad, Zeke, always said about him; a gorilla could be sitting on Randy's face and he'd still see the bright side.

"How do you plan to scare them?"

"Well, the details need to be worked out. We wouldn't rough them up or nothing, just maybe make real loud noises at them, say, or steal their dinners, just to show them your average Joe isn't always such a sweetheart."

"Well, there you have it, folks," said Lyle, closing the interview. "Mayor Randy Anderson's plans to keep the food on your table."

He dialed the Jon Stewart program at TV Comedy Central in New York. "Lyle Stivanski again. Have I got a Zen moment for Jon," he said when a young woman answered. This kind of stuff might even get him back to New York.

Afterwards, Randy thought the interview went okay, he had tried to talk with a smile in his voice the way you were supposed to, but he didn't feel 100% about it. He was happier on TV, big blond guy, chiseled features, little dimple in the chin, people paid less attention to what he was saying.

Well, best forget it; right now he had to help his boy, Skip. Seemed like everybody was looking to Randy at the moment.

"How long didya say that piece a rope was again?" he asked, as he and Skip sat at the kitchen table over Skip's notes.

"Thirty feet," Skip said.

"And how big is the barn?"

"It don't matter how big the barn is. The horse's tied to the corner."

Randy wanted to ask how big the corner was but it wouldn't matter if it was five feet or fifty, he still didn't know how to do the problem. Skip loved Sylene DeWitt and wanted to help her, so Randy wanted to help Skip. He was his only child, and since Sherry died, he was Randy's whole world.

Sylene wasn't right for Skip, but Randy couldn't really say too much. Skip kept saying they were "just friends," but Randy knew what *that* meant. He'd had some "friends" like that, too, when he was a teenager. Boy, just remembering those gals, whoowhee! That Pammie Pettipaw!

Randy had a dream for Skip: he'd go to college, then marry and have loads of kids. Randy would be their ancestor. Skip never even had a brother. Neither did Randy, come to that. Had the stepbrothers, sure, but might as well have had pit bulls. He would have loved to have a good brother. A good father, too. Zeke Anderson was a rich widower, a banker, with two boys when he married Ma, and he never wanted a stepson. A couple months ago, he'd told Randy that his estate would go to his "own" boys: the bank, the real estate development company, the beauty salon, the whole lot. He was giving Randy the old Twi-lite motel right now, while he was still alive. Said he wanted to be around to pick up the pieces. No confidence in Randy, ever.

But Randy's ma, she was the best in the world, and then Sherry, she was the best wife you could imagine, those two, he was blessed. But Sherry was gone now, pneumonia, got her in no time. Sherry's mother, she was still around, Juanetta Wilcox, old Miss Guns n' Ammo 1948. A woman to stay clear of.

"Well, son, it's just like the problem Miss Pettipaw, Miss Viola Pettipaw, not her niece Pammie, give me one time in school: if it takes a man and a half a day and a half to move a box from A to B, how long would it take three men?"

"That don't have nothing to do with this," Skip said. "Not unless the box they was movin' was the barn. I *know* how to do the problem. What I want help with is thinking of all the dumb questions Sylene could ask, like how old is the horse or what if the corner is five feet wide or whatever, and have answers ready for her, so she can see they don't matter. Come on, Dad. Please."

Randy could never say "no" to his boy, but he wasn't sure but what he might be putting himself in a bad light here. Oh, sure, he knew people thought he was stupid. He could read the paper, until he'd cancelled it. He knew he was no genius; fact was, no one ever said he was even average. He'd been a big disappointment to Zeke, and in fourth grade, when they hit long division, Miss Pettipaw gave up on him. Not Pammie Pettipaw, though, her niece, I'll tell you, she and Pammie were as different as night and day. Miss Viola was a dried-up, crimp-mouth old lady, and Pammie was one of them "friends," as soft and hot and juicy . . .

Skip was staring at him.

But he was going to make Skip proud. He had hit the ground running the minute he was elected mayor; he had a transition plan and everything worked out on paper. Okay, he'd lost the paper, but heck, he could think it up again soon as he got a minute.

"Dad, I better go over to Sylene's. She's real upset, her dad going to lose his job and all."

Randy figured he should stay in and wait for the calls that would start any minute now. People would want more details of his plans, and those that missed his radio debut, well, they were probably asking each other, "Where's our mayor now that we're laid up with a recession? What's Randy Anderson doin' about all this?"

Matterafact, he was sittin' at his dinette table, slipping new rubber feet on the chair legs.

Well, forcing, really, and now one just split. He stuck a second one in the microwave for a few seconds, warm it up and stretch it. Maybe he wouldn't answer the phone; some people were plain nasty.

He'd got plenty of angry calls after that newspaper article. One was from Zeke. He forgot that Randy was the only public employee left, so besides doing mayor work, he had to drive that damn city snowplow.

"I'm not happy about that, Dad," he protested. "There's a lot of moving parts to that thing. It's a complicated machine."

"You're the last person should fool around with complicated machines. That contraption cost us taxpayers a pretty penny. But you better learn."

So last winter after a good snow, he was just practicing like, doing some wheelies over in the parking lot of his motel, the Twi-Lite.

"But there was plenty ice underneath," he told Zeke, "and before I knew what end was up, I skid right into Room 18, some guy wearin' a diaper and a baby hat, and a lady with a whip."

The guy had to help Randy outta the plow, and he was madder'n hell when the picture came out in *The Vindicator*. Randy was mad, too. They caught the situation at a trick angle, made it look like Randy was attacking a man in a diaper with a snowplow. Went all over the country. MySpace, Jon Stewart, you name it. Someone here had a hotline to those folks. And the snowplow was nearly a write-off; the whole system, frame and all, got pushed under the truck part. It got folks' goat up, they'd been taxed pretty stiff for that plow, and the City Council demanded he get Leland DeWitt to fix it, seeing as he was the only one around who seemed to understand it. Give Leland credit, he did fix it, free, except for a few parts.

"I don't know how you ever got elected," Zeke said.

Yes, he did, Randy thought. Everybody did. The other two candidates were sent to jail during the campaign, one for murder, one for trying to use a little low-voltage electric chair to motivate kiddies at the summer Bible school.

Randy sat in his kitchen a while more and around about ten-thirty, with nothing doing, no calls or anything, but he'd managed to force one of the dinette feet on and scrape out most of the melted rubber mess in the microwave. He set the coffee up for tomorrow, put Sherry's doily in the middle of the table, set out two bowls, two spoons and two paper napkins, and went up to bed.

Chapter 3

Laurinda

This was the day she'd been waiting for, the Phone Call that would change her life, for good or bad, maybe forever. And her boy Mickey's too, of course, although a mother feels it more. In the next hour, she'd be crying and hugging everyone, or she'd be crying and everyone would be hugging her. Whichever, she'd be doing it in front of the television cameras. She'd stuck the phone under the davenport pillow; she needed a little longer to get herself together. Distract herself. So right now Laurinda Wilcox McCardle was end-up behind that davenport looking for the peep.

The phone rang. She froze. No, it was 10:30 on the dot, thank God, so it had to be her mother, not one of those vicious reporters. Juanetta always phoned at ten-thirty and at one, then at four-fifteen, right before Septus got home from the boiler factory. Or did until it closed down last week. Her sister Sherry had always been her mother's favorite, but after she passed on, Juanetta persecuted Laurinda instead. She fished the phone out from under the davenport pillow.

"I bought me a real nice outfit in McKelvey's basement," Juanetta said. "A pants suit. Sort of a carteroosy."

"I don't have time to be keeping up with Italian designers. I got enough trouble over Mickey." She didn't mention that she had enough trouble with Septus, too, down with a case of depression. No intimacy now for what? Over six weeks and three days. Not that she had much time for intimacy these days, even though she was a hot-blooded woman. "A bleached blonde hottie," that's how the national papers had described her. Nobody mentioned that she was on the City Council, oh, no, although with all this carry-on the last couple years she hadn't attended but once or twice. And, of course, they wrote that she'd lost her job at the boiler factory, not mentioning that everyone else had, too.

"I said to the girl, I said 'I don't think carteroosy will suit me, being so dark-complected,' but she told me it brought out my umber hues," Juanetta said.

"What brought out your umber hues?" What had looked like the peep turned out to be a dust bunny.

"Carteroosy, Laurinda, aren't you listening to me? You got so I nearly have to say everything twice. Are you in The Change? Here, it's on the sales tag: C-H-A-R-T-R-E-U-S-E."

Laurinda wedged the phone in her shoulder and pulled out the Hoover. Dust everywhere, dog toys, a sock, no peep. She switched on the Hoover. Whomp.

She'd sucked up the peep.

"Laurinda? Your vacuuming ain't done yet? It's past ten-thirty. In the old days I'd be on my ironing by now."

Juanetta Wilcox wasn't on her ironing now because she was a businesswoman these days; she'd taken the money Harlan left her and set up the Precious Lambs Day Care Center and Rifle Range. They weren't in the same building, of course. The rifle range was outside, except when it rained. Now she had the Native American reservation at the back; they'd arrived one day and she said okay. Government something or other. That Chief Grey Wolf, handsome as all get-out.

"Isn't this Wednesday?" Laurinda demanded. "Isn't this your Rifle Tots day?"

"Chicken pox," Juanetta said. "The whole class."

"Ma, I gotta go." She put the phone back under the pillow; she wanted a little while longer of not knowing, not having to get all worked up, one way or the other. When she got worked up these days, her ears roared, she couldn't see straight and her knees gave out.

She took the hose off the Hoover and shook it, but nothing. She took out the bag, dumped the dust out on the floor, and the peep plopped out, all twisted, but alive. She blew it off. It had a nasty looking red spot, a hole, really, near its eye, and it looked a bit pale, but it was hard to tell with the blue dye.

She'd got Mickey the peep for Easter, a yellow ribbon around its tiny neck. Turned out you couldn't have a peep in jail, so she brought it back home.

She got some mercurochrome and rubbed it on the red spot. Combined, the dye and the mercurochrome turned the peep's feathers khaki-ish gray.

"Your little feathers are getting in the way. You hold on, I'll just just drop it on with the dropper," she said to the peep.

Laurinda could have been a nurse, anyone could see that. The peep shuddered and its eyes rolled up. She wondered about giving it the kiss of life, but didn't know where to start. "I *told* myself I should of took a first aid course, and now when I need it I don't know doodly squat."

The phone rang again. Laurinda forgot about her phone embargo; she dug out the phone and put the peep in an ashtray to keep an eye on it.

"Ma, did you hear the news?" Her daughter Reenie asked.

She put the phone back under the pillow. She'd take another ten minutes to gather herself. She peeked out into the front yard; nobody there yet.

She couldn't understand these reality-show people; they were crazy, wanting to be on television. Her one and only television appearance on WHAG Action news last year earned her more nasty online comments than she'd got from her own mother in a lifetime. Most of the people she knew had watched it, either that night when it went nationwide, or later on MySpace.

"Just a few words," the reporter had wheedled, thrusting the *National Inquirer* mike at them in their own front yard. Septus looked gaunt and distinguished that night; for days afterward people said he put them in mind of someone famous. "Abe Lincoln on a bad day in a red wig and beard," is what someone said online. Someone else commented that she must have bought her clothes at the Tent and Awning Supply.

But Septus was too shocked to talk that night. Laurinda thought this was ignorant, so she had spoken up. "No, Mickey's not our only child," she'd said. There's Laureen and Septeen and Don, too. Don's away now studying to be a crop duster. Never a minute's trouble, Don. But oh my gosh, the first three! Reenie married three times to the same useless fellow . . ."

"You're losing me, Mrs. McCardle," the reporter said. "How did the *shooting* happen?"

"I'm *telling* you," Laurinda said. "So we hoped Teeny would do better, she's real petite, whereas Reenie and I are on the big-boned side. I sneaked Teeny into every private school dance in the area, and she married a real handsome fellow, looked like something else in his uniform." Problem was, he *was* something else, part of the catering staff at the school, and already married to a couple other women.

"Hello? Ma?" Teeny shouted from the phone somewhere deep in the davenport. Laurinda ignored it; she sat down beside the peep and lit a cigarette.

"Anyhow," she'd said to the reporter that night, "that didn't work out, and the real trouble began later when

Teeny started over. She's Mickey's twin, and they married twins, the Jones kids. Then Mickey's new wife ran off with Teeny's new husband."

The reporter signaled to someone to write some notes. The someone rolled her eyes and drew a circle in the air beside her head.

"So then he just drifted for a while and then he married a nice woman who had a teenage daughter."

"I know where this is going," the reporter said to the camera guy.

"We know where it's *gone*," the camera guy said. "Murder. Our job is to get some color from the parents."

"The nice woman died but Mickey was a great dad to Louise, made sure she ate right, took tap dancing, and so on. Even when she was a lot older, he was a real stickler for her to be home by eleven every night."

Louise was easy going and that was okay with her except when she was on the night shift; she'd become a firefighter so she had to sneak in and out.

"He was so proud of Louise."

"Mrs. McCardle," said the reporter. "How . . ."

"Ms. Wilcox McCardle." But she had no time for gender lectures right now. "So, he was real irritated when Louise took up with Squint Sheehan. That Squint, his baptismal name was Finbar but he went by Squint, he was only doing it to get Mickey's goat. He and Mickey were never what you'd call close. Hated each other, matterafact. So Louise had to sneak out to see him."

"How're we going to edit this?" the reporter asked a skinny bored-looking girl who was holding some wires.

"After a while, Louise decided to marry Squint and asked Mickey to give her away. Mickey said over Squint's dead body. You know Mickey was running for mayor at the time and acting real grandiose . . ."

"Dear God," the reporter said. He tried to get the microphone back.

"So, anyway, one day Louise called Mickey and said, 'Dad, Finbar and I got married this morning, can you find it in your heart to forgive and forget, give us your blessing?'"

"'Sure thing,' Mickey says. 'Come right on over, I'll put the coffee on'. Well, apparently when they got to the house, he kissed Louise, and gave Squint a nice punch on the shoulder. He said to Louise, 'Honey, you go and get the sugar, okay?'"

Laurinda's lips quivered and her voice went way up high.

"Soon's she left the room, he shot Squint dead."

They showed the last twenty seconds on WHAG, and then on most of the national channels. Of course, the whole thing, beginning to end, was on TV. And "Murdering Mickey's Mega Ma;" that's what the *National Inquirer* called her the next day.

Mickey's lawyer said it sure didn't help none. But some local viewers called WHAG to say Mickey oughta get a medal, Squint was Zeke Anderson's henchman and knocking him off was a public service. Zeke fired Laurinda from her job as the receptionist at his beauty salon just when she needed the money, and she had to take a cleaning job in the factory.

Juanetta had offered to give Zeke a good scare, "Just wing him with the rifle some night."

"We got enough murderers in the family right now," Laurinda told her, but she appreciated the gesture.

Mickey was doing life in the penitentiary up in Everton now, but she was hoping the new lawyer could get him out on appeal. She had to sell their RV to pay him; Septus was so down he didn't even seem to notice it was missing.

No reporters outside yet. It wasn't fun, cameras filming you, twisting your words, making you look like a fat washed-up cow in a no-color washed-out T-shirt. The newspapers pestering your neighbors. The *Inquirer* calling you a half-wit, and showing you only from behind. And the bloggers! There were three web sites devoted entirely to her. Since when was VPL a federal crime? And gum? Or blue eye shadow? You'd think it was her who'd committed the crime, not Mickey.

She stubbed her cigarette out in the ashtray and lit another one. She was forty-five-ish. That was nothing these days. If this Mickey thing worked out okay, she had maybe forty more years when she could be doing something useful, Making a Difference, using her brain. Go back to school, maybe, finish high school, go to college, do some good instead of rotting here on the davenport, wondering what Mickey was doing, worrying about Septus, breaking into a sweat and panicking every time some little thing happened.

The phone clicked.

Laurinda stubbed out another butt.

Well, would you look at that peep. She fished it out of the ashes and put it on the floor. It took off walking okay, but it leaned way too much to the left. She blew it off and looked at its little legs. They were all right, about the only part that was. You had to give it credit—it had a pert, cocky air, singed feathers and all.

The screen door banged and Juanetta came in. Never a knock, oh no. Septus could be bare naked if he was here and ever in his life went bare naked.

"Laurinda, what's going on with your phone? I been calling you for twenty minutes." She pulled on the cord and reeled it in. "What's that smell? Why's that chicken walkin' that way?"

"It's got a little cut. I put mercurochrome on it."

"That ain't no cut, that's its ear. You'd walk crooked too, with a ear full of mercurochrome. Should of done both ears, if you was going to do it at all. Anyhow, I'm not here for that nonsense. Didn't you hear the news? Reenie's been calling and calling you. Mickey's appeal's been turned down. Was all over WHAG radio. Reporters all over out there. You want to lock that screen door."

Years later, Laurinda still couldn't look at the old chicken staggering around the house without remembering the minute she heard the news. It was like where were you when you heard Kennedy was shot, or the time she caught her foot in McKelvey's escalator. As clear as the day it happened. She stepped out onto the porch.

Laurinda was too busy to dream; she never bothered, she had enough on her hands as it was and she needed her rest. But what was it in her sleep that night? People were paying attention to her, writing down what she said. Was it sneering newspaper reporters again? Mean-looking police? No, maybe they were students or something. Next day Laurinda still remembered how good she felt in the dream. She'd always wanted to be a teacher when she was a kid. A petite teacher. She wanted to Make a Difference. She got to wondering if any petite person in history had Made a Difference. Was Napoleon petite, or just short? Anyhow, not much chance of anything for her now, she thought; I'm famous as Murdering Mickey's Mega Ma.

Chapter 4

Bert

What the hell was that thing on his face? It wasn't a mole, it was skin-colored; it was more like a floppy piece of dough stuck to his forehead. He wondered what would happen if he pulled it off. Probably bleed to death, no one around but that girl.

Bert Whump could see her looking at him in the mirror behind Winkle's counter. He was on a stool at the counter eating home fries and hot Italian sausage, and she was alone in a booth against the wall.

She was interested, he could see that. Problem was, she was looking at him like he was a warthog or something, a grandfather warthog even, kinda fascinated and horrified at the same time. He didn't like to meet her glance in the mirror, embarrass her, but she sure was studying him.

Huh. Lotta those girls will have beam ends like a bus long before they ever hit his age. But right now, this one was beautiful, and Bert felt like a warthog, only not as happy.

Kids all thought old people were born old. He'd thought that too when he was young; did he think he'd have these ropy veins in his hands, these big brown spots, the veranda belly, or that he'd have to pee every ten minutes? No, sirree. Never even gave a thought to peeing. What he'd thought was he could hold up two lawnmowers, the push kind, over his head, one at the end of each arm, forever, like he did once for a photo. He'd thought he would be able to stay up and dance all night; hell, he'd thought he would *want* to stay up and dance all night.

But he'd had a fine time, all right, when he was a young man. He could remember walking along with his head up, belly tight, legs with muscles like springs, arms pumping. In the service, in his Navy uniform, late sixties, all the girls going wild; wild was the right word. A pimply kid with no hair on his chest one day, and the next day, almost like Glenn Ford, Clark Gable, one of them. It was the uniform, of course, not him.

Boy, it was pretty romantic. Them girls thought he'd be dead in no time flat, killed in action. But what kinda action did a cook see in San Diego? Sure, he got shot in the leg by some damn recruit on the single day sailors get their gun training. Didn't matter to the girls, though; wounded-hero, they thought. They liked the way he looked and the way they looked, too: how they had gone from being bony, freckled girls to real pin-ups, beauty queens.

It was only at the end that he got sent to Europe for what was just a few weeks, in Berlin. Cookin' again, not one minute of action.

He was the only Navy man in three counties; his model had been John Lane, over in Zirconia, a man who seen some real Marine action in World War II on Guam and them places with the Marines. Lane said whenever he came home on leave he'd had himself quite a harem.

Well, Bert hadn't been a saint, either. Mrs. Bert would be the first one to tell you that, and she didn't know but a tenth of it. When you came home on leave, the girls here, thinking they owed it to their country or something, not like those city hippy girls protesting on the streets. He didn't have to sweet talk them much at all except of course the lovely Nora, and Susie, too. And Juanetta, although she didn't know what sweet talk was; she liked to talk munitions. The three of them, they wanted him to be happy as he went off to God knows where and what. Bert looked at the mirror and sighed. Of course, his skin wasn't this cement color then.

In the end, he and sweet Nora had been as good as engaged, and even then, she was no pushover. But by the time he was discharged, not long after, all the girls were married. He'd thought Nora, or even Susie and Juanetta would wait for him, but they married pretty quick.

He'd tried to put things right over the years, but it was turning out to be a sorry legacy. Worst of all, Nora had written to him in Berlin but somehow it went astray.

That girl, she was looking at him again. Beautiful dark blonde hair, huge dark blue eyes. He still remembered what it was like to have pretty girls look at you. But who looks at an old man?

His eyelids—in this mirror, he looked like a lizard. Somewhere he read Aristotle Onassis had to prop up his eyelids with toothpicks, some kinda disease he had. Well, Bert wasn't going to put out his eye with a toothpick; he made two little pillars of paper from a corner of the menu and they worked okay until they fell off.

When he got out of the Navy, he should have gone to college. They would have paid. He could have been a high school teacher, he was real good at math and loved kids, but he thought he was way too old to go to college. And people didn't plan careers so much in those days. They just sorta fell into things.

So he drove for a motor freight company, bought his own truck with his money from the service, and met Mrs. Bert when she came to visit her cousin in Hope And Glory. Wasn't like those other girls, she never heard you were supposed to make a war effort, and wouldn't let him go below the line of navigation, so to speak. That's why he married her, he guessed. If he'd just got that letter from Nora in time. The local girls, they'd always had a bit of life in them. Just look at Juanetta. Armed to the teeth, even today. But Mrs. Bert, she spends all her time keeping people off her white davenport. Fussing over her roses. Paring her corns. Last week she sent him out for bat guano for them roses, she read it in some magazine.

You shoulda seen the look the guy at the store gave him. Like "Where's your dignity, man?"

His nostrils—were they always that wide? They damn near filled up his whole face. They were really stuffed with hair up there. He tilted his head back to see them. Disgusting.

And that spot on his forehead, the one beside the dough, not as big as Gorbachev's, more like a map of Cuba. He pointed to where he thought Havana was.

He and Harlan Wilcox, the guy Juanetta married, God rest him, bought the old movie theater, threw out the moldy old seats and put in second-hand davenports until they could afford seats. People liked the davenports, kids liked to neck on them, so did worn-out young parents, so they stayed. He remembered their opening show in 1980; they had a movie about a guy who thought he was a puma, or vice versa, he couldn't recall. Then they bought the bowling alley over in Cairo, too, fixed it up, and it became the place to go on a Friday night. Made good money.

When Harlan passed, it was too much for one guy. The City Council asked him to be Chief of Police, thinking he'd been an MP in the Navy. He cleared that up and then had some real good years on the force. But the Council never should've closed the jail when he retired last year; a jail was a kind of focus point for folks. Now Hope And Glory was just part of Chief Earl Arbogast's penal empire over in North Vienna.

That was his career in a nutshell. Everybody else here spent their life in the boiler factory except Butch Winkle

here in the diner; Zeke Anderson, who made a killing out
of his various ventures; Mitch over at the gas station and
"Bob" Matthews, with that Union Dollar tax scam thing
down the road in Cairo. They'd all be gone soon except
Butch, who was thirty years younger.

He wondered how long the diner would stay open in a
recession. He was safe enough, himself; his police pension,
a nice three-bedroom split-level all paid off, and a little
boat he took out on Beaver Dam.

He had a nice family, too, Mrs. Bert and his girl Kimi
Lynn and the grandkids—that Danielle, she was a real
corker. Why Kimi married Chief Earl Arbogast in North
Vienna was beyond him. Why the Hope And Glory City
Council let him have the jail was a mystery.

But if he'd got that letter from Nora in time, things
would have been a lot different.

He'd tried his best to look out for Nora's little boy,
when he found out; it had been too late to do much else.
By the time he'd got the letter, she'd married his pal Buck
DeWitt, and later they had a couple little girls and another
boy. Buck was crazy about Nora and good as gold to all
the kids, made no difference between them. Susie married
pretty quick, too, Al Hamilton, nice enough guy, he died
in a rooter accident, and she was left with little Randy.

"Bert." Bert swivelled and got a curt nod as Zeke
Anderson marched past and through the swinging doors
to the kitchen. That was another guy'd been crazy over
Nora. He ended up married to another girl, had two boys
and then she'd died, just like that. Bert was never too clear

on that. Zeke was left with a couple of uncontrollable boys. He married Susie then to take care of them, and of course little Randy came with her. Zeke didn't take to Randy, by all accounts. But he'd always been nasty, even brutal, to most people, except those two spoiled boys.

Funny thing, that girl didn't even look at Zeke as he passed through. Even his worst enemy, and there were plenty fighting for the title, would admit Zeke was a good-looking fellow, still. Looked like one of those silver-haired sheriffs or judges in the old westerns. That's probably how he got away with so much—nobody expected a man who looked like Lawrence Welk to steal your pants off. Or worse.

These days, Bert was a godfather to half the town and pretty near a full-time pallbearer. He and Buck DeWitt, who worked out the geometry of the situation. Bert was tall, Buck a little shorter, and then, depending on the other guys, maybe one a squirt, and whether there'd be four guys or six, ABCD or ABCDEF, Buck would have it all laid out. In really complicated situations, they'd get together and rehearse it with a table and some possible shifts in the center of mass. Buck always got kidded; he usually wore black. Joked he was a Lone Ranger fan. He had cancer now but they still depended on him for the math. Mayor Randy was going to have to step in, only for the grunt work because he struggled with the times tables, to say nothing of geometry.

He was on the City Council himself now. Big deal: when they weren't closing jails they had nothing much to do but pass a hat for this one or that one, a young widow or a kid who needed money to go to college. Laurinda's idea, to give her credit. She was picking herself up, despite all that trouble over Mickey.

He should do more for those poor kids, too; he didn't get any advanced education, but he shoulda. He shoulda run for mayor, too; even at his age he wouldn't have sat on his hands while the boiler factory got closed down. Not that he blamed Randy; after all, it was a recession. But what was he, Bert Whump, doing to help? Nothin'. In the end, biggest thing was he shoulda married Nora. People think you forget when you get old, but he didn't.

That girl was still looking at him. He would just like to tell her he wasn't always this old. That maybe her grandma would have thought he was swell. Well, no, you couldn't say that to a young girl.

I still got some life in me, though, Bert thought. I could still do a lotta things, as long as I could pee regular. I could go to Hawaii. I could teach math to immigrants, if we had any. I could mentor some teenagers. Some boys, he said to himself as he caught sight of the girl again. No, sir, Bert Whump was not finished yet.

"Finished?" asked the waitress.

"Yup," said Bert. "Real good, them sausages."

"Uncle Bert?" the gorgeous girl was coming over. "I couldn't make out if it was you in the meer. My dog chewed the side thing off my glasses. Sylene DeWitt, Leland's daughter, remember? I'm your goddaughter? I know, yeah, I look different—I grew my hair long last winter and got these awful highlights. Well, you're looking real good, now I can see you. How's Mrs. Whump and Kimi Lynn doing?"

Ah. So she's Nora's granddaughter. *His* granddaughter, when it came to it, which it did. Leland's kid.

Okay, he really was going to do something. Help his kids, all his kids, if he could, maybe broaden his horizons, too, get on some mailing lists, do the crossword, reach out a little, make up for a few things. Stop being such a stupid old fart. Speaking of which, the Pope was on TV not too long ago, the holiest person on earth, and he was man enough to apologize for the Holocaust, and for your Crusades, and the Inquisition. Well, Bert could maybe make some amends, too. Not on the same scale, but still. The problem was how to do it without dragging up a whole lot of stuff better left buried.

"Bert?" Butch Winkle came out through the kitchen door, "How's tricks? You okay?"

"Real good," said Bert. "You?"

"Oh, pretty good. I could do without visits from Zeke, though. Never take out a loan from that guy, no matter how tough things are. Listen, you sure you're okay? Gonna wash this mirror. You know, a lotta folks don't know it's a two-way glass, so's when we're in the kitchen we can see if anybody at the counter wants sumpin'. We just wondered in there were you okay. And the Mrs., how's she doing?"

Chapter 5

Zeke

Zeke Anderson squats on the edge of the septic tank, thinking about the jump. Septic tank, hell, what's he saying, it's a three-stage White Water Bio-Waste, the god-damned Rolls Royce of waste management systems. It shouldn't be acting up like this. Installed it all by himself, too, except for the electricals, he let that dim-wit preacher Dwight Wayman handle that. People laugh, saying he treats the system like a baby, and to be extra vigilant he throws in a dead jackrabbit once a year. Right now, though, there sure as hell is something wrong with it. But in the dark it's hard to tell what, and brother is it cold tonight. He's depressed. Thank God for whiskey. Anyhow, here goes.

Hold it, someone's coming, crunching down the gravel path. A limping sound? Must be that fool preacher

Reverend Wayman, always fussing about how he should go easier on the wife, Susie, and her pride and joy, that idiot Randy. A real bonehead, Wayman. Lousy electrician, too. Well, he'll just hunker down here till the old geezer gives up and leaves.

Boy, never saw such a mess. Keeps up, next thing he'll be knee-deep in turds. No wonder it's so dark, though, he forgot the electricity is off, another disaster today. And just a half hour earlier he had his head down the toilet, baited for bear. Everyone knows how he gets when he's mad. But is he sorry? No sirree. It would teach Susie a good lesson. But just thinking about it all makes him want to . . .

Well, for sure, whoever is clomping along that gravel path will try to give him an earful of useless advice. The steps sound more like Randy. Maybe he was still sore from yesterday. Came here without an invite, bringing his kid Skip and his mother-in-law Juanetta. He called Randy a bastard right in front of them, but wasn't it right? In the true sense? Old Juanetta went for him with her crossbow. Said she'd call back and make a better job of it next time. Well, whoever was coming, he didn't need them.

Lookit now, that dead jackrabbit floating around in the first chamber, doing nothin'. He'd yelled for Susie to call the so-called expert from the septic tank company. No sound, so he goes in and calls the guy himself; Susie must have gone out somewheres. If she thinks he's running after her, she's crazy. She wouldn't even know how to run, or where, knew what was good for her.

He feels his way back to the Bio-Waste and stands on the edge, rocking on his heels. He'd pick the guy's brains and then pack him off; the guy is a friend of Bert Whump's and he isn't going to be shooting the breeze with any crony of Whump's. All his life Whump had everything too easy. Oh yeah, everybody loved Bert, the big man, the "war" hero, ha, and Zeke was always the bad guy. Of course people always hated a successful man. Okay, someone's comin' along the gravel, that must be the expert, maybe Whump's with him. What a pain in the neck, just as he thinks he can see now what's wrong. That guy better not expect to be paid.

Nope, looks like there he goes, just missed the house going ninety miles an hour.

So who's that on the path now? Well, he was goin' to hide the whiskey; too good to waste on some goddamned fool. Unless it was Septus McCardle; he didn't drink. Yep, sounded like Septus, all right, heavy step for a man with such little feet. Anyhow, any fool could see what was wrong: the rodding eye. Who woulda thought a little thing like that . . . shit, he cracked a piece off the lip of the bottle on the edge of the tank. Someone put their hand down there, they'd get a nasty cut, probably end up suing. People were miserable cusses.

One thing he had to say for himself, Zeke Anderson, he was a smart man. Maybe no saint, but smart. He'd made his big money hauling garbage for the city. It paid by the pound, so it was only sensible to water it. Sometimes the garbage was nearly floating, and soon he was able to build up a fleet of trucks. Now he had a hand in nearly everything in town. He didn't need help from nobody, but naturally the minute you get it figured out, somebody else is tramping across the gravel, probably thinking the sun shines outta their backside, they know so much about septic tanks, more than him, a professional waste expert.

Sounds like high heels. Stupid things to wear on gravel. What was that "zing"? A crossbow? Juanetta in high heels? Now that'd be a sight. He stayed low, just in case.

Dammit! It was nearly getting too dark to see what was going on, but he wasn't so sure now that the rodding eye was the trouble. Lookit that mess. What the hell, he was a garbage expert, a garbage magnate, actually, not a septic tank expert. Buck DeWitt, his septic tank always worked like a charm. You could brush your teeth in it. He hated Buck DeWitt, no guts. Not a real man. No real man would bring up somebody else's kid, be as nice as pie to him. Buck shoulda slapped that slut Nora the way he himself slapped Susie when he learned her whole story. And now, would she even appreciate what he was doing for her this minute? Blast! Who was that now, coming down the gravel path? This place was like downtown New York. Never knew he was so popular. Well, whoever, if they didn't know anything about septic tanks, they could get the hell out.

Good thing he had a little more whiskey to keep the circulation going. He was getting awful light-headed, nearly forgot why he came out here in the first place. He bet it was Buck coming along, although it was a light footstep.

Probably a queer. Well! Maybe that's why Buck put up with all that stuff of Nora's. He'd never thought about that before: Buck DeWitt a queer. Hid it real good. But no, sounds like work boots, might be Buck's boy Leland. Smart fellow, Leland. He's pretty sure Leland hates him but still, he wouldn't grudge giving a hand.

He wasn't really crying—Zeke Anderson never cried in his life—a septic tank will do that. It was like a woman, really: a good woman, strong but a little fickle. You needed a firm touch, but with the right treatment she'd work her heart out for you. Whoever was coming down the path—God, the whole world was coming down his path tonight—he was gonna share that thought with them. Him. Or her. Boy, he was getting dizzy. Better lay off the whiskey for a while. One thing about drink, though, it clears your mind.

Well, he wasn't ashamed to admit it, he was sobbing. This was a beautiful system, nothing in the world wrong with it; it was clear as day now what had happened. Could be fixed easy enough, although God knows the fumes would take a while to go away. Okay, now he could get on with what he started out to do. He hoped Susie would be satisfied. Maybe old Suse wasn't so bad after all. Had he been too hard on her? And on that idiot Randy? Maybe he should go in the house and tell her he was sorry? Yeah, it's never too late to . . .

THE HOPE AND GLORY VINDICATOR

Volume 232 Issue 25   Hope And Glory, Ohio

Groundhog Day Debacle

In a shocking development yesterday, the Groundhog Day celebrations were disrupted when Hope And Glory Hal, the beloved local groundhog, made his appearance and was eaten by Mrs. Laurinda McCardle's wolfhound, Pixie. Dozens watched helplessly as the mayor, unaware of the atrocity occurring behind him, gave a lengthy address on the plight of the space aliens in Roswell, New Mexico.

Afterward, small children were led away sobbing. Mrs. McCardle, who goes by her maiden name, Wilcox, said Pixie had been brought up vegetarian. The mayor said that one of the most unfortunate consequences of the fracas was that we would not know whether we were in for more winter, or were having an early spring.

Mayor charged under ancient law

Chief of Police Earl Arbogast of North Vienna has charged Mayor Randy Anderson with uttering a profanity under a 90-year-old law which forbids cussing in the presence of women and children. According to the chief, the mayor made an excretory remark in the presence of Mrs. Laurinda McCardle upon seeing the mangled groundhog parts behind the podium from which he was speaking. Mrs. McCardle was wresting a leg from her wolfhound Pixie when the offense occurred.

Mayor Anderson's office denied the charges and announced last night that this was just one more example of why Hope And Glory needed its own police presence, with officers who understood the local culture.

Social

Zeke Anderson, the wealthy garbage magnet and stepfather of Mayor Randy Anderson, was found dead in his septic tank last night. Chief Earl Arbogast deferred, temporarily, to Bert Whump, who was Hope And Glory's former police chief when we had one. Apparently many people visited Zeke Anderson on the night of his death, and it was better to leave Mr. Whump to track them down, because the Chief is laid up with heel spurs.

INSIDE THIS ISSUE

2 High hopes for Grey Wolf Casino!

2 Where's Canada? Answer and Win!

3 Making flavored wallpaper paste

4 Nebraska entirely under sea water

5 Septic Tank Safety: wear that life belt!

Good by and Good Luck, Hal

from Mrs. Kimi Lynn's 5th grade class at Chester Arthur Grade School

---

DRYWALLING. MCCARDLE. 330-0186

GUTTERS CLEANED. ASK FOR RYAN. 330-1358

REPAIRS, ROOFS, ATTIC. REASONABLE. LELAND L. DEWITT. 330-1358

REPAIRS. JOHNNY G. 330-8950

ELECTRICAL AND PLUMBING. CALL MURPH 330-6450

LIGHT HAULING. ANGELO. 330-9435 ANYTIME

DRAINS CLEANED, YARD WORK. BILL McG. 330-6020

FIN 'N FUR KENNELS AND BIBLE SCHOOL—30% OFF.

NEW PIANO. CALL RYAN. 330-1358

Chapter 6

Leland

"Hold it, hold it, I said HOLD IT, dammit!" Lyle Stivanski's voice interrupted Vaughn Monroe's "Racing with the Moon" on WHAG's "Famous Singers from Ohio."

"I always thought Monroe sounded like he had somebody else's teeth in," Buck DeWitt called out from the depths of his plaid recliner to Leland, who was outside getting ready to put new screening into the screen door. Buck nestled deeper into the chair and pulled a fringed blanket over his knees but Leland thought he still looked cold.

The radio music halted part way through "mooooon."

"Folks," Lyle squeaked, "I got some breaking news." He paused and resumed with a more authoritative tone. "As you've heard, Zeke Anderson, local nabob, was found dead in his septic tank. The North Vienna police say it just maybe could be murder."

Leland stood up from his toolbox. The screening rolled off the front porch and got caught in the rose thorns.

"We'll have a special, right after the noon news, 'Zeke Anderson—Pushed, Jumped or Just Fell In?' That's it for this month's 'Famous Singers From Ohio.' Next time it's Roy Rogers."

Buck's fingers traced the paisley pattern on the blanket over and over. "Huh," he said, finally.

Leland waited a bit but nothing more came out. "Well, when Bridget gets home I'll run Susie over a pot of lima beans. Or maybe a casserole."

"Bert Whump'll be there, making sure she's okay," Buck said.

"My money's on 'jumped,' Juanetta called, sticking her head through the top half of the screenless door. "Couldn't stand his own miserable ass anymore."

"I guess a lady like you picks up some awful language at your Rifle Range," Buck said. "Son, you could send that casserole over to Randy, maybe. He might take this hard, he couldn't help but feel bad even if Zeke *is* a monster. Was."

"Yes, sir," Juanetta said. "I went over there last night ready for blood but by the time I got there it seemed like there wasn't much point."

"Yeah, I went over, too," Buck said. "I gave him hell. I forget who all I met, coming and going. My memory isn't what it was. I used to know all the state capitals."

Leland was a baby when the trouble started between Zeke and Buck, but a few years ago Bert Whump told him some of the story.

"When your dad and ma got married," he'd said, "they bought a rickety little house on Garfield Street and Nora fixed it up really nice. Your dad worked double shifts every chance he got so they could sell and move to a better place out in the country. But old Zeke, even though he had the money to buy anywhere, he bought the house next door to your dad's, got it rezoned and set up a twenty-four hour wrecking and scrap yard."

Leland remembered some of this. By the time he was six or so, he was aware of the dirt, the racket, the machines, the searchlights. Once he had to have thirteen stitches in his knee because he fell on some sheet metal in the backyard grass. His mother had to wash the windowsills in the house every morning. Leland was twelve before Buck could make a down payment on the house they were sitting in now, way out here on Route 123, a nice house shaded by maples and fruit trees, and nothing but fields behind it. It was like heaven to Leland to lie on the porch on Sundays in June and listen to the gentle swish of the leaves and the buzz of a light plane heading to the North Vienna airport.

Leland looked over now to see Juanetta hauling Buck out of his chair for a game of cards. "Strip poker," she said to Leland; Buck, beaming, hustled to the table, dragging the blanket around his feet. He dealt Juanetta their usual hand of cards for canasta.

There was another time that Leland did remember, though. Randy's stepbrothers always beat up on him, but later one of them, he was about nineteen for God's sake, started picking on Leland's brother Ralph, when Ralph was about twelve. One day he twisted Ralph's arm so hard he put his shoulder out. Buck and Leland walked over to talk to Zeke but Zeke ran them off the front porch, waving a window sash-weight at them. "You're nothin'," he yelled at Buck. "You're a loser and you're always gonna be a loser."

Buck never talked about that, and he and Zeke never spoke again. Leland was surprised that once in a while Buck would bring Randy over to their house, give him some dinner, take him to a game with Leland.

But now, what did Randy do but start the whole thing up again, more or less saying Sylene wasn't good enough for his boy, Skip.

Still, tonight after everybody in town had a say about what happened at the septic tank, Leland knocked on Randy's door and handed him a sweet potato casserole with crusty golden marshmallows on top.

Chapter 7

Laurinda

To be left for another woman was one thing, but to be left for a muskie? Septus was off all the time, fishing, fishing, fishing. All her plans for Making a Difference went pfft as she brooded. Was she losing that special something that drove a man crazy with love? Like they said in the magazines?

Dr. Sherman gave her a prescription. "You're depressed," he said.

"I'm not depressed, I'm irritated." She pushed the prescription across the desk.

"Oh, well, then, you're in The Change," and he pushed it back.

Now she really was irritated. She looked better than she ever had in her life, almost trim, buffed (she'd got some weights from a yard sale) and radiant from exfoliating her face with an invention of her own, oatmeal, ground almonds and a few frozen strawberries she'd found at the bottom of the freezer.

"It didn't look very good on," Randy Anderson said one day when he and Skip stopped in. "But you look great now that you've got it off, and the leftovers, mm-mmh!" He kissed his fingers. He and Skip both dipped in. Laurinda's heart went out to them; when Sherry died, all Randy knew how to cook was cinnamon toast, and he still probably couldn't cook much more. To see the two of them him sitting happily over that bowl of exfoliant, it would gladden any heart.

But here she was, looking good, and she'd started getting really active in the City Council, and look what she got for it—her husband off cutting up worms all the time and her getting accused of being in The Change, at her age, just in her mid-to-latish forties. Unbelievable.

Well, maybe she'd have to get more interested in the kinds of things Septus liked, more outdoorsy? Until now, she hadn't liked to get too involved with the environment; she didn't appreciate it getting too involved with her, either; who needed hurricanes, tornadoes, mosquitoes? But maybe she should look up "muskie" on the Internet. She was going to get really good on it, she had really nice tapered fingers. Since Skip was sitting here in her kitchen now, a flick of oatmeal on his cute face, she asked him to help her.

"OMG!" Skip gasped as a dagger-toothed, black-spotted monstrous face filled the screen.

Laurinda studied her competition. "Oh, yeah, that's a muskie, I remember them. Can't see the attraction, though."

"But wait, this next thing sounds good. A course on 'How to Become an Outdoors Lady!' Think you'd like that?"

She didn't think she'd like that.

"They have a little test you can take to see if you could be one. Here's a question: did you bag your Thanksgiving turkey yourself?"

"I been a vegetarian since way before Thanksgiving."

"Oh. Okay. Here's another one: Have you ever given yourself a manicure with a rock?"

"Skip . . ."

"Do you think you would be able to pee in a . . . oh, sorry! Gross!"

"Skip, you're talking to a real lady. You should be ashamed," Randy said.

After Skip and Randy left with her recipe, Laurinda went back into the outdoorsy site and bookmarked it: it might be something a little different for Juanetta's next birthday.

And instead of brooding, she asked herself when was the last time that anyone had called her a real lady? Or any kind of a lady? When was the last time anyone told her she looked great with the oatmeal off her face?

She knew Randy never cared that much for Septus—he'd told Juanetta once that Septus was too booky for a man. Randy probably never opened a book but what she liked

about him was he was so calm, even with all the ferment
he faced as mayor. Some said Randy's calmness was just
a way-subnormal IQ, but Laurinda thought he was sweet
and fun, and for a minute or two he could take her mind
off Mickey locked up down in Everton.

The next day, Randy gave Laurinda a call. "We oughta
put our heads together, me being Mayor and you on the
City Council. We have a responsibility to come up with
some plans to save Hope And Glory, now the factory's
gone." She hoped the plans didn't involve mooses. She'd
heard that program.

They met in Randy's office and afterward they often
went over to the El Dorado.

In years to come, some people wondered how the hell
the idea for the town's new garbage facility got started in
the first place, and the simple truth was it was born right
during those conversations. In fact, Randy, who was a
generous man, freely admitted in later years that Laurinda
had been his garbage Muse. "Moose" is how he said it,
so it confused some. Of course, garbage was in the blood,
too, his stepdad having been in the profession and all?

Chapter 8

Leland

"Look at that poor organutan doin' that laundry," Leland said to his dad.

"This is why you need your unions," Buck gasped, but before he could launch into the sorry history of the labor movement, he was scoured by a raking cough that left him mouthing wordlessly, making his point by jabbing his finger in the air and signaling with his eyebrows.

Leland was over home at his ma's house, watching a nature show on TV. Buck hunched in his recliner, wrapped in an old afghan, with a hunter's hat. He had the fur ear lugs down most evenings, he was so cold now. Crepuscular chilliness.

The program was about whether animals could think or not.

"Of course they can. What else have they got to do all day? They'd go crazy, otherwise."

Leland agreed. His Arthur Leroy, now there was one of your exceptions. You couldn't find a nicer dog, but he had a wind-up egg-timer where his brain should be. But take this orangutan on the show. He was living in Borneo, in one of them camps where they send zoo animals to re-train for the jungle, learning to climb trees and such. After that, they were supposed to go and live in the jungle.

But now here he comes, trudging back out of the jungle every day to do the camp laundry. Can you believe it? Nobody asked him to, he just does it, sitting on a board by the lake, right alongside one of the camp workers, scrubbing T-shirts and shorts with a big brush, rinsing them in the lake and wringing them out. Nobody talks to him or anything because he's not supposed to be back in the camp at all. Night time, he trudges back into the jungle.

"The poor bugger." Buck drew the afghan closer around him. "The saddest part is it isn't even his own laundry. Way he walks back reminds me of the years I trudged into that factory with my lunch bucket. Wonder what he does about lunch. Doesn't seem to have a banana with him or anything."

His dad was a soft man, everyone always said that. You couldn't show him a newspaper article on kids in refugee camps or even the dog pound's adoption ads. Leland wondered what he thought now, his time nearly up, lived his life from one paycheck to the next, and now here was Leland, his son, washed up. It must break his heart. He had so many hopes for his kids.

He put down his eyeglasses to wipe his eyes and got the eyepiece caught in one of his ma's crocheted doilies, damn near took down a china lady in a ball gown.

"Whoa!" his dad said. "You break that collectible, your ma'll kill you."

"What's a collectible?"

"Beats me. S'what Nora calls it."

Buck had had a lung taken out, a thing he said he wasn't going to do again in a hurry. Leland was spending more time over here because his ma needed a break and his dad liked the company. They did a little drywalling in the basement when his dad was up to it, although his dad wouldn't let him do much but hold the tools.

Leland really enjoyed these times. His dad was the smartest man he ever met. Oh, he had his oddities, didn't have a lot of time for your blacks or Hispanics or Asians, or whites, for that matter, and he was real aggravated by what he called the Judeo-Christian power bloc, and as for your Moslems, Hindus and Buddhas, forget it. The elderly, the handicapped, gays, rich people, glee clubs, Chilean pines, the Marriott Hotel chain, and Lech Walesa, among others, all came in for special mention, too. Sometimes Leland got a little lost, but so what? The thing that was good about Buck was he liked *individuals*, every individual of every race and religion he'd ever met, practically, except Zeke Anderson. It was mainly groups he couldn't stand, and with the pines, species.

The phone rang. Buck struggled from deep within the depths of the old recliner but sank back, exhausted, muttering. Leland picked up the phone from its doily.

"Leland?" The voice sounded a little desperate. "Randy. Bridget said I could get you there. Hold on a minute, this phone, I don't know, I think I'm taking a video of myself. That's better. Listen, how you doin'?"

"Pretty good. Can't complain."

"Me neither. Listen, I just got a call from Laurinda, she's over in the supermarket, there's some kind of problem. Reverend Wayman just ran out, says he heard God talking in the Baked Goods aisle. Laurinda says this might be a Disorderly in Public. She called me right away." Randy sounded pleased at this bit.

"Well, maybe he did."

"Nah. Not possible."

Well, if God could do anything and be anywhere, why couldn't He be talking to a man of the cloth in any aisle He liked? But Leland decided to let this pass; it was Randy he was talking to. "The manager got on the phone and told me it's a machine gone haywire. I told him I knew just the man."

"Well," Leland said. "I'm here with my dad, and . . ."

"Something about thunder and rain, I don't know, he got all technical . . ."

Leland put his hand over the receiver. "You up to a little trip to the supermarket, Dad? There's some kind of problem down there. Thunder, rain, God in the Baked Goods aisle."

Leland hadn't seen him move so readily in a long time; he rocked the recliner backward and forward until he had enough momentum to scramble out and prop himself up against a chair. Standing, he looked like a broken stick insect, but he waved impatiently to Leland. "C'mon. I'm all ready," he rasped, untangling himself from the afghan and revealing the winter coat underneath. "Let's go." He had the wicked grin that Leland remembered when he was little and Buck threw his special knuckleball; no one could hit it, no one could catch it. Leland loaded him into Bridget's car.

Not much was happening outside the supermarket. Once inside the doors, though, thundery booms reverberated off the walls and he brightened up. Cyndi Lynne Poot, red-faced at the checkout, was shouting into a microphone.

"EEE-VAC-U-ATE THE BUILDING!!! EVACUATE!! CODE ONE! Or is it Code TWO? CODE TWO, YEAH."

Reverend Wayman pushed her away from the microphone. "It's the Rapture! Lord Jeezuss," he bellowed, eyes squinched shut. "We're comin'."

"It thunders okay but it don't rain," said a deep disembodied voice. Everyone looked up into the ductwork. Even Leland, not much of a churchgoer, was impressed.

"Fools," Buck said. "God don't say 'okay.' What's goin' on here?" he demanded of a man wearing a name badge. The man pointed to the fresh vegetable display. "Rain machine's broken," he said. "The thunder's okay but the volume's way too high."

"Oh, yeah, Leland, I seen that before, these little nozzles up there spray mist on the greens."

"Are you Leland DeWitt?" the man asked. "I'm Jim
Casey, I'm the produce manager. Randy Anderson said
you were on your way to see could you fix this."

"Good of Randy," Buck sniffed.

But Leland was already up a stepladder and poking
behind the fascia above the vegetables. He adjusted a
nozzle. Nothing. He tried the others. A boom of thunder
sounded again, and people who were watching from the
lettuce area moved back a little.

"Clear this area," Buck ordered Jim, who snapped to.
Buck yanked at Leland's pants leg. "Let me have a look
up there." He shoved the stepladder closer to the display
and started up.

"Whoa!" Leland shouted to Jim. "Listen, grab ahold
of him, he can't come up here!"

"Get on down outta there, Leland," Buck said.
"I'm comin' up." Leland stepped back on some zucchini and reached down. No stopping Buck, he should
have known that. Buck looked happier than he had in a
long time.

Buck twiddled the nozzles. "Hand me one of them
things, them plastic wire doohickeys," he ordered Jim. He
stripped the bag twisty down to its wire and poked at each
nozzle. "Okay, let her rip," he said. He got a resounding
clap of thunder but no rain.

"You go turn off the fuses, Leland," Buck shouted,
cupping his ears.

The store manager, a new guy in town, came out of the stockroom. "Can I help you?" he asked Buck, who was now squatting in the green bean tray.

"Not unless you know more'n I do about hydrodynamics."

"He's the manager," Jim said, a little nervously.

"I know that." Buck handed the manager a zucchini. "What's your name? Speak up! Rick? Okay, Rick, when I say 'tap' you tap that along this main pipe here. I gotta do some acoustic diagnostics. Leland, you man the controls." Buck clambered up on top, behind the fascia of price signs. "That won't hold you . . ." Rick shouted. "You gotta . . ."

"Do you wanna do this or will I?" Buck asked. "It'll hold. I'm real slender." He disappeared above, tsking occasionally. "Tap!" he said, finally.

Rick tapped. Buck's head shot up, and the whole fascia shook, sending a shower of price signs down into the celery hearts.

"What'd you want to do that for?" he cried, massaging his head. "I told you to wait until I said 'tap'." He shoved his upper denture back in.

"You said 'tap'," Rick said.

"I said 'trap'," Buck was invisible behind the fascia. "I were you, I'd shut off this thunder, it don't do your hearing any good, going off like that all day. What I said was the trap in this valve don't open. Now tap."

Rick tapped. There was a lurch in the system. "Aha!" Buck said, jiggling something. Mist shot out. Thunder clapped. Lightning flashed. The little crowd huddled near the salad croutons cheered.

The vegetable aisle went dark.

"Hell's bells, Leland, you were supposed to wait till I gave you the word to turn the power back on. Not supposed be any lightning. You blew the damn fuse. Nearly fried my behind." He climbed down and hobbled off to the fuse box. "Always the same old story," he groused. "If you want something done right you gotta do it yourself. Okay, Rick, you can let the customers back in, emergency's over."

"You gotta admire that technician," Rick told Jim later. "He's getting on but he knows his stuff."

On the way home, Buck seemed happy, but he looked drained. "I hope you were watching," he said, as Leland pulled into the driveway. "I can't always be around to get you out of fixes."

Chapter 9

Laurinda

Laurinda got a little thrill as she pictured Septus, masked, his surprisingly dainty feet in little bootees, with a girl dropping a tempting chocolate tidbit into his mouth. Or even a guy, maybe, she wasn't fussy. She'd do anything at this point to save her marriage.

Both of them were a little down, considering all that had gone on with Mickey, but Septus was worse now that he'd not only lost his job, but also put his back out flycasting for steelhead on Lake Erie. "Dead-drift nymphing" he called it, but she didn't care for the sound of that and covered her ears.

Septus spent a lot of time these days sitting on the toilet and plucking hairs out of his nose with a tweezers.

"You gotta get you a hobby," she'd scolded.

"This is it," he'd said.

She'd looked for a job, but it was a joke in this climate. The day they both went down to the unemployment office, they met dozens of guys from the factory, every one of them looking for work. Septus's claim went right through, but when she didn't get hers, she went back.

"Says here, when they looked into it, that a former boss, Mr. Zeke Anderson, states you were fired for misconduct. You wanna dispute that?"

"Course I do, Mary Ellen. You know he fired me for Mickey's misconduct."

Mary Ellen said she'd put it through again, with a nice little personal note. She'd been one of the people who'd said Mickey deserved a medal.

In the meantime, she intended to make some of the life changes she'd promised herself: every two weeks she took a dog from the dog pound and gave it a Schnauzer cut, no matter what it was. The pound people took its picture for the newspaper as the Dog of the Month and it was always adopted. Sometimes people were surprised when the dog grew out to be something else. But at least she was renewing her spirit and even starting to Make a Difference.

But Septus couldn't take his mind off Mickey. He became remote, a thing the magazines warned you against. Laurinda fought for her marriage: She gave him surprises for lunch, such as tuna fish sandwiches with pimentos, and one time she dyed his hard-boiled egg with fancy stripes, the way she saw on TV. But Septus didn't notice, or if he did, he didn't say anything, except for the time he said he didn't care all that much for tuna fish.

One day when she was passing the airport in North Vienna, she got a great idea for his birthday. She scooted back into the airport and found the manager. When Septus opened his birthday card, he found a certificate entitling him to 20 VIP pagings at the North Vienna airport.

Septus had never been in a plane in his life, and wasn't about to start now, not after all these crashes and such. Hell, he'd only been in the airport itself a couple times. "What's a VIP paging?" he asked.

"It's like when a plane lands from somewhere, say Pittsburgh, the manager will announce 'Will Mr. Septus McCardle please proceed to the First Class Lounge?'"

"But I'm not going to be on any plane from Pittsburgh," said Septus.

"Don't be silly. You're not going to be on a plane at all. You're not even going to be in the airport."

"Then what's the point?"

Nitpicking, always nitpicking. "The point is people getting off the plane will wonder who this important person is. Over the twenty times, thousands of people will hear it."

Laurinda had had to convince the airport manager, too. "First of all," he said, "it might be against the Federal Aviation Agency or Authority or whatchamacallit, or even the balloon people, who use the airport when things are quiet. Of course, that's a bit hush-hush: not s'posed to have other things in the air when planes might be flying.

So high and mighty, the FAA, they're getting so they think they own the air or something."

Laurinda agreed this was unfair, although she did like the idea of *somebody* keeping track of things up there.

"Second of all, we don't have a first class lounge. Or any lounge, matter of fact. We have a cubbyhole we keep the little bootees and masks and stuff they give to the folks in Business Class. "S'pose if we had to, we could put a chair in there. I could bring one from home. All the ones here is bolted down."

She liked this. Septus might perk up with a pert stewardess fussing around him but she went over and saw there was scarcely room for one person in the cubbyhole. Anyhow, she didn't actually need a lounge. "It's the honor of the thing that counts," she said to the manager. So they discussed the wording and all. They tried "Would Mr. Septus McCardle please report immediately to the First Class Lounge?"

"No," Laurinda said, "'Report' is no good. Sounds like you want him to come and clean it, or something. How about 'proceed?' And how about 'Dr.' Septus McCardle?"

"Is he a doctor?"

"No, but his momma always hoped he'd be one."

"Well, I don't know. Do you want it to be a Ph.D. or a medical doctor?"

"Medical doctor," Laurinda said.

"Oh, well, I think that would have to be extra," said the manager. So in the end, they just settled on the 20 pagings, excluding flights from New York City, and the manager would read it out himself. She made him rehearse it a few times, and gave him some tips, like having a smile in his voice. On Sundays, it was time and a half. So six days a week for three weeks at three dollars a time, and two Sundays at four dollars and fifty cents. Not cheap.

But now, Laurinda could see Septus had no interest in this, or in her, as far as she could tell. He went around moping for the rest of his big day, and turned in early.

She waited until it didn't look like she was after sex or anything, and then went to bed herself. Septus was still awake.

"I been thinkin'," he said in a tired voice. "You and me, we'll take a run on over to North Vienna on Sunday and sit in that First Class Lounge. Maybe have a few drinks and some peanuts. Be like it used to be."

But on Sunday, he went back to fishing, alone. Laurinda had the Easy Hamburger-Rice Casserole at Winkle's and turned in early.

Chapter 10

Laurinda

Making a Difference. Laurinda had so many ideas about it, her brain was nearly afloat. She should go back to school first, though, maybe even get her Ph.D. She could be Dr. Laurinda on WHAG radio. The idea had a couple drawbacks, of course. One, she didn't have a college degree; hadn't even finished high school because Reenie came along in her senior year.

Two, the drug problem. A few years ago, some addicts broke into old Dr. Sherman's house looking for drugs. Of course, being a Ph.D., she wouldn't have any, but your ordinary burglar wouldn't know that. What to do?

"You think too much," Septus said.

"Well, it works because I got an idea. I'll get some little letterheads printed up with my name on the top, but not our real phone number. I'll put the number of the police station!"

"Uh huh."

"So if they break in and threaten to tie me up, I could write them a fake prescription, and when Blumetti's drugstore called up about it, Mr. Blumetti would get the police station. Simple."

"Sure is."

"But," she added, "I'll wait until I'm nearly done with my Ph.D. before letting the police in on the idea, or they would maybe get on the radio and tell all real doctors to do it, and pretty soon it wouldn't be all that effective."

Septus looked exhausted, she hadn't noticed how worn he looked before.

This idea made her mind easier. Now all she had to do was finish high school, go on to Jim Bob Bagby Community College, and then get into a good grad school somewheres. She owed it not only to herself but to Septus; he'd brought in most of the money down the years, and her heart broke every time now when she saw him sitting at the kitchen table, cold coffee, cigarette out, just staring, dead-eyed.

"You got to go see Dr. Sherman," she told him.

"Laurinda, I don't have the money."

"We could . . ."

"And what's wrong with me can't be cured, anyhow."

So Laurinda just kept herself focused, centered, eye on the dream.

She was not a dummy. She'd had plenty of other good ideas in her time. The rope, for example. She kept a rope tied to the foot of hers and Septus's bed, because they slept upstairs. If there was ever to be a fire, the rope was knotted every few feet and they could climb down from the window, easy. Plenty of people who laughed at the idea would be laughing on the other side of their face if they got caught in a fire upstairs. She met Leland one day in the post office; he was an inventor, he was smart and would appreciate her idea, so she mentioned it.

However, according to Septus, who couldn't see the good in anything any more, the bed would be pulled through the fancy French doors she'd made him install, go over the little fake balcony, and whomp her as she lay on the ground gasping for air. He said you had to take gravity, the size of the bed, and even the size of Laurinda into account before you could tell whether it would work.

A few days later, she slept in late and woke up to find a note on the kitchen table, and Septus gone. A grocery list? Or maybe a note saying . . . But no, the note said:

L *m*. G> B *m*

Not Septus's writing. And a code of some sort, no two ways about it. She took it straight to Randy Anderson. After all, he was her late sister Sherry's husband, sort of the man of the family now that Septus was down with depression. Plus he was the mayor, and no police were situated in Hope And Glory itself; you had to ride over to North Vienna to find a policeman.

"Yep," Randy said. "It's a ransom note, definite. I can't put out an all-points alert, no police, but I can send it over to Chief Earl Arbogast for fingerprinting."

"A ransom note! Well, whoever wrote it is pretty stupid—we got absolutely no money right now. Last year's when they should have sent it, if they had any sense. People!"

Randy faxed it to Chief Arbogast.

"Looks like some kind of email address," the chief called back. They could hear computer keys clicking. "But I just tried it with a dot com and without. No luck. I'll keep on it though. Meantime, Laurinda, you keep the doors locked, hear me?"

Randy drove Laurinda home. "You don't worry," he told her. "We'll find him. Not too many people look like Septus. And we have that photo of him from the *Inquirer* we can use."

Septus was sitting on the back porch, gutting a fish. He looked a little less depressed, a little livelier now that his back had picked up. "Hey Randy," he said, and to Laurinda, "You missed Leland this morning," he said. "Dropped in before you were up to say hey, see how we're doing. Took him fishing with me." Laurinda threw her arms around him.

"They let you go!"

"No, I let some of them go," he said, gently pushing her away. "Not this one, though. What'd you think of Leland's formula?"

"Formula?" Randy asked.

"Yeah. About Laurinda's mass, gravity and the mass of the bed? He wrote it down on a note somewhere, it was here this morning."

Normally Laurinda would have kicked up over any suggestion that she had mass, but she was so relieved she let it pass. Anyhow, where was the balcony in that formula?

Randy slipped away.

Later, as she thought about those smart-aleck television chefs who could make supper out of three ingredients— hers were applesauce, baking soda and a can of corned beef—she knew something big had happened today, not to Septus, to her. How come her very first thought, when she found that note this morning, was that Septus might really be leaving her? Simple: she'd known it deep in her mind for months, like a canker sore in your cheek you know musta been there a long time but just all of a sudden you feel it.

Now, when she woke at night, she'd look over to make sure Septus's form was there. In the morning, if he was already gone fishing, she'd just check his part of the closet, which was always nearly empty anyway. He smiled a little more these days, and he touched her arm a few times, tentatively, when there was no real reason. Sometimes she caught him looking at her, almost studying her. She'd lost forty pounds since Mickey was gone; she couldn't eat, thinking about the awful food he must be getting. Someone told her the *Inquirer* had published a cute photo of her from behind, calling her Luscious Laurinda. She hoped Septus noticed; she was nearly petite now, as petite as a big-boned woman was likely to get.

She studied Septus, too. He still had those broad shoulders, well-shaped for such a thin man, and since he'd started getting his hair cut again and shaved off that awful beard, she could nearly see, if she squinted, the handsome, carefree young guy she'd married. Maybe this is the way it's supposed to go, she thought. You get older and you get comfortable together. The passion isn't there, but you got something else. Be grateful.

One night when she'd woke and couldn't get back to sleep again, she went down and made some hot milk. It was 4:30 a.m. by the stove clock. She carried the milk into the living room with a box of crackers and sat in the blue chair. Her eyes adjusted to the dark.

Septus was sitting across from her.

"I didn't hear you get up," she said.

"No."

"Are you okay?"

His face twisted. Was it a stroke? She could see he was trying to speak. He said something; she couldn't hear.

"What? Septus, what's wrong?"

"I want to leave." He bent his head. "It's not me, it's you. You're a beautiful woman, I don't say that often enough. But I can't keep up with you, you're like a comet or a one-man band, a I don't know what—maybe a one-man band tied to a comet."

None of that sounded too bad to Laurinda, especially the beautiful part. The rest made no sense. She was never a woman to sit down when something needed done.

"All this stress over Mickey, the reporters, picketing the prison, the freedom marches. And now, it's a Ph.D. I really want you to have a Ph.D., Laurinda, it's just that I can't keep up with you. I know I'm holding you back, and I'm ashamed, but there it is. I just want to live in a little cabin and fish."

"Cabin?"

"Yeah, somewhere I can catch largemouth bass, crappie, maybe a little muskie. Yeah, I haven't caught muskie in a good while. A forty-pounder—that's my dream."

Laurinda was speechless. Septus hated fish—or was it just canned tuna? When the sun came up, though, he packed up a few things, all plaid as far as she could tell, a fistful of socks and a couple old warm sweaters, and went off to live in a fishing shack up by Lake Erie.

Chapter 11

Leland

When the worst happened, Leland was over at the Job Center in Leetonia doing a mock job interview. "I'm Gerald Robertson and I'm interviewing you for a job at the municipal water facility," the tall mustached man told him.

"Howdya do, Gerald?" Leland said, shaking his hand.

"No," the man said, irritated. "I'm Bill Lavelle, I'm just interviewing you as Gerald. A stage name, if you like. Okay, a check: No toeless or backless shoes, sitting forward, no overwhelming perfume, fine, all good, but DON'T AVERT YOUR EYES, LOOK AT ME."

Leland looked at him. "Now," Bill said, "not a no-no, but you're wearing brown, and brown is still considered a questionable color for an interview. Navy is best."

"I don't . . ."

"NEGATIVE SOUND BITE," Bill shouted. "Never say 'I don't' in an interview. Wear navy for the next interview and get a hook, so the interviewer remembers you later, something different from all the other interviewees. A red tie, being born in Patagonia, anything memorable."

"Will a Leland DeWitt come to the front desk," a voice called over the address system.

Leland half-stood, looking at Bill.

"Have you sent a pee sample to a lab? Or a strand of hair for analysis?" Bill demanded. "I'm doing it for all my job interviews these days."

"Isn't this your job?" Leland asked, scraping his chair back.

"Nope, this is volunteer, to pass the time until I find a job. Now those hair samples, they can show drug use four, five months ago, so get clean first."

"Will Mr. Leland . . ." the announcement repeated.

Leland shook Bill's hand, promised to write a standard thank-you letter for the interview, and made his way to the front desk.

It was Leland's ma.

"Your dad told me you were going over there. I'm with him in the hospital, we came in an ambulance. They asked me did I want the siren on, it was $50 extra, and I can't afford it right now, I hope you think I did right, Leland."

"What's happened, Ma?"

"Well, I don't want to bring you back for nothin'," she said, "but I'm trying to get a milkshake into him now and his face is blue. He's got a bad rattle in his throat. Will I hold the phone to it, see what you think?"

"I'm comin' back right now, Ma. My truck's in for a new windshield, but there's a bus goes every hour from East Leetonia. I'll get the next one."

As he stood at the bus stop, an old boat-sized driverless car rolled slowly toward him. The window creaked down and a thin voice inside said, "Bus just left, and the other one's broke. Where you goin?"

"Hope And Glory, but I'm okay, thanks."

"Hop in. Me, too."

Leland looked around. If he asked Bridget to leave work and come over, it would take a couple more hours.

Leland got in.

A wizened little man about eighty was down behind the wheel. "John Lane," he said, jabbing his finger toward Leland. "Chicken Shit John." They rolled off at something under twenty miles an hour.

"You tell me if I give off a smell," the old man said. "I know a lotta people smell when they get old. I try to keep myself clean. I can still put my socks on standing up, too."

"No, sir, you don't smell a bit," said Leland, thinking how much older this man was than his dad, and here he was, driving around.

"I'm passing through Hope And Glory on my way to Zirconia, helping my daughter put up some chilla sauce and piccalilli. Well, I do it while she golfs. Only chance I get to see her. She's married to Dentist Brown over there, but he don't care for home-canned goods. I got two dozen

Mason jars in the trunk. What takes you to Hope And Glory?"

"Live there. My dad's bad in the hospital, I gotta get back over there."

"Who's your dad?"

"Buck DeWitt. Used to be in the boiler factory."

"Buck DeWitt? That's like saying Hank Aaron used to hang around the outfield. Buck is sick? You're who, Leland?"

"Yes, sir. Buck's got lung cancer."

Leland's neck pretty near snapped as the old man revved up, hitting close to 75 in under a minute. "I seen guys playing baseball on TV weren't as good as Buck. We all went down to Pittsburgh for the World Series in 1960. Pirates beat the Yankees 10–9? Bill Mazerowski hit the ball into left field at the bottom of the ninth? Well, Buck coulda done that."

Leland didn't like to think about that right now. "How'd you come by that name, outta curiosity?"

"Well, my dad was a Lane. My ma's side were Foleys and my dad was a Lane . . ."

"No, I mean the 'Chicken Shit.'"

"Makin' hooch. Used to ferment it in chicken shit. Ideal medium. Guy taught me that when I was on Guam. Most useful thing I ever learned."

"Guam? What were you doing there?"

"Marines. Don't want to brag, but I made myself a name out there."

"Chicken Shit?"

"Naw, did a little bit of marriage counseling in my spare time. Them Guamese men, they didn't know their ass from their elbow. Told them to try a little tenderness. Made all the difference. So they shared their fermenting secrets."

When they lurched to a teeth-rattling stop at the hospital, Mr. Lane told Leland to call him Chicken Shit and to tell Buck he'd come to see him when he got out, they'd slam down a few boilermakers at the El Dorado.

But Leland worried about what he'd say to his dad, himself. He never said anything deep to him and didn't want to embarrass him now. He decided he would see how it went.

He found someone else in the bed number his ma gave him, a big smiling guy in a smock. He looked in the rooms on both sides, but nothing. "Where's my dad?" Leland asked the man.

The man got a wary look. A nurse came by. "What room is Mr. DeWitt in?" he asked. She edged him out into the hallway and didn't say anything, just looked at him. Finally, she said, "I'm real sorry. He passed away this afternoon."

"Thank you," he said. What else was he supposed to say?

At his ma's, Bridget, his brother Ralph, his two sisters and Sylene were sitting around a table full of casseroles, with more arriving every few minutes. "We didn't want you to find out that way," his ma said. "Ralph waited at the hospital a long time but in the end he left a message at the front desk. You musta walked right on by."

"Then," Ralph said, "I thought you might do that and so I should I go way out to where Route 123 starts, you'd have to pass by there for the hospital, and maybe put up a sign. But then I thought no." Leland wondered what the sign would have said.

He eased himself down at the Formica table. Sylene produced a crooked cake from behind the casseroles and started singing "Happy Birthday" and they all joined in, crying. It was his birthday. He forgot. Forty-nine. Before bed, Bridget gave him some socks from her and Sylene.

Next morning, Leland was back over home first thing, but his ma had already been to the funeral home and back; she got a real nice coffin. Not the very best, she said, but good; sealed and waterproof, and two urns of roses for beside it, and a pillow of flowers from the grandchildren saying "To Poppa," and a couple bouquets.

"Ma, you don't buy all the flowers. Other people send them."

"Well," she said. "I'll tell you." She looked a little embarrassed but held her ground. "I was afraid he might not get many. He never mixed that much, just worked. I wanted there to be some there."

Leland went up to look for a shirt for his father for the funeral. He found his work pants and shirts folded in a drawer, and in another, his underwear and socks. In his "good" drawer, he found his dad's upper teeth, two cloth handkerchiefs, his wallet with a quarter in it, the watch he got when he retired, and a buffalo nickel. Three shirts hung in the closet, a white and two light blue, a couple ties, and a suit he wore when one of Leland's sisters got married. That was it. He took the suit and the white shirt.

At the funeral home, the rooms were jammed with flowers from other people. Leland never saw such a display. The room was filled with neighbors, relatives, the bishop, a congressman who had been accused of stealing 60,000 books from the Library of Congress and keeping them in his basement. Old Bert Whump was crying, didn't care who saw. Bert kept patting his ma's hands, saying, "Nora, Nora, he was a real good man. The best." Middle-aged guys Buck had taught to play baseball when they were kids. Women, too. Buck always said women were some of your best baseball players, long as they didn't try to throw a ball or catch or run. Guys he'd given a bed to when they were down on their luck, and a fellow he'd joined the AA with, even though Buck never took a drink. Kids he'd taken out of the detention home to go fishing, give them a little boost. A couple of nice foster kids that Leland was delighted to see again, all grown up, they flew in from Chicago for the funeral. Guys shoved up a seat as John Lane from Zirconia came in, to admiring whispers of "Here's C.S.!"

And Randy Anderson, sitting on a hard chair, shoulders slumped.

Three tiny old men in stiff bright blue suits waited just inside the door. Sylene saw them first. "I think those men worked with Granddad," she said. Leland went over.

"I'm Briggsy," said the one with glittery faded eyes, sticking out his hand. The bones moved like slipped gears, but Leland's hand felt like it got mashed.

"I'm Griff," said another. "And this here's JimBaker. JimBrown, he's laid up, but he said to say he's awful sorry. All of us worked with your dad before we retired."

Leland knew these names like he knew the names of giants or heroes of old. "Old JimBaker hid my lunch bucket yesterday and boy did I pull a good one on him;" "Griff got called home today . . . boy killed under a truck . . . ;" "They fired old Briggsy today; found some tools in his lunch bucket, it didn't matter they were his own and he brought them in to fix the lathe." Here they were, finally, angled like coat hangers, turkey-skin necks, twisting their hats.

"He always bragged how smart you are. He was real proud of you, Leland. He talked about you all the time."

Months later, Leland said to Sylene, who was painting eyeliner out to here, "Remember those three men at the funeral home?"

"Yeah," said Sylene, without asking which three.

"How did you know they worked with Granddad?"

"They seemed all broken, like Granddad." She blew upwards on her eyelashes.

The morning of the funeral, Leland thought of the day before him, all that had to be done, and no matter how you looked at it, wasn't no good going to come out of it. All that effort, and his dad was still going to be dead. His glance fell on the encyclopedia A to K belonging to his dad. Nobody ever touched it, and it was kept on a special little table he built for it. He stopped for a second. Well, it didn't belong to his dad now; anybody could come in and muss up the pages, or put a wet coffee cup on it. He felt a funny kind of thrill, first time he ever really thought about what it meant to be dead. Irrevocable.

The funeral was the sorriest thing Leland had been at in a long time. Dust beams floated across the yellow pews. The organist played with her shoes off and fell asleep during the eulogy. The pall covering the coffin was wrinkled and kept slipping off. His dad wasn't much of a churchgoer but every Sunday since they were married he gave Ma money they didn't have to put in the collection. Well, it didn't buy much of a funeral. Leland slumped a little.

He felt a hollow thunk on his right shoulder. Laurinda McCardle sat in the pew behind the family with a box of Kleenex, passing it up and down the row, and banging it on the shoulders of anyone in front who looked like they might be sobbing. Leland came to dread that thwack and tried to remember his posture and keep his mind off the fact they were burying his father. He had a shot at one of the hymns.

Buck's sister Virginia, down from Buffalo, was sitting next to Leland and had set up a kind of litany with the priest:

"Father, forgive the sins of Thy servant, John Paul . . ." the priest said. Leland's boy Ryan swallowed hard. He'd been named for Buck, but changed his name to Ryan when he figured out he was John Paul II, not John Paul Jr. Laurinda passed him a tissue.

"He *had* no sins," Virginia hissed. She was deeply anti-religious and had recently become a minister by mail for the hell of it.

"Father, forgive . . ."

"He was a *saint*," Virginia shouted. "A living *saint*."
The priest, a mild man, a cousin of Bridget's who had
offered to say the Mass, backed down. Later, in his sermon,
he mentioned, tentatively, that Buck was now blooming
as a flower in the Lord's bouquet. Virginia stayed quiet.

Finally, a reading. All through the service, Leland's
brother Ralph had been grunting instructions to Ronnie
Zweig, his old Jewish school buddy: "sit," "kneel," "up."
But Ronnie was the only one among them with any real
grasp of the New Testament, or the Old, for that matter,
and he had taken the time to choose the reading.

*Behold the hour cometh, yea is now come, that ye
shall be scattered and shall leave me alone. In the world
ye shall have tribulation but be of good cheer, for I have
overcome the world. John 16:32,33.*

That's it, thought Leland, but instead of giving him
good cheer, it just bore out what he had been thinking:
his dad's time over forever, that one encyclopedia the
only luxury item he owned, precious little to show for
his tribulations. Sure, he'd overcome the world, but lookit
how. Was this all that was in front of Leland too, year
after year gone, no job, a stretch even to send flowers to
his own father?

The ceremony limped to a close. Bert Whump led the
pallbearers, mismatched because Buck wasn't there to do
the geometry.

That night, Leland had that Dream. Even when he was
having it, he knew he had dreamed it many times before.

Somehow, his dad and ma and them had lost the new house on Route 123 and had to move back to the little one beside the scrap yard. It was an awful dream; they all kept trying to make the little house nice and cheer each other up, but it was even worse than before because now they could remember the shady lawn way out on Route 123, the porch swing, the peach tree.

He woke up, knowing it couldn't be true; Buck paid the new house off a long time ago, no chance of losing it. For the first time, he wondered if his dad ever had that dream, too.

Then, just as he was falling asleep again, he remembered that waking up wouldn't fix it any more. He could lose his *own* house, easy. Once again, he saw himself and Bridget and the kids in a shack, sticky little kids running around crying. He didn't know whose kids they were, but it was awful.

THE HOPE AND GLORY VINDICATOR

Volume 234 Issue 2   Hope And Glory, Ohio

Keep the Feedback coming!

In a happy development, readers love our craft hints so we decided to put a few right on the front page. Enjoy!

You also enjoy our page 2 craft hints so much we thought we'd put a couple right on the front page. Enjoy!

Making a simple candle holder out of a branch

A romantic gift for that certain someone! A beginner's special!

What you need: a circular saw, a mitre saw, a pizza box lid, a drill with a ¼ inch bit, an awl, a router, a glue gun, your leatherworking kit, decals, T-square, a grommet punch, masonry nails, 80 grit sandpaper and a yard of chenille. Remember those safety goggles! Begin by (cont'd on page 2)

New Grub At Winkle's!

Teriyakii Shark is just one of the dishes now available at Winkle's, along with Tartiflette Au Poulet. To add a nice twist, a Peruvian dish, there's Cuy, or guinea pig, roasted over a fire, with a nice dipping sauce.

First reviews have been mixed. Mayor Randy Anderson reported that guinea pig tastes almost like chicken. Later it emerged that the mayor had been eating Lomo de Saltado de Alpaca, which tastes like alpaca. Septus McCardle said phooey and brought his own homemade favorite, pickled pigs' feet (pieds de porc marinés).

Mrs. Laurinda McCardle said she preferred her own potato casserole topped with s'mores.

Divorce Granted

Mr. and Mrs. Septus McCardle have been granted a no fault divorce . Mrs. Laurinda McArdle was restored to her maiden name and received custody of the wolfhound Pixie.

Laurinda McCardle, who goes by her maiden name, has announced her engagement to Mayor Randy Anderson. The future bride's previous marriage ended in divorce. The groom was previously married to his fiancée's young sister, the late Sherry, who died four years ago. No date has been set for the wedding.

Brain Teaser!
Here's an odd fellow. The last president he voted for was
Kennedy. Doesn't like music but loves jazz—his favorite is
Dizzy Gillespie. He's a sensitive man—he prefers the poor to
the rich, but he likes tycoons and good businessmen. He hates
gardening, but he doesn't mind cutting grass. What's his story?

INSIDE THIS ISSUE

2 Pasta and Frosting Delites

3 Doilies for the Dying: a true
   story

3 Anderson wants rest of Dad
   back

4 Norway recovering from
   armadillo invasion

FOR SALE. PROM DRESS. CALL
SYLENE 330-1358

YARD WORK. McCARDLE 330-9554

WHATEVER. RYAN DEWIT

Chapter 12

Laurinda

"It's illegal," Juanetta, said, firing off a few practice shots at the Rifle Range. "He was married to your poor late sister."

"In some cultures like Africa," Laurinda bristled, "a widower is *entitled* to his dead wife's sister. It's called the levirate. Or the sororate, I forget which, but I better know by Friday for the test."

In the months since she and Septus had parted, Laurinda had got her high school equivalency in no time flat and was now studying anthropology at the Community College over in North Geneva. Already, she was feeling she was Making a Difference. She was a lot more sensitive to your Ethnics, now, for one thing.

"Well, here it's called incest," said Juanetta. "Sherry was your baby sister. Move aside, you're in the line of fire."

Laurinda ignored her. Sooner or later Juanetta would have to find out for herself her aim wasn't what it used to be, and Laurinda wasn't about to baby her. "No it ain't called incest, and anyhow, I can't help it. I love him to bits."

Laurinda was besotted. She had been on the City Council, what, three years now, and had wrangled with Randy at practically every meeting she'd attended. She'd only seen him as Sherry's husband, and later, as Sherry's forlorn widower. But when Septus was kidnapped, or nearly, Randy's cool head really bowled her over. That *Vindicator* thing about Randy cussing was ridiculous: anyone would cuss if they saw a wolfhound eating an innocent groundhog. Anyhow, after a visit from Laurinda and Juanetta, the judge postponed the jail time until Randy had finished his mayorship, but he warned Juanetta to carry her rifle concealed the next time she came to the courthouse.

The magic of it all was that Randy was crazy about her, too, although as a brother-in-law, he had never paid much attention to her. But with all that weight gone, she was nearly cute, like one of the country and western singers. She also wanted to be a mother to poor Skip.

"I wouldn't say motherhood is your strong suit," said Juanetta, thinking of Reenie, Teeny and Mickey, "although Don is okay." Privately, though, Juanetta thought it was the crop-dusting job that had saved him. "It's a good thing Skip's nearly eighteen and his disposition is already set."

Laurinda had gone out to the fishing cabin where Septus was living now, playing his old 45 collection, fixing his boat, writing to Mickey's warden. They agreed the song was ended, though the memory lingered on, and Septus said he wouldn't be happy unless she was happy, too, so she should follow her star. He intended to devote his time to the kids until at least one more of them came out normal. This could be a while. Okay, Don was going to be a professional man, but the rest, just thinking about them brought on hives.

"But I'll miss bed," Septus said.

"What?"

"Those soft old sheets. I love them, like clouds around your ears while you're sleeping."

You never really know anybody, Laurinda thought.

They got a quiet, peaceful divorce, and went out for some fried fish afterward. It was a real nice occasion. Afterward, she sent him the sheets.

Naturally she and Randy faced a few problems, only to be expected with second marriages. Randy said the one thing he wouldn't do was sign a paper promising to bring up any kids they might have as Catholics. Laurinda said neither one of them was Catholics so that was okay. Sure, her kids were, because it was Septus who was the Catholic, and it was her who had had to sign the paper bringing them up Catholic. Randy knew all four of her kids still thought the rosary beads was a necklace, and that clinched it in his mind: if Laurinda was that weak on religious knowledge, he would have to bring them up Catholic single-handedly, and he just was not equipped to do it. That's all there was to it, end of story. Laurinda thought Randy was masterful.

But maybe he really expected kids? Her oldest, Reenie, was thirty now. She doubted if she had the last egg left. Not that she was old. She kept herself up; nice highlights, Jergens morning and night, aerobics when she could remember, although she never had a minute to herself.

A second problem about the wedding was Laurinda couldn't dance. She tried once, out at Mosquito Lake with Septus years ago, and he'd liked to die laughing at her. She had heard somewheres recently, she couldn't remember who told her, that one party not being able to dance had led to a festering resentment in a marriage. Well, she sure didn't want that with Randy. The trouble was, no one in her family could dance, not even step one. Take Juanetta. She used to hit a bullseye at fifty yards no bother, but dancing just confused her. Also, Laurinda resented the idea that the woman had to go backwards and guess what the man was going to get up to next, just like in real life. But for Randy, she would make the sacrifice.

Juanetta said well, she would learn too, since Laurinda was getting married and they had a lot of dancing at these Polack weddings. Laurinda said who was she calling a Polack, although there was nothing wrong with your Polacks. Randy was of Scottish extraction, and was only having Slavic Yankovic play at the wedding because bagpipes got on people's nerves. They went off to the Arthur Murray Studio in East Liverpool.

Along about the foxtrot section of the course, Laurinda started not being able to leave the house. It got really bad in the Beaver Dam Shopping Mall one day when she was in Penney's looking for a lilac commode cover and surround. Suddenly, the lights were flashing at her and her knees turned to jelly. She got a knot in her stomach. She was going to throw up.

"I got a knot in my stomach and I'm gonna throw up," she said to Juanetta. "I got to get out of here."

"Oh, sweet Jesus. I told you to be careful. I told you you wasn't through with The Change yet."

Laurinda gave her a snippy look and bolted; after a few more incidents like that, she decided it was better to stay home, not go out at all. Randy came to call every evening and for a while he thought it was kinda cute and old-fashioned. But when he had his pants let out at the dry cleaners and Laurinda couldn't pick them up, it was a whole nother story. And when they tried to go for a walk, she was so tense she sank her nails into his arm and drew blood. Fortunately, she was still able to go over to the dog pound and take out a dog for trimming, like the old days. Only difference was now she couldn't get out of the car; the people at the pound had to hand a smallish dog in through the window and take it back the same way. Whatever they handed her, from a Pomerian to a Collie, it came back as a Schnauzer, but they were used to that.

Finally, she went to Dr. Sherman. It took two glasses of whiskey to get her there. He asked how many units she consumed a week, but Laurinda was Temperance, so in the end he told her she had probably caught agoraphobia. Dr. Sherman said you sometimes got that with The Change. Laurinda said she hadn't come down with The

Change yet, she wasn't near old enough. She figured it
was delayed stress over Mickey.

She tried one failed cure after another. Randy was
anxious to get married; this was the slow season for his
motel, and for mayor as well, and he wanted to have the
time to show his new bride a good time. He intended
to kill two birds with one stone, take Laurinda to New
Jersey for a honeymoon, and also look up some garbage
people, because he maybe had sort of an idea about how
to bring some new employment to Hope And Glory. And
since that moose radio interview, no one had come to him
yet saying save us, Mayor, save us, but they would, and
when they did, he wanted to be ready.

Reverend Wayman had expected to do the wedding,
Laurinda being a lifelong member of Muddy Branch Bible,
but after that little tiff about Catholics, they thought it
best not to start off their new life with another theological
hullabaloo. They said they'd go for non-sectarian. The
Sheriff could do a non-sectarian, so that was okay.

What was not okay was Randy's family. Most of the
Andersons didn't think of the Wilcoxes as people you'd
put the good dishes out for. They had finally reconciled
themselves to Sherry, particularly since she was dead, but a
divorced mother of a murderer, with one of her daughters,
Teeny, marrying a brother-in-law, and another, Reenie marrying the same idiot three times, no sirree. They wouldn't
come to the wedding, pure and simple. Susie couldn't; after
Zeke's death she'd gone to her sister over in New Nirvana
and now had a septic foot that the doctor didn't like.

"Pshaw," Randy said, which was one of the things Laurinda loved about him. She had seen "Pshaw" in books but had never really known anyone who said it. Anyhow, Laurinda didn't care about his relatives. Old Zeke had been a real piece of work, picked on Randy something awful, and as for those spoiled stepbrothers, one of them had bullied her and plenty others, even Leland and Ronnie Zweig. In Zeke's eyes, those boys could do no wrong. Didn't stop one of them having that huge fight with Zeke the night he died. Apparently, he wanted Randy's Twi-Lite motel on top of everything else he was going to inherit. Anyhow, it was okay by her if the Andersons stayed away for good.

Juanetta was getting edgy. She wanted to visit her sister Twyla in Ashtabula before all the Valentine's Day hubbub started up there. Her nerves were bad enough already, and since no one knew when Laurinda would be able to go out, if ever, it was hard to set a date. What Juanetta had noticed was if you sprang something on Laurinda, like saying we're going to East Palestine to take in a show, here, get in, she would. She explained this theory to Laurinda and they agreed Juanetta would set a wedding date, keep it secret from all but Randy and the Sheriff, and not let on to Laurinda until a couple hours before.

Anyone who plans a wedding knows a million and one questions have to be settled. Would Laurinda have to be married at the dog pound, or would she be able to make it to the county Sheriff's office? The Sheriff was told the whole story, and he said sure, if he was on duty the day of the wedding, whenever it might be, he could call the vows through the car window to Randy and Laurinda if need be; or, if they liked, they were welcome to come into his office. He seemed doubtful about the sanctity of doing it at the dog pound; also, he'd got a Schnauzer from there and was beginning to suspect it was part Bichon Frise.

Then the witnesses. Juanetta was one, but they couldn't ask a friend of Laurinda's or Randy's since they couldn't tell anyone the wedding date for fear it would get back to Laurinda. Juanetta had asked Bert Whump; he'd been good to her from the start, and he looked swell at ceremonies. But Bert was old-fashioned, a little like Juanetta, and said Randy and Laurinda shouldn't be getting married at all because of the connection. She said she had mentioned that in a vague way to Laurinda, who had thrown something about Africa back in her face. Bert said Africa or not, he sure hoped they weren't planning on kids; they could be monsters. Sometimes as people get older, Juanetta thought, they get funny notions; she didn't, herself, but that thing about monsters was a little far-fetched. Plenty of people marry an in-law. Anyhow, Laurinda was in The Change, she was sure of that.

Laurinda herself definitely did not want to involve outsiders because she didn't want anyone to know about her problem. She didn't want people thinking she was mental. So they couldn't get a witness, or guests, for that matter. The only possibility was one of Laurinda's kids; they would understand. Unfortunately, Reenie was up in Ashtabula with husband #one, two and three, expecting twins; Mickey was still down in Everton, and Don was just about set to do his crop dusting exams over in Altoona. He said he would come back in a shot, but Laurinda said no. Don was really her only hope for the next generation.

What about Teeny? Teeny had gone to Charlotte, North Carolina to show her friends and them back in Hope And Glory she could make it on her own in a big city. She was willing to come back, she said, but if she couldn't say she was coming to her mother's wedding, people might think she was crawling back home on her belly. Trouble was, she was; she had a little bit of culture shock. People in North Carolina weren't like people in Hope And Glory. She couldn't understand a word they said, and they were cold. "You hold out the hand of friendship to these people and they crap in it," Teeny complained. Also, life was too hectic there, all go all the time.

They could ask Septus, of course, but that would be in questionable taste.

In the end, Teeny agreed to come. Juanetta and Randy set a date.

So far, so good. Now the complications set in. It was ridiculous, but Juanetta had lost her driver's licence renewal the day she got it. She had run over Reverend Wayman's foot—he was the tester—on the way out of the testing station. He was hopping mad, and he tore the license up right in her face. But, of course Laurinda could still drive as long as she didn't have to get out of the car and as long as it was within in her comfort range, which was the vicinity of the dog pound. So Juanetta had to find flowers for a

bouquet and headdress, and a cake, with no transport but
Laurinda, since no one else was supposed to know. Still,
it would be a high-wire act, hiding all that stuff from her.

Laurinda and Juanetta set out the day before the wedding (of course, for Laurinda, it wasn't the day before the
wedding, it was just an ordinary day); Juanetta to get the
cake and flowers, and Laurinda to do a dog. Juanetta
found she was pretty limited in the choice of bakeries and
florists handy to the pound, and had to plan carefully.
Anyhow, it came off okay, and Juanetta was shoving the
cake in the trunk just as Laurinda got handed a pair of
beagle-type twins.

But that Teeny beat all. She had set out from Charlotte
and planned to be in Hope And Glory by four a.m. She
telephoned from the Ohio border about one a.m. She had
got as far as Marietta and couldn't face the humiliation of
coming home. Go ahead without her. About an hour later she
calls and says she isn't going to let this thing get the better of
her; she would sleep in the car awhile and get there around
noon. Her place was beside her mother; surely people could
see that, and Juanetta was to hold off till she got there.

Juanetta put the cake in the basement freezer and put
some aspirin in the flower water. She saw that on TV.

The next afternoon Teeny called to say after a good
rest she was on the road again and in fact had decided
to brazen it out in Hope And Glory. Juanetta should call
her old boss and see if her job was still there, and help
her find an apartment that afternoon. Juanetta said the
wedding was supposed to be in a few hours, and Teeny

said it was high time people stopped saying "the wedding this, the wedding that" and paid a little attention to *her*. Juanetta would have to go apartment hunting with her because all she had with her were shorts and it wouldn't look respectable to a landlord.

Laurinda was kind of mopey. She had sensed some tension and excitement that day at the pound, and was obviously expecting the wedding any day. She got into bed with a donut and some aromatherapy oils, and said she was going to beat this, she was going to get in touch with the goddess in her and lick it.

The next day, Juanetta got all set again, took the cake out of the freezer and hid it behind the old sewing machine in the basement. Teeny had arrived, and Juanetta had sweet-talked her old boss and found her an apartment. "When all this is over," Teeny announced, "I'm going to come home at night, turn on the TV, drink a Bud, and not do shit for no one."

On the wedding day, Juanetta planned to break the news quietly, fitting it naturally into a conversation. Laurinda was in a crabby mood, even though she had managed to get in touch with her goddess. Something from last night was bothering her: she never dreamed, she was too busy, but there was something about Crosby, Stills, Nash and Young, and it made her have second thoughts about Randy. It was a kind of omen.

"Who is this Crosby Stills?" Juanetta demanded.

Apparently, in the dream, or whatever, she and Randy were watching the noon television news, and the announcer said one of the group was killed in a crash. She and Randy spent the whole afternoon waiting for the six o'clock news to hear which one. She hoped it wasn't Stephen Stills, although she liked the others pretty good, too. The suspense was killing them.

"And then," said Laurinda, "I said to myself, 'Way mint! Who do you think is going to be writing the six o'clock news, anyhow? This is *your* dream. You already know which one it was, or you wouldn't be able to write the news. Why do you have to wait till six? Grow up.'"

"Ah huh," Juanetta said.

"Well, it really grated on me. Such a shock, and then wasting all that time worrying because Randy made me wait for the six o'clock news. He said he wanted to hear it officially."

Juanetta couldn't see any way to bring the conversation around to weddings in a natural way. "Laurinda," she said, "this is your wedding day."

"Well, okay," she said, but it was clear she was still worked up. After the wedding was out of the way she was going to make it clear to Randy she was planning on Making a Difference, and he'd better not get any notions about coming on all patriarchal.

At one forty-five they set out for the Sheriff's office above the fire station. Laurinda had one of Reenie's wedding dresses on. Teeny had her shorts. A few volunteer firemen were polishing the truck and they cheered. They went up, and Randy joined them. The Sheriff read out the ceremony. When they left the building, the firemen were gone out on a call, and Laurinda looked a little disappointed. They went back to Laurinda's, and she stood on the front porch for a while, but no one happened by, and eventually they all went in.

Laurinda kept her wedding dress on for the rest of the day. At one point she offered to ride over to the store to get some more ginger ale, but there was some down cellar. Teeny showed some video footage of North Carolina, and it was true, you really couldn't understand the first word. Laurinda moved in with Randy next day, and Juanetta went up to Twila's in Ashtabula. Ashtabula was a hectic place, almost bad as New York, some said, but Juanetta was too tired to care.

Chapter 13

Leland

"You need to let that rag alone," Leland said to Sylene, who was wiping out the china closet. "I don't think this is the day your mother dusts."

"But, she asked . . ."

"Just let it alone. Ryan, put that pot back. Did your mother say you could take that pot out?"

"I was just going to make myself some . . ."

"You better wait till she gets home."

Leland was out of work three months now. For the first few weeks he kept hoping the factory would re-open, call them all back, but now a lot of the machinery had been moved out. He saw his own lathe being loaded onto a truck one day when he was standing around the gates, and another day he thought he saw his old coffee cup in a dumpster.

That last day at the factory, he'd locked up the battered box of tools he and his dad collected over forty years. Every tool had his dad's initials or his own scratched or burned into it and the handles were worn to a deep shine, deeper and finer than any piece of furniture. The little drawers and compartments were filled with metals that made his mouth pucker with their sharp, oily blue smell. He brought them home and put them in the old root cellar in the basement.

Once, in the middle of the night, Ryan heard something, a burglar, he hoped, and crept down the cellar stairs armed with a window sash-weight. But it was Leland in the root cellar, going through the tools, hefting their weights and brushing off metal filings that stuck to their oil.

Ryan felt a little funny, almost jealous. It was almost like . . . well, suppose if Leland brought a new kid of his into the house, one he loved and hadn't mentioned before. Like that.

Bridget got a job, first time since they were married, working for Butch Winkle as the cook over at the Party-Pak. No benefits, and Butch couldn't promise it would last the way things were going.

Leland answered every ad in the papers in Hope And Glory, North Vienna and Cairo. Mostly he never heard back. Jim Price, who'd been looking for a guy to do duct cleaning, called to say Leland would have been great, but the duct business had gone kaput, ducts were at the bottom of peoples' lists when times were tough. He was closing down at the end of the week.

"Make yourself a CV," one guy who answered the phone for a janitor's job advised him. "Get yourself on Facebook."

He and his old workmate Dutch went to a Job Fair over in North Vienna. Young guys, slick dressers, full of pep, talked to them in a kind of rehearsed way. Talk to your mortgage company. Use your health benefits before they run out. But Leland's and Dutch's had run out the day the factory closed. Consider plastic surgery if you're older, one guy added, as he looked around at the mostly over-50 battered-looking factory crowd. Shorten your CV; most people's are too long and irrelevant.

"Yeah! You go, guy!" a new speaker said, patting the last one on the back. "And you gotta network. Expand your channels. Plaxo keeps it all organized. Develop a compelling storyline for your channel. Pick out just a few topics you want to emphasize and stick to them—try to show you're witty or expert. Get yourself out there on LinkedIn."

Leland signed up for unemployment.

"What's KinkedIn?" he asked Sylene. "You got that on your computer?"

"No!"

"I gotta get myself on Facebook or Doohickey or something to get a job," he said. "Time was, you'd go over to the school and ask if they needed a janitor."

"I feel like I'm caught in a Mix-Master," Sylene said to her best friend Danielle Arbogast one Saturday as they sat on the back steps plucking each other's eyebrows in

Audrey Hepburn shapes. "You should see me sneaking around the place, trying to get the housework done."

Danielle's eyes watered as Sylene removed a little forest from under her right brow. "Up till now I never saw you even wipe a dish," she said.

"I know," Sylene wailed. "And now, lookik, I should be in there ironing doilies and I'm not allowed."

When her dad first lost his job their only problem was what to do with him. Where were they supposed to put him during the day? After five o'clock he had his chair, or the garage, or his place at the kitchen table, but during the day, her mother needed to clean the living room or cut out a dress on the kitchen table, and when Ryan got home from school, he needed to practice his drums in the garage or his piano in the living room. Wherever, Leland sat right there, beating the time off-tempo. Helping.

He got nervous if Ryan opened a new box of garbage bags or Sylene hauled her sheets down to wash them. "Did she say you could open that?" he'd say, or "I don't think this is the day your mother washes." He didn't seem to understand what each of the rooms was *for*, either: one day when he'd pulled his back but was supposed to be watching a meatloaf he brought a velvet armchair into the kitchen and used the dog's bed as a back support; another day he took the microwave and the coffeemaker into the living room while he was watching the game. He pushed some of the good wedding glasses in the china closet aside so he could keep all the little Hoover brush attachments in one place.

"You and Ryan need to keep on top of your chores," Bridget said one night when she got home from a late shift and found the pickup's carburetor in the sink. She smelled like Sloppy Joes. Sylene didn't like to say that they weren't allowed to do much while she was gone.

When Sylene tried to explain that she and Ryan, or she, anyway, wanted to help with the house, Leland talked to her patiently, as if he was explaining something to a six-year-old. "We want to keep the place the way it was when your mother left. You know how particular she is. If she wanted us to fool with something, she would have said so."

When Bridget shuffled in at night, exhausted, he'd give her a cup of coffee while she made dinner. He was so happy to see her; Sylene told Ryan it was like a second honeymoon. Ryan told her not to turn his stomach.

"Now that I'm out of work," Leland said to Sylene one day when she was home with the flu, "I thought I'd be out of *work*. I thought I might be able to do a little reading, or fix Ma's gutters for her. Ha! Not a chance."

Sylene hadn't heard him use the words "out of work" before. It hurt her in an odd way, the same way it did when she noticed his fingernails were clean now, for the first time in her life.

She wandered around in her bathrobe with some hot tea.

"Your mother left me a frozen pan of meatloaf I gotta put in the oven at four," he said, writing it down on a piece of paper towel, "and she wants me to empty the washer."

He didn't ask about her flu; in fact, he seemed to pretend she wasn't there. She could tell he was afraid it was female trouble. This suited her; eventually he forgot about her for a while and she was able to watch him.

Four or five times that morning, maybe more, he looked in the ice box to make sure the pan was defrosting. He checked the pilot light on the oven. "I might as well go down cellar and read the gas meter while I'm at it," he muttered. Up again in no time, adjusting the temperature on the icebox, and a couple hours later when the lettuce was frozen solid, changing it back.

He set the rock-hard meatloaf out on the counter.

When she came into the kitchen next time to get more tea, he was flicking the stove burners on and off. ("Want to make sure that pilot light isn't gassing us all.") He had the cookbooks spread out on the counter.

"I'm looking up the temperature for the meatloaf—I can't find the note your mother taped on the pan. The book says 375. I'm sure she wrote 350. Where the heck is that note?" He went through the wastebasket.

"And what the heck is that racket? Sounds like the high school marching band."

"I think it's the washer," Sylene said.

"A real cacophony," he said. She thought it was nice he was back to his Word for the Day. He rushed down cellar again; the load was unbalanced.

"Come down here a minute," he called up to her, while she was fixing herself a hot water bottle. "If there's one thing that shows how this here country is going to hell, and what the clowns in Washington have got us into, it's this washer." He looked disgusted. Or satisfied, she couldn't really tell.

Back upstairs he called Bridget at work and dangled the receiver down the laundry chute so she could hear it. He saw some of Ryan's friends out in the back yard, and made them come in to listen. He called them all "Eddie." They all agreed instantly that materials and workmanship weren't what they used to be, and Ryan stomped upstairs to Sylene's room to tell her he was leaving home. One Eddie went up and told Ryan that they all had a lot of strange conversations these days now that their fathers were out of work. "Suck it up," he said, laughing, cuffing Ryan on the shoulder.

The meatloaf was burned black. Leland made Ryan come down and help him open all the windows. "Don't touch your mother's good drapes," he warned.

So the next few weeks, Sylene just sneaked around behind him fixing things up the best she could, and Bridget did some other things, like taking the washing over to her mother's.

One day when Sylene was on the school bus she'd seen something really awful. They were stopped at the traffic light by the boiler factory, and Leland was standing there, hands in his pockets, just looking at it, not moving.

"My dad's so smart, why can't someone see how smart he is and give him a job?" she'd said to Danielle, who was penciling in thicker eyebrows, using her reflection in the bus window.

"My dad's smart, too," Danielle said.

Okay, Sylene knew a lot of girls thought their fathers were smart, but she knew some of these fathers, Danielle's included, and yeah, they were nice and some were even fun, which Leland was not, but they were not smart.

"My dad knows a lot of big words," Sylene said. "and he can fix anything. He could fix our car or our washer, easy."

"Your washer's broken," Danielle said, which she knew because she was carrying Sylene's gym clothes home to wash.

"That's just because he wants to keep it the way it is as an example."

"Of what?"

"I forget of what, but he could fix it if he wanted to."

Danielle looked unconvinced, although even her own dad said Leland was the smartest man in town.

"And he can do horse problems," Sylene said. "Some girls' fathers can hardly do long division and yet they're making a lot of money."

"Yeah," said Danielle. "Some of the smartest people we know, like Sister Magdalen, don't make much money. And then just look how rich that Paula Shipsky's father is."

"Who has to have an IQ below zero." He wasn't even nice, either.

So that was what negative numbers meant, Sylene thought. If Paula Shipsky's father was just two points below zero, he wouldn't be all that stupid. But if he was 25 points below, which he probably was, he'd be way

more dumb. Why didn't they explain it that way? Come
to think of it, the same went for temperatures. Why do
teachers do all that messing with X's and Y's and people swimming up and down streams? Bring in her dad,
Paula Shipsky's father, and, say, her dog Arthur Leroy,
and stand them all side by side. Students would grasp the
idea in no time flat.

Sylene and Danielle didn't like Paula Shipsky very much.

"Talkin' about her sex life on Swap Shop that time,"
Danielle said.

"And prancin' around at the prom in that peach chiffon
dress, yards and yards of it that she got in exchange for
an electrolysis kit . . ."

"That she shoulda kept." Danielle also knew, but didn't
say, that she'd seen Paula snickering at Sylene's dress.
Danielle and her mom, Kimi Lynn, had helped her pick
that dress out at Lerner's.

"Well, *my* dress was nice. Skip really liked it," Sylene
said.

She didn't mind not having a lot of money. Danielle
wasn't much better off than she was, and anyhow, nobody
in town was *that* rich except a few of the Andersons, something to do with Skip's dead granddad, Zeke, and garbage.
Sylene remembered when she was little, Leland painted
her old toys for Christmas. He and Bridget thought, still
think, she was too young to know the difference. But money
didn't matter; the other kids liked to come to her house
because there was always something interesting going on,
like the time Leland installed motion-activated sprinklers

on the roof of the dog house because Arthur Leroy was awful nervous of raccoons. Nobody ever went to Paula Shipsky's house, or to Skip Anderson's, either. In Skip's case it was just because people were afraid they might have to converse with Mr. Anderson. That was another father they could bring in the day they did negative numbers, and yet he made pretty good money. Thank God Skip was smarter than Mr. Anderson. Skip was completely different, more like Sylene herself, a sort of soulmate.

And what was really great about her dad was not only could he answer anything, he didn't look at her like she was crazy, the way Bridget did. She remembered the day she asked Bridget the simplest question.

"Is the Pope Catholic?"

Bridget put down the iron on the ironing board so hard it almost collapsed.

"How old are you, anyhow?" she demanded.

Okay, by this time she was thirteen but you could see how she would wonder. In her *Catholic Exponent*, naturally they wrote all the time about the Pope deploring; "Pope Deplores Poverty" or "Pope Deplores Crime," but she also saw that the *Hope And Glory Vindicator* would write "Pope Deplores Stress" or suchlike.

"Why would they say "Pope" if he isn't everybody's Pope?"

The iron hissed. Or Bridget did. Something did, anyhow.

"Do they say 'The Queen' in the paper when they mean the Queen of England?" No, they did not. She figured she had Bridget there.

"I don't know why your dad works his fingers to the bone to pay for Catholic school if this is what we get."

But Leland, he understood a person might like to ask a question without getting their head took off. She'd been asking him about the horse problem for three years now, and each time he'd explain it. It was nice; after they gave up each time, they'd just sit and talk. Now that he was out of work, she'd bring the problem to him more often, and sometimes he'd talk about how he and his own dad worked side by side in the boiler factory for years, and the good times they had.

But she hoped he would be happy again sometime soon. She remembered one time he must have been happy. She was lying in the shade in the side yard near the cellar window, playing with Granddad's's cat. Her dad was banging around in the cellar most of the day, working on the furnace. She thought maybe he'd finished, because it got so quiet down there. But no, there he was, with the furnace front still off, all by himself, his arms stuck out, waltzing, humming a little song. She remembered that song, Little Sir something. Little Sir Echo; her granddad Buck used to sing it to her all the time when she was a baby. Leland wasn't much of a hummer, but he was a good dancer, for a man so bulky. Not fat. She pretended she hadn't seen, but it was nice.

The days passed, no job for Leland, no prospects, three reminders from the mortgage company, and now, this morning, a new blow.

"Don't move," he said to Ryan. Ryan had no intention of moving, except maybe to pass out with boredom. "Just stand there." Ryan stood.

His own boy, and not one iota of sense about how to repair an automobile.

They needed two vehicles now, with Bridget working and him looking for work, but the carburetor went in the pickup a few days ago, and he was still looking at it. And after he took Bridget to work for the 6:30 shift yesterday, her Ford started to kick up, too.

He could fix most cars, but he couldn't figure out what was wrong.

"Hear that 'shmweeeeeee' noise?" he asked Sylene and Danielle when he drove them to a dance, but they hadn't heard any shmweeeeeee.

What the devil could it be; he never heard anything like it. It wasn't rod knock, nothing like that, a whistle, sort of, but not exactly. "Shmweeeee." It was driving him crazy.

He made Ryan take the day off school to help. Leland believed with all his heart in education; if you didn't know something, you always thought it was because you didn't go to college, but these days over at Chester Arthur High they were teaching things like French Toast and Feelings and how most of your great figures in history had been perverts and such, so he thought a day one way or the other wouldn't hurt Ryan's chance of getting into college. If they could ever pay for it. But right now, he might as well learn something from his old man. Hands-on experience would do him some good. They went out to the garage.

"Don't touch them tools," Leland said. Ryan put down a screwdriver. "Don't touch a thing. Stand over there, outta my way."

They worked together all morning, Leland adjusting the engine timing and the idle speed, pouring top cleaner down the carburetor, cleaning the battery posts while he was at it. He took off the wheels. He checked the differential. Ryan leaned against an old bedstead. Inscrutable, that was the exact word for him. Inscrutable ennui. Week 12 of the correspondence course, and it came in handy around Ryan.

Leland took the car for a spin but the noise was still there and he was irritated when he came back and Ryan was gone. He went into the house and complained to Bridget. Ryan re-appeared.

"Stand over there," Leland said.

The feeler gauge slipped into the works and he cut his hand fishing it out. He dropped the oil pan to get at the main bearings. He checked the universal joint and repacked the wheel bearings. You name it: oil pump, rocker arms, carburetor float, belts, he looked at everything.

Just around dark, the car was basically stripped down and reassembled. Ryan looked bored and sighed a lot. (Years later, Ryan was proud to be able to do the same thing for his own boy, although not as well, of course, because Leland was a genius, Ryan knew that much by then.)

This time Leland took Ryan with him for the spin, more to keep an eye on him than anything else because it was now obvious he was irremediable, mechanically. A little lazy, too, thought Leland. He hadn't done a damn thing all day long.

"Hell!" Leland shouted as they drove out Rt. 123, past Randy Anderson's Twi-Lite motel. "It's still there."

"I was you," said Ryan, "I'd roll that back window up tighter. You got an awful whistle coming in there."

Some days, Leland stayed up until Bridget went off to work, and at 7 a.m. he'd go down to the El Dorado to meet the few guys coming off the night shift at the factory, Wilkie and Al Kemp and them, the ones who were finishing off the last orders in the factory. Soon they'd be like him, trying to figure out what the hell a resume was. That first day he went in, he stopped at the far end of the bar; it sounded like they were making fun of him or talking about him, or something.

"There's this guy, see, he goes into a bar, and he don't have enough money for a beer, so he gives the bartender what he has and he says to him, he says . . ."

Leland felt sick. Maybe he'd just pretend he'd come in to get some cigarettes out of the machine at the door and go. The voice droned on, and someone snickered.

". . . so finally, the guy says, 'No, you owe me such and such an amount back.' So, Wilkie, how much did the bartender owe him?"

"Shit, I don't know," said Wilkie. "That's algebra or something."

Leland waited a little bit, but he really couldn't help himself. "Fourteen cents," he called down to them.

"Hey, Leland!" Al called out. "Hey, Einstein, sittin' up there in the dark. No fair, this stuff's kid's play to you. Park your butt down here, buddy. How the hell ya doin'? How's tricks? I heard somewheres that Sylene got herself a horse."

The guys would also talk about how old Murph or Jonesy was doing, they were still hanging on in the day shift, and how the Whoop and Holler, one of Leland's old machines, was doing, too and whether his drill press was acting up. Leland knew exactly how to fix that drill press, but no one was asking him to. And sometimes the guys would try to buy him a drink and he couldn't buy one back, so he stopped going.

Then almost no one went into the El Dorado because the whole factory shut down and those last few guys were gone, too. Old Bert Whump dropped in sometimes because he had the money, and he also had Mrs. Bert waiting at home. And fat cats like Randy Anderson went in once in a while to slap people on the back and tell them things would pick up, but who the hell wanted to drink with Randy Anderson? Even a chimpanzee wouldn't wreck a snowplow three, four times a winter. Bert was okay; he was a real nice guy, real interested in everything Leland did, but still, Leland was embarrassed that he couldn't buy him a drink.

A few of the latest firees came over to the house one Wednesday afternoon. Leland made them coffee and explained LinkedIn when Murph asked, and then they all sat for a while.

Winkle's Party-Pak and Live Bait

B ert Whump watched Bridget DeWitt cleaning up behind the jumbo bloodworms. She looked real tired. He was poking at some fried mush and maple syrup.

"How's Leland these days?" Bert asked her.

"Oh, fair, you know, it's hard for a guy like Leland to be outta work. Hard for anybody, I guess. And not getting any jobs; everybody's looking. But he does some fishing with Septus. I get them the jumbo night crawlers half price."

"Well, maybe he got time to do a little remodeling for me? I need some stuff done, urgent, and my back ain't what it was."

"What do you need?" asked Bridget. "Your house is already swell."

"Well, I thought maybe I'd, ah, well . . . sure, there's lots of stuff."

"You don't really need anything done, do you?" Bridget laughed.

"I *do*," said Bert, indignant. "I need one a them porches you put in the middle of your back yard." He raised his eyebrows and jabbed a finger at Bridget. "*And*, I thought I might surprise the missus with a sump pump. Water in the basement's her worst fear. Not that we ever had any. Yet," he said, knocking on the Formica.

Randy came in, and plumped down next to Bert.

"Who *is* this guy they're taking about in *The Vindicator*, do you think? The one that likes the poor? I like the poor, come to that," Randy said. "How come he don't vote for president? I wonder if he voted for me for mayor?"

"Nope," said Bert.

"You know him, huh?" Randy asked.

"Nope."

"Oh, so you just think he wouldn't vote for Randy Anderson, no matter what?"

"Nope," said Bert. "He wouldn't vote for Mickey McCardle or Dwight Wayman, either. *Or* Earl Arbogast, come to that."

"Well, phooey," said Randy. "Is anybody good enough for him?"

Bert thought for a second. "Yep," he said, "Matterafact there is. Juanetta."

"Juanetta? Is he crazy, or what? Juanetta's armed, half the time. Is he a gun nut?"

"Nah. Likes six-shooters, though," said Bert, fishing a long fellow out of the night crawlers.

Six-shooters. It was the Lone Ranger, thought Randy. Obviously Bert didn't know he knew the Lone Ranger personally. That the Lone Ranger had taken the trouble to turn his life around. *Acourse* the Lone Ranger would vote for him.

"Did I ever tell you how I wouldn't be where I am today without the Lone Ranger?" Randy asked.

Chapter 14

Leland

Trothless. Friday's word, and he had learned it in the nick of time. It described Bridget exactly. Her and her inamorato. No job, and pretty soon he'd have no house and no wife. All he'd have would be his dad's encyclopedia.

He'd been sitting in his pickup with his dictionary on Christmas Eve waiting for William F. Buckley to come on a talk show. He couldn't go home; they were blacktopping his driveway, so he had no place to park. He had given it—the blacktopping—to Bridget as a surprise Christmas present. It wouldn't be that much of a surprise now, because the Party-Pak closed early and she was blocked in the house.

He had got a coupon for it from a flyer, so it only cost $39.95, and they said he could pay it off over time. Bridget had been ashamed of the driveway, it was gray and cracked and made the house look bad. This flyer seemed like a good idea, and anyway, he had no money for anything else except little things for the kids.

Bridget usually gave him new steel-toed work shoes for Christmas, but since he was out of work, he told her not to bother getting him anything.

He didn't know what he was going to do. He had put up a couple signs on telephone poles: "Gutters Cleaned—362–1358" and "Repairs." Maybe that'd get something; nobody replied to the ad in *The Vindicator*. When he got the new carburetor in the pickup, he was going to put up "Light Hauling" as well. Trouble was, everyone in town was doing it. Besides fixing the city snowplow four times in one month, he'd had exactly one job, roofing Bert's shed. He built a new cellar trap door for Ronnie Zweig's ma over on Garfield Street and it came out real good, invented a nice remote control for it and all, but he wouldn't think of taking money from a nice old lady like Mrs. Z, let her yell all she wanted, she even tried to stuff it down his pants. Since he was over there, he helped Angelo next door to finish his basement. Couldn't take money from him, neither, he was as bad off as Leland. He drew up some house plans for Angelo's sister while he was there, and Ronnie Zweig's kid asked if he could teach him calculus so's he could understand it, his teacher sure couldn't. Amazing how that stuff comes back to you.

Well, between one thing and another, he just moved from house to house on Garfield Street, putting in a furnace, doing some roto-rooting, and painting and such. They were all set up over there, now, nice and snug for next winter. He would have to get some paid work, soon, though, and then he was going to do Angelo's roof for him or he'd be lookin' at the sky. Bert had asked him to give him a hand putting up a gazebo, and he'd start in a couple days. Be a little something comin' in, anyhow.

But right now, Leland was trying to figure out what had gone wrong in his life. Seemed like you were a boy one day, all full of ideas, and then things just started closing in. His own dad getting hurt at the boiler factory when Leland was in tenth grade. His ma, she went out to work cleaning nights at the boiler factory office, and his dad felt terrible, you could tell. Leland was more than glad to go to work and help out until his dad was on his feet again but that was the end of school. When he and Bridget got married, he paid for a correspondence course in engineering but he was too worn out after work each night to do much, and after a few years, Arthur Leroy's mother ate a couple books. And now lookit, no job, God knows what going on with Sylene, and now Bridget having an affair.

About nine pm, he was able to pull the pickup onto the end of the driveway. It looked better, all right, but when he got in the house, Bridget was furious. She didn't have any warning, she said. She could have parked next door and been able to get out; instead she'd parked the car behind the house to load his mother's turkey roaster, and by the time she saw what was happening, it was too late. She'd been trapped all day, just when she had last-minute shopping. She had run out of wrapping paper. The turkey had no giblets, and the stores were closed now. What about the gravy? What about his own mother, who was waiting on the turkey roaster to cook her own bird? Was Leland going crazy, or what? He should get ready for Midnight Mass, which started at 9. They'd be back by 10:30 and she would run the roaster over. The kids had walked to the earlier Midnight Mass.

When Leland and Bridget came back, Sylene was finishing a gold lamé tie for Leland that had already flunked as a Home Economics assignment. She knew something had happened: Bridget began banging the cupboard doors even before she took off her hat.

"He never has a good word to say about anyone," she snapped.

"I can have an opinion, same as anybody else," said Leland. "All I said was 'All they ever think about is money' is all. If it ain't the missions, it's the roof or the football team or paving the parking lot or school uniforms or I don't know what all. They should be talkin' about doing unto others and such, 'specially on Christmas." He could nearly hear his dad talking, he sounded just like him.

Bridget never liked to hear this. She believed the priests were there to guide us through the fine print of the Church's regulations, not to be going on about doing unto others. Her ma once dragged her to the front of the church and got a priest to say whether Bridget could go to Communion after she swallowed fluff off her blanket during the night. That's what they were there for. Those churches that went on so much about doing unto others, the next thing you found one of their ministers up in court for doing something unto an animal. One fellow was caught interfering with a chicken.

"Who are YOU to be questioning the priest?" Bridget snapped at Leland.

Sylene could see this was not going to blow over. Usually, the worst thing that happened was a temporary chill; then, after a while Leland would go into the kitchen rubbing his hands and saying, "Hmm. What's cooking?" even when nothing was. This time he took the car keys from on top of the icebox and slammed out. Bridget ran upstairs.

Arthur Leroy jumped into the pickup with Leland. He was a morose looking dog, usually quiet, but he seemed thrilled to be out alone with Leland at this hour and kept jumping from the front seat to the back. "Whoa, boy, you're happy to be with your old man, aren't you?" Arthur Leroy jumped into his lap and leaped up, licking Leland's face over and over. You knew where you were with a dog, thought Leland. Faithful. And when you gave him a name, he was content to leave it be. "Ryan," huh.

Leland didn't know where he could go; everything was closed. Would the Croatian Club over in Bessemer be open at this hour on Christmas Eve? He'd gone there a couple times with Johnny Novak from work, but he wasn't really familiar with the habits of the Croatian people, and it was thirty miles away. One thing was sure: wherever he went, he wasn't going to blow all his money on drink. Too many guys were doing that already. He was still the main support of this family, at least until his money ran out. He would take some of it out of his wallet and lock the rest in the glove compartment. He took out six dollars and put the nineteen away.

When the little light in the glove compartment went on, he saw Arthur Leroy had walked in the driveway tar and spread it all over the car and him, too. The upholstery was filthy. His shirt was black. His crotch was the worst of all.

He backed out slowly. He was not normally one to feel sorry for himself, but here he was, a man with a wife who didn't love him, no job, six dollars in his pocket, his front covered in tar, maybe his daughter in trouble, running away from home to the Croatian Club in Bessemer at eleven pm on Christmas Eve. Did he even have any clean work pants in the trunk?

Sylene caught up with him as just as he was starting down the road. "Where're you goin', Dad?"

"To the Croatian Club," Leland said. "They always have a big do." He was a Class B member of the Club. Novak told him Non-Croatians had to be Class B members, except Bert Whump, who for some reason was made an honorary Croatian and had Class A privileges. The Class A members had right of way at the toilet door, going in or out, didn't matter. No one liked to lord it over anyone else, so in fact the Class A members always stood back. The Club had a Formica bar and two billiard tables.

"Come back in," Sylene said. "She didn't mean anything."

"Did you hear her? She's been talking to me that way for a while. I have an ego, too, you know."

Sylene was stricken. "Of course you don't. Who ever said a thing like that to you? You don't pay any attention to them."

Leland paused a moment. "Your mother is no good. Why," he waved his hands, "I've got more morals in my little finger than in my whole . . ." He stopped a minute. "Anyhow. She's been carryin' on. Right in front of me. I'm outta work, and here's her rollin' up her nose at me. She flirts all the time."

Well, Sylene, thought, if this don't beat all. She couldn't even imagine anything you could say that had her mother and "flirts" in it together. And normally, Leland was so quiet; he reminded her a lot of Arthur Leroy, and she loved Arthur Leroy to bits. He just went about his business, not a peep out of him.

"Yep," Leland said. "She got no control over herself anymore. Everybody's talking about it. She's fooling around with a guy out at the El Dorado. Stanley."

"Stanley?" Sylene yelped. Stanley was a corner short of a square, a neat, harmless fellow who stood at attention when they played the national anthem on television. He once asked Sylene why puppies didn't have belly buttons. Sylene would have liked to know that herself. She had turned Arthur Leroy upside down, but nothing. He, Stanley, had "bad days" sometimes when he thought he was leaning to the left, so he leaned to the right and felt perpendicular.

Leland's eyebrows were nearly up in his hair. "I'll tell you. I go in there Thursday morning when the guys were coming off night shift and first thing I see is a guy nudge another guy. I heard them laughing and talking behind my back."

Sylene knew for a fact Leland couldn't hear a thing behind his back after his years in the boiler factory. "Well, maybe they were talking about something else?"

"No sirree. They were talking about her. Whenever your mother and I go into the El Dorado, Stanley gives her a big wave and says 'Hi, Bridget, how's my girl?' Sometimes she invites him to sit in our booth. Right in front of me."

"But, Dad," said Sylene, "She's that way with everyone. Stanley's like a little kid. She wouldn't want him left out."

"What about me?" Leland asked, for the first time Sylene could ever remember. They sat for a minute.

"Hold on," Leland said. "Wait till you hear this. We went dancing with Septus and Laurinda out to Mosquito Lake and when they got up to dance, I said to your mother, I said, 'You want to dance?' and she says 'No.' And when Septus and Laurinda came back, Laurinda says 'How come you're not dancing, Bridget?' and she says, *she says*, 'Nobody asked me.'"

Leland folded his arms. He had a look of bitter satisfaction.

Sylene was lost here. Septus McCardle *dancing*? And Leland rarely left the house except to go to work and to do odds and ends for neighbors. All this talk of drinks with Bridget at the El Dorado; it had to be no more than two times, maybe three in all. And dancing?

"When was this, Dad?"

"The August before we got married."

Sylene figured this had to be eighteen, nineteen years, at least. "Come inside and we'll talk in there. It's freezing. It's after midnight."

"She won't talk to me."

"She will. I'll get her downstairs. Change your pants, though."

"I'm not coming down," Bridget said. "I've had it. I don't mind him out of work, but he's driving me crazy. I think he's watching them soap operas in the afternoon, going on all the time about the meaning of life, and me up to my elbows in baloney, making you kids' lunches at six a.m."

"You've got to come down," Sylene said. "He says he's running away from home. Just come down and talk to him for a minute. Say something nice. His feelings got hurt. He thinks he's got an ego."

"Didn't get it from me," Bridget snapped. She came down and sat at the kitchen table, whacking the newspaper into shape. Leland sat alone in the living room, waiting to have something nice said to him. "Please say something to him," Sylene begged.

"All right, all right. But I'm taking the Deaths with me." She picked up the obituary page she'd been reading.

A minute later she was back. "He doesn't want to talk. Didn't even answer me."

"What did you say?"

"I said, 'Does anyone want a sandwich?'"

Sylene and the boys gave Leland his Christmas presents and he sat on the sofa, with half-opened sock packages, pretending to be interested. For the first time, he spent the night on the sofa, on top of crushed paper and the battered gold lame tie. Ryan and Sylene took turns sitting halfway down the stairs, and later Ryan quietly took the bolt out of Leland's rifle.

Bridget came down in the morning, looking wan. She snatched up her pocketbook and said she was going to see her sister. "I'm going with you," Leland said. She didn't seem to pay any attention, and Leland had to trot to keep up with her.

Sylene never did find out what happened. When they got back, Leland was smiling and rubbing his hands together. "Put her there," he said to Ryan, shaking his hand heartily. "I'll have to put on this fancy tie of Sylene's." When he sat down at the head of the Christmas dinner table, hair combed with water, face shining, it almost looked like he was going to say grace. Instead, he surveyed the table and said, in wonderment. "Wow! Napkins."

That evening, they were sitting at the kitchen table drinking coffee while the kids played cards in the dining room with Bridget's mother, who wondered how Sylene had learned to shuffle like that.

"There's a thing I been meaning to ask you," Leland said to Bridget. "How come you said to Laurinda that time that nobody asked you to dance?"

"Leland," she said, without a pause, "I don't know how to dance."

He paused a bit. "I never thought of that."

That night, he dreamed he said to Sylene, "Today I buried a cemetery and planted a rose garden." When he woke up, he decided to keep on planting, maybe something would come up. Fecund.

Chapter 15

Randy

A fter this, no one in Hope And Glory would dream of snickering at him. He'd heard the jokes, all right, and the editorial in *The Vindicator* even made some mention of an IQ in the low red numbers, etc., etc.

"What kind of a way is that to talk? What about your handicapped who really do have IQs in the red numbers? How do they feel when they open their newspaper and read something like that?" he had asked Laurinda at the time. He might mention that at the next City Council meeting.

Forget about that, though, because the big news was that Randy was finally moving ahead on his brilliant garbage plan.

They'd gone on their honeymoon to New Jersey and had a swell time. Laurinda was a swell woman; completely different from her younger sister Sherry, but swell. They booked into Patel's Super 8 Motel in Perth Amboy and one of the first things Sherry—what was he saying, Laurinda—-wanted to do was go to the mall there. She was looking for a lilac commode cover and surround. Nearly got there, too, before she got a pain in her stomach and they had to come back. But he was workin' on it. She'd be fine. She'd made the trip all the way to New Jersey and she'd be fine. Some kinda goddess helping her. He hoped she wasn't going Catholic on him; they were fine people, Catholics, but their religion was awful complicated, using a thermometer during their sex and all, and he just wasn't up to it, not with this garbage business occupying him full time.

So he was sorta free, with Laurinda not able to go out and all. First thing he did, of course, was to contact the motel management; it was only professional courtesy since he owned a motel himself. Off-duty pilots did the same thing; if they were flying as a passenger, they went straight up to the cockpit and introduced themselves. Sometimes they even got to fly for a bit, especially if the pilot or co-pilot died. Randy didn't expect to run the motel for a bit; hell, he didn't really even want to, he was on his honeymoon. But he introduced himself to Mr. Patel and gave him some complimentary shampoos and body lotion. He wondered if he should have waited until the real boss showed up, but hell, he had bigger things to think about now.

He got busy on the phone and contacted a name he'd been given, the one they called The Garbage King.

Woowhee, big deal, he thought when he first heard that, but hey, the guy really was impressive. He explained to Randy how advantageous it was for a town to become a sanitary hub, *the* place where other towns transported their garbage. A premier destination. Trucks, ocean-going barges, sometimes even trains, all full of garbage, moving in and out of Hope And Glory, the place humming with activity, no more tears over the boiler factory. No more cracks about snowplows, whips, what have you. Randy particularly liked the idea of ocean-going barges, sort of romantic. Maybe he and Laurinda could go on one; maybe they'd celebrate when she got over this problem. Sounded to him like The Change, but he didn't like to say anything, Laurinda seemed touchy about it. Too bad in a way; he'd always wanted a big family. Well, Skip would make him a grandpa someday, he'd love lots of little grandkids running around.

The Garbage King had important connections in the waste world, and said he would talk to a first-class big shot. Randy should call him in a couple days.

When Randy got back, Laurinda was buffing her nails. She had found these new lifetime nail files in the motel gift shop and bought a few, in case. They went down to a romantic booth in the bar and he outlined his plan. He built a model on the table: the matchbooks were vehicles carrying garbage, and the ashtray was the quality garbage facility. The matchbooks with the matches torn out were the empty vehicles returning from the dump. The tore-out matches were the citizens. As mayor, he couldn't forget

the citizens, no sirree, and there they were, lined up. He
thought they might be watching a parade, maybe even a
parade in his honor.

He was whizzing the matchbooks around the table,
making truck or train noises as applicable, when the
waitress came to take their order. He ordered a good old
American beer; Laurinda said her stomach was still queasy,
and ordered a Virgin Mary. This upset Randy a little; she
was more entrenched in her beliefs than he had thought.

Well, but the great thing about Laurinda, religion or
no, she was going to be a wonderful helpmeet. She was
all for the garbage idea, praising him for his initiative,
and counseling caution when necessary, like when she
pointed out Hope And Glory was landlocked, so don't
let them talk you into any ocean-going barges. They say
behind every great man . . . and it was so true. He could
see them having power soirees and all: "Mayor and Mrs.
Randy Anderson request the pleasure . . ."

Except Laurinda wasn't so hot on changing her name.
He forgot that. Well, how was that going to work, anyhow? Was he supposed to be Mr. Laurinda Wilcox? Did
you ever hear of anything funnier?

"Listen, Laurinda," he said, trying it out on her; she
needed a laugh.

"What's so funny about that?" she snapped. "You think
'Mrs. Randy Anderson' sounds any better?"

Well of course it did. It sounded natural. Boy you had
to be careful around Laurinda, but once she got through
her female trouble she'd be fine. The problem was she was

studying that anthropology too hard. What does a woman need to know about that stuff, anyhow? Randy would get her an exterminator the minute she needed one, that went without saying. He took pride in being a good provider.

They rounded off the evening with Randy calling for some karaoke. The motel people said they usually didn't set up the system when there were only four people in the lounge, but after a while they went ahead and cranked it up. The rest were too shy, but Randy said he would sing a song he'd known since he was a kid, "Little Sir Echo." It was too bad they didn't have the karaoke for that, but he said he would sing accopello. It made him all glowy to see Laurinda, sitting there staring at him.

"Where did you learn that?" she asked.

"Some old guy, a real nice man, used to sing it to me when I was little."

"Zeke?"

"Zeke! Not a chance. Bert? Buck? Can't remember, it'll come back to me."

A couple days later, when they were back home, Randy called The Garbage King and the guy said he'd send him some full color promotional material. He couldn't take a meeting with Randy right now because he was having a little liposuction done on his tush and wouldn't be able to sit for three, four days, but he'd be in touch, and not to do anything he wouldn't do. (Randy had let him in on the fact he was on his honeymoon. What a guy!)

So back they went, Randy full of plans and Laurinda backing him up one hundred per cent. That was the difference between Randy and other folks in Hope And Glory. Randy had giddyup. He could give courses in giddyup. Bert Whump, he had it too, but people like Septus, or even Leland DeWitt, it didn't come natural to them to look on the bright side and hustle a little.

People thought he didn't like Leland DeWitt; not true. That was their dads that didn't get on. And that Sylene, Skip's "friend," she was a lovely girl. Not the girl for Skip, though. He really thought Skip should get out with the guys in his class more. He was going to suggest to Skip that he take up football or something.

Anyhow, first thing, he would have to call a special meeting of the City Council. Laurinda could entertain the wives of local power brokers, get them on his side. She could be his sidekick, and a mom to Skip. Already, they looked like a family. Sherry had had dark hair, but Laurinda was blonde like him and Skip. And Sylene. When Sylene was with them, strangers thought they were Mom and Dad and the kids on an outing.

Another thing. He had to get some kind of police presence in Hope And Glory. Not that the town had any crime to speak of, but just for the dignity of it. Hell, they used to have a jail here when Bert was Chief of Police. Still did, it was just closed up. It would have looked real bad if he'd had to ride that ransom note of Septus's over to Chief Earl Arbogast in North Vienna. So la-di-da about it. Thank God for faxes.

Hope And Glory should have at least one policeman. Policeperson. He'd have to be careful about that kind of thing now, with Laurinda. And they had to get somebody who could maintain and operate the snowplow. It wasn't right, the mayor driving the snowplow, and when anything went wrong, he sure as hell couldn't fix it. Jeez, he couldn't even put air in his own tires: that time when the gauge said 100 and he thought it said 10, whoa, man, that was something. Although, to be fair, those air machines could be a lot more user-friendly. A lot more. A voter could get hurt. Anyhow, he was going to put the whole thing to the Council.

That night, Randy got so tangled in the bedclothes he nearly put his shoulder out. Awake, dreaming, awake, all night long. He was walking along, a little kid, crying. He was hurt. His ma was hurt, too. Somebody came along and gave him a Klondike ice cream bar. Told him he'd be okay, that he was a good boy. And smart. Took him and his ma to Grandma's.

Who was that? He was all in black and he gave Randy a toy silver bullet. Did he wear a mask? Did he whistle "Sir Echo"? He only remembered being happy.

THE HOPE AND GLORY VINDICATOR

Volume 232 Issue 24   Hope And Glory, Ohio

A FLIER, HOT OFF THE PRESS

Factory Shock!

The Vindicator has just learned that BriarHill Associates, the corporation that recently bought and closed the Hope And Glory boiler factory, was owned by Zeke Anderson. Articles of incorporation registered with the Ohio Secretary of State list Susan Anderson (Mrs. Zeke Anderson) as the Statutory Agent. No directors are listed. When Mrs. Anderson was contacted, she said she had no idea what a Statutory Agent was, but that she knew her husband and his two sons, Brock and Ken, were the directors. (The official form does not require directors' names to be listed.). The stated purpose of the corporation is to create upscale luxury gated housing on the six acres of land at the corner of Garfield Street and Hillman, the location of the closed factory. When contacted, the mayor, Randy Anderson, said why was he always the last to hear stuff like this? Others wondered if regrets may have driven Mr. Anderson to his demise, or whether one or more of the many threatened homeowners, concerned about their property rights, might have taken the law into their own hands. *Where are our police, we ask you?*

Chapter 16

Leland

"Any luck with the job search?"

Leland was watching today's episode of *Love Forever* when Bert phoned, just at the moment when Clint and Vanessa were put on support machines.

"Nope. Tried every place that was hiring between here and Cleveland. All three of them. So did everybody else here." At this rate, his unemployment would run out.

"Well, 'Bob' Matthews just opened a new store over in Cairo," Bert said. "I was over there yesterday and he said he could use somebody like you to take care of the place."

"Janitor?" He could do that, easy.

"No, running the store. Management. Said to give him a call."

Management. "But there's people out of work around here that got some experience in management."

"You call him, Leland," Bert said.

"You really think so? Okay, I'll think about it. Appreciate it, Bert."

He didn't know what else to say, so he said, "I'll let you know how it goes," and Bert didn't know what else to say, so he said, "Let me know how it goes," and they hung up.

Leland felt a little awkward, he only knew "Bob" Matthews as the husband of Mrs. Herman "Bob" Matthews. He's heard that Bob had dropped his first name when he started to do TV ads, too German, but Mrs. Matthews said "Bob" was undignified and always signed her letters to *The Vindicator* with her full married name. Still it wouldn't hurt Leland to give him a call.

"Just back from getting my diploma at the Academy Institute Foundation for Entrepreneurial Leadership in Cleveland," "Bob" said when Leland called.

"Congratulations."

"Man, a tougher three days I never went through. The speakers! The workshops! The ice! You think 'Cleveland' and you think 'lakeside beach' and 'cocktails' and all, but you don't think ice storms! I missed one whole day because I got iced in at the Rock 'n' Roll Museum. So anyway, Bert told me about you, your situation and all, and I says to myself, I said 'I have just one question to ask that guy.' Do you have any experience in retail?"

"Well, no, can't say . . ."

"Bingo," "Bob" said. "Just what I want. A fresh mind. A Mindful Mind. An 'In The Moment Guy.' Welcome, Retail Associate! Can you meet the unforeseen challenges of this Recession? Can you?"

"Well, I guess I could," Leland said. Then, proudly, "Yes, I can."

"Now you're talking! Let's liaise Sunday morning and get ourselves over to Hidden Lake in Cairo."

Retail Associate. It was a start.

On Sunday morning, they liaised at Winkle's Party Pak, "Bob" in his church clothes, his impressive paunch emphasized by pants up to his nipples and a sheepskin coat that couldn't meet in the front, Leland in his winter jacket and vinyl trapper hat with fake fur earflaps. "Bob" had rimless glasses and seven or eight strands of hair, grey at the roots, orangey-black on the ends.

They drove over to Cairo, "Bob" in his Ford Crown Victoria P71 Police Interceptor and Leland close behind in Bridget's car. Leland knew Cairo pretty well—the one business street, East Federal, with its bank, a couple clothing stores, the insurance office, a coffee shop and a Woolworth's that always had peeling yellow cellophane on its windows. But Hidden Lake was new to him. He liked the sound of it, a lot better than your old-fashioned names like East Federal Street. Then he saw the Woolworth's and realized Hidden Lake *was* East Federal Street, pedestrianized, benched and abandoned, except for two guys sleeping under dirty tarps beside the broken fountain. A Vacuum Cleaner Repair, a Dollar Pawn and that Woolworth's seemed to be the only businesses left.

"Don't need that fountain anymore," "Bob" said, hurrying Leland past it. "We got ourselves a new central Artistic Focus now. Right around this corner. It's a real head snapper. We call it the Spirit of Hidden Lake."

"Where's the Lake?"

"Bob" looked at him, stunned. "Hidden, of course."

"But hidden where?"

"Just hidden," "Bob" said. "It's one of your metaphors or proverbs." He marched Leland around the corner.

A rusting, multi-pointed metal sculpture, about twenty feet high, stood in an angle formed by two closed stores. It looked like a cross between a blender and the kind of industrial crane used on old city docks.

"*The Spirit*," "Bob" said, saluting.

Leland walked around it, staying well clear of its many sharp prongs and spears, saying nothing. When it came to Art he had very few standards, but one of them was First Do No Harm.

"Bob" tightened his lips and marched Leland back around the corner. "Here's my store."

Leland wondered if Union Dollar was hidden, like the Lake. "It says 'Woolworth's.'"

"It was Woolworth's." "Bob" pointed to a new "Union Dollar" sign propped up against a cracked window. "My sign guy's got an ankle tag right now, says he can't climb above knee level or whatever." "Bob" looked doubtful. "But I got it all custom-fitted inside."

Inside, though, it was like every faded-town Woolworth's Leland had ever seen.

"Sixteen thousand items in here," Bob said, beaming around happily at the Small Electrics, the Travel Sizes, the Picnic and Party Ware. He escorted Leland to the Analgesics and then on to Incontinence.

"*This* is where you'll learn management. This is Seat of the Pants stuff, you won't get it from some half-assed course, and this here," he said, pounding on the cracked counter, "this here is the coal face."

An ancient computer, listing a little, sat on the counter beside the cash register. Leland didn't know much about computers but this one looked like an old Delco tube radio. "You'll want to check this regularly for email messages. You'll have your messages from Regional Office all the way down through District Office, to Line Manager's Office. They all come to the Retail Associate, that's you, but you only answer the ones from Line Manager. That's the protocol."

"Okay," Leland said.

Bob showed him how to work the cash register, and illustrated the use of the gun thing that stuck prices on items. It didn't work, so Bob took it apart and peeled off some red ninety-nine-cent stickers. He stuck a few on things in the nearest aisle: an electric toothbrush, some hemorrhoid cream, a Fresh Day douche. "Like so," he said. "Remember to peel those off, okay?"

"Isn't everything supposed to be ninety-nine cents?" Leland asked. "Being Union Dollar?"

"Bob" looked at him, flabbergasted, then shook his head as if to clear it of such idiocy.

It was all simple enough, and Leland was satisfied that he could figure out what to do. It seemed a little arid, maybe, compared to heavy equipment mechanics, but there was no place for romantic nostalgia in this economic climate.

Bob locked up and gave Leland the keys. They passed the Spirit of Hidden Lake on the way to their vehicles. It *was* an industrial crane, with some flanges and blades soldered on.

On Monday, Leland opened the door at eight and set his lunch bucket underneath the counter.

Bob had an old kitchen stool here, but Leland stood so he'd be ready to help whoever came in. He straightened his tie a little and polished his right shoe against the back of his pants leg.

But at nine, no one had come in, so Leland went over to the drink machine and bought a bottle of water, in case anybody needed a drink. He moved the kitchen stool out beside the counter, in case an old person needed to sit down. Then he moved it back again; an old person could kill themselves hoisting their bad hips onto that stool. Bandages—that's what he needed, in case anybody fell. He bought some, and some wound cleanser.

He was in Nose and Throat when Juanetta came in. He hurried forward.

"Your dollar pack of kids' erasers," she said. "A dozen. What if I only want two?"

"Well, let's see if they come in twos," Leland said, shepherding her toward the Stationery.

"They do, but not in this yellowy green shade. Only mauve."

Mauve. What was that? He'd write it down in his Word notebook, but right now he was stumped. He reached Stationery and picked up a couple packs to show her some that maybe weren't mauve, but she'd darted off somewhere else. He caught up with her in Feminine Hygiene, and backed up hastily into Canned Goods. Juanetta stayed in Feminine Hygiene. Leland stood on tip-toe and waved the denture-colored two-pack erasers at her.

"Those are mauve," she said. Leland broke open the bigger package, and took out two yellowy-green ones. The rest fell out of the torn package and skittered under the shelving.

"Twenty cents," Leland said. "Ten to a dollar pack, so twenty cents."

"Yes, but they're not in a package now." She wandered off into Small Electrics, and tore a toaster out of a box, checking it feature by feature against the identical display model. She pinged the bread lever up and down about a dozen times. "I always said I was going to do this next time I bought a toaster," she called. "You can't make but about ten pieces of toast before this part gives out." She slammed the lever down hard with the palm of her hand. Most people needed a twenty-pound mason's sledge hammer to get that kind of force, Leland thought. He heard the lever break.

By the time he got there, Juanetta had jammed the toaster parts, minus the protective Styrofoam form, back into the box, and was standing on the Styrofoam trying to put the box up on the highest shelf. The Styrofoam crumbled, and he caught her, but the contents of her handbag emptied all around his feet. They included a new Fresh Day Douche and some Warming Personal Lubricant, both of which "Bob" had stickered at ninety-nine cents yesterday, and Leland had forgotten to change.

Leland was shocked. Juanetta watched him, chin jutting, waiting.

Leland unfolded the torn eraser wrapper and put the two erasers in. He ran a fingernail across the top to make a neat closure and held it out to her.

"Well, I don't really care to buy damaged packaging. Anyhow, I was only looking. I'll come back some other day when I got more time." She re-packed her handbag and left.

No one else came in. He remembered that Bob told him to be sure to check for email messages. He supposed now would be a good time to crank the computer up and give it a shot. He got out Bridget's glasses and perched on the stool.

"HEY THERE TEAM!" the message shouted. "WE GOTTA MEET OUR MONTHLY TARGETS!! CHECK YOUR STORE'S TARGET NOW. AND REMEMBER, HAVE A HAPPY UNION DOLLAR DAY!"

AND A HEADS UP, GOOD MERCHANDISING IS GOOD BUSINESS! CHECK YOUR MERCHANDISING!!!"

What was his merchandising? He poked around under the counter and all he found was a magazine showing a woman and two guys with huge . . . Well, that really surprised him, he'd always thought of "Bob" as a family man.

Four kids of about eight or nine came in. Candy, he thought, and went over to the candy bins, little shovel in hand. Bob had warned Leland that the candy wasn't self-service; otherwise they'll eat straight out of the bins, robbing you blind and spreading cold sores. Bob said he weighed each candy bin every night on the scales, and that way he was always on top of his through-put. Leland noticed one of the kids had a runny nose so he snatched a packet of handkerchief tissues, two for a dollar, and put it in his shirt pocket. People appreciated a gentleman offering a hanky, he'd noticed that in the old movies.

While he was opening the packet so it was easy- access, one of the kids put a handful of something into the orange spider bin and crammed a handful of orange spiders into his mouth.

"You want to put them in a bag and get them weighed first," Leland said, with a kindly chuckle.

"No I don't," the kid said.

A fat, red-faced boy chugged by, waving a little plastic man from Toys and Seasonal. "Here's what it looks like," he called to the first kid. "I'm gonna hide it and you and Jason have to find it." He lumbered off, and the candy-eater covered his eyes.

"Okay!" the fat boy called, and all the other kids raced through the store, pushing stuff aside on each shelf, jumping up and ducking down, looking for the plastic man. Things rattled on the metal shelves; glass crashed to the floor. One kid grabbed a battery-operated kitchen whisk and screamed as it caught in his hair and stuck.

"Got it!" the candy-eater shouted, waving the little figure. "Awwwhhh," the two other searchers groaned, disappointed. They all slumped out. "Thanks, Leland," Whisk-Hair called politely. The nametag, Leland had forgotten he had one.

He bought some aspirin.

The place was a mess. The computer pinged. A message From Regional Office.

RE: POLICY
PLESE REFER TO THE CORPORATE MANUEL.

Regional Manager

The phone rang. "Leland. It's 'Bob.' How's it goin?"

"Fine. I just got a message from the Regional Manager."

"Yeah, well you want to pay attention to those. Leland, we got a complaint on our hands. Juanetta, she filed one and it's already shot straight up to the Regional Office."

"What about?"

"She says she wasn't greeted right."

"Treated?"

"*Greeted*. She says she walked on over there and you just said 'Hi, Juanetta.'" "Bob" sounded like he couldn't believe anything so unlikely.

"I did."

"Leland, you read the Policy Manual? Under the counter?"

Whatever you wanted to call that magazine under the counter, it wasn't a policy manual.

"What you do, when people come in, is you say to them "Hi, My Name Is Leland, We're Having A Wonderful Day Here At Union Dollar, May I Help You Find Something?""

"Every time? All that?"

"Yep. And she says you didn't compliment her scarf."

"What?"

"You have to compliment them on something as soon as they get in—their scarf or purse or tie or whatever— say you like it, or that you used to have a favorite one exactly like it."

Leland thought this was ridiculous. "What if they're carrying a gun and wearing a mask?"

"There's no room for levity in this economic climate," "Bob" said.

"I could have complimented her on her purse but she'd filled it with shoplifted stuff."

"What kind of stuff?"

"Stuff."

"Oh."

They were both silent for a moment. "What's the policy on shoplifting?" Leland asked.

"Let 'em walk."

"Walk?"

"Loss Prevention Policy says you can't take your eyes off a suspect at any point. They might have put the thing back, and then we'd get our heinies sued off. So we let 'em walk. You want to kind of give them A Look. If you get your Look right they catch on and don't do it again. But if they take something, you gotta pay for it outta your wages."

"My wages?"

"Yep. But it's better than causing a kerfluffle by wrangling with a customer in the store."

Leland pictured himself wrangling with Juanetta over a douche; he had to agree.

"Anyhow, isn't this Monday?"

"Was, this morning," Leland said, and then remembered about levity avoidance.

"Monday. Lady Shots day. I wouldn't fool with Juanetta when she's got eight or ten rifles on her back seat."

"Listen, what about this Regional Manager? What am I supposed to do?"

"You don't communicate directly with the Regional Manager. This is a Line System, Leland; you communicate with your Line Manager. He in turn communicates with the District manager and eventually it goes All The Way Up to the Regional."

"Okay."

"Just click on Line Manager, and pass on Regional's message. Line will get back to you."

"Okay." Leland hung up and looked around. The place was a mess, bits of crushed Styrofoam, broken glass, shelves all every which way, a box of plastic men broken open and scattered.

Sixteen thousand items, "Bob" had said. The store closed at six but he was still straightening up at eight-thirty. He must have got a little light-headed after a while or maybe he even fell asleep and dreamed a little because there he was, clear as day, back in his old job, heavy equipment mechanic at the boiler factory, lying on a golden pallet, being fanned by maidens and borne along by young men in togas as he plucked tidbits from his lunch bucket. Leland shook himself; probably he was just hungry.

When he got home, Bridget was making ham and lima beans. Their bouquet unmanned him; he collapsed with relief and gratitude. Bridget looked up, worried.

"How'd it go?"

"Fine," Leland said.

Tuesday was very quiet. Randy Anderson came in for some new rubber dinette feet; he said he'd melted one last week and then his aunt gave him some but somehow he couldn't find them. Anyways, he only needed three.

"But what the hey," he said, "I'll take the pack of four."

Leland hadn't forgotten Randy's nasty objection to his Skip going out with Leland's Sylene, but today, after some of the characters who came into the store, he welcomed Randy's reasonableness.

"What brings you over here to Cairo?" he asked.

"Oh, Gus's sells old comics, thought I'd look for some Lone Rangers."

"We don't sell comics."

"No, Gus doesn't either. I see he closed down. Everything closed down around here." Randy looked around. "You need to keep on top of your merchandising."

Leland was mildly annoyed that someone as dumb as Randy knew a word that he didn't, but Randy made up for it by straightening some cans, so at least he was making himself useful.

The computer pinged.

"CHECK WITH YOUR LINE MANAGER FOR TODAY'S SPECIALS!!"

Leland called "Bob." "Who's my Line Manager?"

"Me."

"Well, what are Today's Specials?"

"Um. I'll have to check and get back to you."

Leland decided now was a good quiet time to look in the stockroom for the policy manual. A Silvertone television console with a tag advertising two-knob tuning blocked his view but when he squeezed behind that he found some ladies' church hats in cellophane and a box of Flame-Glo lipsticks, orange, marked 39¢. Past a poster of a lady who used Ipana so she didn't have Tell-Tale mouth. A bigger poster of a couple kissing at a fancy ball with an arrow pointing to the guy's underarm, saying, "Are you *always* lovely to love?" Poor bastard. Or maybe it was pointing to the lady's underarm, it was hard to tell. Some Father John's cough syrup, dried up, and a bottle of Prince Matchabelli. No policy manual.

When he came back out, the store looked like a new place. Nice arrangements of canned goods, a few baskets filled with perfumed soaps, a display of flowerpots filled with seed packets and trowels. A market umbrella was hanging upside down from the ceiling, and below it were a table and some beach chairs, napkins, plates and martini glasses all set out.

Randy was over in Seasonal now, dressing an old Halloween skeleton.

"Hey," he said, "Lookie. A Lone Ranger mask." He put it on.

"Thanks," Leland said, waving at the new arrangements.

"Sure," Randy said. "I guess I'll take these rubber feet." He pushed the mask up on his forehead. "We should get together sometime," Randy suggested. "Little fishing, maybe go to Akron and take in the sights." Bert came in as Randy left.

"Whoa!" he said to Randy. "Don't shoot."

Randy looked baffled and left.

Leland added a Lone Ranger mask to his own tab.

Bert had a pile of garish-colored clothes slung over his arm. "I gotta return these, Leland," he said. "The wife was here a couple weeks ago, she likes a day out, and she bought all this." He dumped them on the counter.

"What is this?"

"Cruise Wear. But see the thing is, we ain't goin' on a cruise. She didn't know it was cruise wear."

It looked like circus wear to Leland, but he didn't know much about clothes.

"She couldn't wear it around?"

"What I said, myself. Those big old house coats she goes around in, 'specially first thing in the morning with her hair all sticking out, she looks like an asylum patient, but . . ."

The problem was, Leland didn't know how to make a return. "Bob" hadn't shown him that, yet. Returns were only on Wednesday, and this was Tuesday. The computer pinged, a new message coming in, but Leland also noticed a box on the screen that he hadn't seen before: "RETURNS."

He clicked on it. "NO RETURNS EXCEPT ON WEDNESDAY. COMPANY POLICY. CONTACT YOUR LINE MANAGER."

Leland phoned "Bob." No answer.

The new message was from Regional:

"URGENT!!! CHECK TODAY'S SPECIALS! RE-TAG ALL SPECIALS IMMEDIATELY!!"

Leland called "Bob" again. It just rang, couldn't even leave a message.

The hell with it, he hit "REPLY" on Regional's message. "What are the specials?" he wrote. "And what do I do about a Return on Tuesday?"

"Leland?" Bert shifted from one foot to another.

"Well, I don't know what to do. Give me your receipt, maybe it'll give me some kinda number I can cancel on the machine."

Bert searched his pockets, back, front, jacket, inside jacket, all his wallet compartments. Then he did it again. When he'd finished the third time, he said, "Think it might be in the car. I'll go see." He went out into huge empty parking lot that used to be downtown West Federal Street. Bert always parked at the furthest point away, for the exercise; it caused a lot of fuss between him and Mrs. Bert, particularly when she had the crutch.

Leland waited. It would take Bert a good seven or eight minutes to make the trip. He gave him credit, though, an old man like that, little bit of a limp, still trying to take care of himself.

Leland saw Bert's keys on the counter at the same moment that he saw Bert jerking at the car door.

The fat kid from yesterday came in. He looked around, delighted, at Randy's changes.

"Don't move," Leland said.

He picked up Bert's remote car key, held the metal part against his chin, and pushed the unlock button. Out in the lot, Bert gave one last tug on the car door and it flew open, throwing him off balance. He staggered back toward the open door and looked in.

"You're weird," the kid said.

"I just made my head into a long-distance antenna," Leland said, pleased that this trick had come in handy for once.

"'S what I said. Weird." He left.

All those numbers and codes on Bert's receipt weren't helpful. "You might have to bring these back tomorrow," Leland said. "On Returns Day."

Bert gathered them up, a little bent now, but resigned, and as always, gracious. Leland didn't have the heart to make him come all the way back.

"You know what?" he said. "I'll buy the stuff off you and return it myself tomorrow."

Bert handed over the clothes and the receipt, and Leland handed him the money he was saving to replace Bridget's tires.

"Thanks, Leland," Bert said. "Anything I can do, you know to call me."

"Sure."

A flood of messages awaited Leland as he opened the store on Wednesday morning. Some were from Regional, some from District, none from Line. "HAVE U GOT 2DAY'S SPECIAL'S TAGGED?"

"TODAY IS RETURNS DAY. WE DON'T TAKE BACK ANYTHNG FROM K-MART OR WAL-MART OR TARGET UNLESS IT'S BETTER THAN WHAT WE HAVE."

Ping! A new message. This one really cheered him up, the first time in three days that he'd felt happy. "EMPOYEE OF THE WEEK IS LELAND DEWITT!!!! LET'S ALL GIVE A SHOUT OUT TO LELAND!! MORE SALES THAN ANYONE ELSE! RECORD SALES ON MONDAY! WAY TO GO LELAND! GIVE YOURSELF A HAPPY PAT ON THE BACK." A little leprechaun danced on the screen.

Leland didn't have time to work out what a Happy Pat was because when he looked up he saw a line of eight or ten people waiting for the store to open. Every one of them was carrying something: lampshades, a garbage can, a crockpot, an electric foot bath, Juanetta Wilcox with a rusty rake, and at the front of the line, a blonde, familiar-looking middle-aged woman struggling with a ripped lawn chair. Returns. Further down the line, he could hear a woman talking. "Huh uh. He's waaay too good to come in and get anything himself. Oh, no. Sits there all day foolin' around on the computer. If I had to pay a dollar every time my husband got up off his butt, I'd be a rich woman."

Leland pondered this. His math was slipping, or maybe he was just tired already.

"I need to bring this back, sweetheart," the blonde woman said to Leland, tapping on the counter. "I want a yoga mat and a blow-up yoga ball instead. Right over there." She smiled.

Right. Leland took the lawn chair, entered it into the computer, and brought over the mat and the flattened yoga ball.

"Could you blow it up for me? Please?"

Leland looked for a little pump. Nothing else in the box.

"You gotta blow it up by mouth," the only man in the line, said. He had a box of furnace filters.

"I'm very little, my lungs aren't big like yours." The woman laid a lovely, manicured hand on Leland's arm.

Leland started to blow.

The woman with the lampshade had struck up a conversation with another woman who had a lampshade, too, and a garbage can. "That's how my Arnold died," she said now. "Blowin' up one a them things."

"Oh, yeah. That's a direct ride to the hospital with an aneurysm, doin' that. Lookit, his face is a little blue."

"And that vein."

Leland jammed the plug in and leaned on the counter. Black dots floated in front of his eyes, and he thought one of his lungs might be torn. His heart was going like a ten-piece drum kit. He panted, unable to speak.

The lady pursed her glossy lips. "Weellll, I wonder. Now that it's blown up, it's the wrong shade of aqua. I have to keep it in my living room, my other rooms are all filled with my craft projects . . ."

There'd been a little buzz in the line when she'd started speaking, but when she said "craft projects" the whole place erupted.

"That's Lelia Pusser!" one of the lampshade women cried. "From WHAG TV! Cute Country Crafts!"

Leland and the lone man, who had a furnace filter, looked baffled, but the rest, except for Juanetta, circled Lelia Pusser.

"She's soo petite!" one cried. "I always thought she'd be a full-bodier woman than that. Didn't you?" she asked, turning to Juanetta. But Juanetta, who was pretty full-bodied, looked frosty.

"Lelia! Will you autograph something for my mother? I got a piece a paper here, wait, no I don't . . . oh, here, just autograph this." The woman shoved the lampshade at Lelia, who signed it with a flourish.

"Your funeral," Furnace Filter said. "Now you can't return it."

"I'm not returning, I'm buying."

"Wrong line, then."

Lelia moved through the group, autographing. The woman who'd been complaining about her husband reached the counter. It was Mrs. Herman "Bob." She plunked an encrusted crock pot and a bag of candy on the counter. "I wanna exchange this crockpot for a pressure cooker." She hoisted the pressure cooker. "I ain't got time to be sitting around stirrin' a crockpot."

"You don't need to stir a crockpot," Furnace Filter called out. He looked at his watch and sighed loudly.

Mrs. "Bob" turned and looked him up and down. "I won't even dignify that with a reply," she said.

"And these orange spiders," she said, "I got a bag of them just now and they're half gravel."

"I've been trying to reach "Bob" for two days," Leland said to Mrs. "Bob."

"Ohhh no," she said. "No sirree. Waaay too good to pick up a phone."

"Here you are, honey," Lelia said, stretching to pass an autographed shade back to Lampshade #two. Leland saw her raised left foot, saw it about to come down on Juanetta's rake, saw it come down, heard the thwack of the handle on her skull. Everyone heard it, although later some said it sounded like a heavy blow to a melon. Blood poured down the left side of Lelia's face and she crumpled backwards.

Her fall was broken on a display of roto-tillers. Leland could see she had a gash on her head, and now her arm hung funny, too. The two Lampshades turned on Juanetta. "How come you got that dirty old rake with you?" one asked. "You nearly brained a notoriety with that thing."

Leland called 911 for an ambulance. Furnace Filter snatched the phone and kept yelling, "We got a elderly lady here hurt bad, Code One, Code One!" in a shrill voice.

Leland was impressed. "What's Code One?" he asked.

"They all say that on TV."

The idea of Lelia Pusser being an elderly woman seemed to infuriate most of the female customers, all of whom were older than Lelia. Mrs. "Bob" got her charge card out of her pocketbook and snapped it in two right in front of the counter. The Lampshades at the back said that they wouldn't bother with the garbage can or shades now. Furnace Filter just rolled his eyes at the women and helped himself to a different package of filters. He left with both packs.

When the ambulance came, Leland helped Lelia in, and Juanetta packed the yoga ball and mat in beside her. "She'll be fine," the paramedic said. "I seen this same thing so many times you wouldn't believe it."

Back in the store, Leland surveyed the morning's take: a broken lawn chair, the autographed lampshades, a sticky crockpot and a roto-tiller that would have to be completely scrubbed down and disinfected. He was missing a yoga ball and mat, a pressure cooker and a package of furnace filters. On the other hand, he was one garbage can and a dirty rake to the good. He decided to enter the exchange for Bert's cruise wear. Where was the receipt? It had been right there on the counter when he opened for business this morning.

The computer pinged. Regional.

"LELAND'S FIRST-DAY SALES!" followed by a list of items. "LELAND, SEND OUR OTHER SALES ASSOCIATES SOME VIGNETTES ABOUT YOUR CUSTOMER TIPS!!"

Leland looked around at the items sitting on his cluttered counter—the still unoffered water bottle, the bandages, three of which were applied to Lelia Pusser's head; the broken toaster, the tissues, the aspirin, the kitchen whisk. What else was on his sales list? The Fresh Day Douche and personal lubricant, he'd paid for those, too, and the orange spiders. All in all, $96.50, minus his three% Retail Associate's discount, so $93.60. Oh, and the Lone Ranger mask, $1.98, on sale for $1.59, unless it was a Today's Special, so that was $98.01, discounted to $95.07. He'd only worked two full days so far, at $7.25 an hour, Ohio minimum wage, so let's see, $116 for the two days, minus $95.07, so that was $20.93, or $10.46 a day, with three extra hours Monday night, no overtime pay, so $1.10 an hour before taxes.

Still, it was nice to get a little recognition.

Chapter 17

Leland

A lady, Leland wanted to think "elderly" but decided against it, came in to Union Dollar. She'd come in the day before, too, stayed a while, and then left without buying. Today she had a ragged scrap of a dog with her; they both looked a little down and out. One of them smelled like mildew.

"Hold this," she said to Leland, thrusting the dog into his arms. So it was the lady. After two weeks in the job, Leland was used to this kind of thing. One man, elderly, because it was okay to use "elderly" for men, had asked him to hold on to a plastic case of dentures while he'd shopped. The dog nipped his thumb.

"I need to buy a toothbrush." Unlike the dog, the lady seemed to have no teeth. Her face looked like a sock puppet's. Leland edged her toward the denture brushes.

"Are you implying I have no teeth?" she demanded. She snatched a water-squirting electric toothbrush and shoved it at him, hitting the dog and causing it to bite Leland again. "I want that, and I want to return this set of rubber dinette feet that I bought last week."

"I don't think you got these here," Leland said, turning them over. They were bright green.

"Course I did! You gift-wrapped them for me yourself. Be careful with that wrap, I want that back. I need to send my neighbor some of my zucchini, want to arrange it in a basket."

Leland refunded her money and started to gift-wrap the toothbrush. "It's for me, stupid!" she gummed at him, snatching it away. She told him to mind the dog while she went over to the cash machine in the pawn shop for money.

In the hour she was gone, Leland had to take the dog out twice to pee. When she came back to get the dog, she left without thanking him.

He was dealing with a second old lady when it occurred to him that the first hadn't paid him for the toothbrush. She had also reconsidered the dinette feet, and taken them, too. This new old lady was the way old ladies should be: soft, pink-powdered skin, clothes a little musty, a sweet veiled hat on her silvery permanent.

"Hi, My Name Is Leland, We're Having A Wonderful Day Here At Union Dollar, May I Help You Find Something?"

"Oh, yes," she breathed happily at him. "I like this place. I'll be coming in here often."

"Pleased to have you. Look around."

She did, item by sixteen-thousandth item, picking each up and putting it back down exactly in its place. After about an hour and a half, she came up to the counter. "Do you mind if I stay a little while?"

"Not a bit."

"I get a little lonely. My daughter made me move here from Florida and I don't know anyone. She's out all day, and I don't think she likes me, anyhow."

Leland thought this was shocking.

"She's planning to get married for the third time, to an unemployed wrestler, and I just think she wants me here to pay for the wedding. But after the last one, to the sandwich board fellow, I don't have a penny left. And I'm a little woosie right now. I'm a diabetic," she said, looking frail and sad.

"Here," Leland said, offering her a Twinkie from the shelf. "You eat this, right this minute. And let me get you something to drink from the coffee shop. Tea, maybe?"

"Oh, yes, please. Prince of Wales."

Leland blushed.

"That's the kind of tea I like, if they have it," she said.

Late in the afternoon, they were joined by a wiry, battered-looking guy, mid-forties, thin stringy black hair plastered to his skull. He stood in the open doorway.

"Hi, My Name Is Leland, We're Having A Wonderful Day Here At Union Dollar, May I Help You Find Something?"

The man studied him, like Leland was a frog he was
planning to squish, then turned away and leaned against
the door frame.

"May I Help You Find Something?"

The man plucked a straw from the broom Leland had
been sweeping the sidewalk with and picked his teeth.
"Security guard," he muttered, scratching some eczema
under his chin stubble with the straw.

"Security? For what?"

The man seemed to weigh the need for the slightest
expenditure of energy before making it, or, in this case, not.

"For what? Where's your badge? Your credentials?
Your uniform? Gun? Night stick? Anything?"

The man flickered his lizard-like eyelids and lit a
cigarette.

Had Leland Come Face to Face With Evil, he wondered?

"Looky," the man whined. "Be reasonable. What I
hear, kids are chasing around in here, you got disorderly
lines for your Returns, gravel in your Spiders, and I don't
know what all else. 'Bob' sent me." He scratched one
grubby sandaled foot with the other.

"That an ankle tag?" Leland asked.

"Yeah!" the man brightened up. "How'dju know? You
got one, too?"

"No, I don't got one . . . haven't," Leland snapped.

"Oh. Well, you don't want me here, you gotta check
it out with 'Bob.'"

Leland emailed Line. No reply. He called Line.

"Ain't here," Mrs. "Bob" said. "Gettin' his feet done."

"I don't hear from him in an hour, I'm calling District. Maybe Regional. I got special offers I don't have any idea what they are, I got some character here at the door, you wouldn't know what he'd do . . ."

"Barnabas," Mrs. "Bob'" said. "That's his name. Old Reverend Elkins' boy. Seen some hard times."

At four, Leland wrote to Regional.

COMMUNICATE DIRECTLY ONLY WITH LINE, the reply said. What if pirates hijacked the store, Leland wondered?

LELAND, YOUR NOT MEETING YOUR NEW SALES TARGET. SALES

TARGET IS YOUR BEST DAY, MONDAY, PLUS TEN PER CENT. A RETAIL ASSOCIARTE GETS A PAY CUT FOR NOT MEETING TARGET. TWO HOURS AND ELEVEN MINUTES LEFT TO MEET TARGET! ATTABOY, YOU CAN DO IT!!! YEAH, LELAND!!!

At five, "Bob" came in. The old lady wandered off. "Leland, Leland, Leland, Leland, Leland." He looked despondent. "I go on like this, I'll be bankrupt. And I got all these messages you sent to Regional."

"I know. I been trying to reach you for two, three days now. How do I sell specials if I don't know what they are? And what about this guy in the doorway? How come Regional can always reach you and I can't?"

"I *am* Regional."

"What about District?"

"Hell, yes. You got to turn your hand to everything in a small business. There's me, killing myself, and here's you, sitting pretty, not selling anything yesterday or today."

"Why couldn't I just reply directly to whatever Office sent me a message? Since they're all you, anyhow?"

"Directly? *Directly?* Think I went all the way to Cleveland to the Academy Institute Foundation to talk to you like we was just kicking back on two front porch chairs?" He laughed pityingly.

"And then," "Bob" said, voice shrilling, "and *then*, I gotta shell out for a security guard and a Mystery Shopper and Loss Prevention Officer to help you."

Leland looked around.

"Mystery Shopper?"

"The dog lady. Tests your customer handling skills."

"What about my dog handling skills?" Leland bristled. The two bites were stinging and he'd used up most of the wound cleanser on Lelia Pusser. "And what Loss Prevention Officer? Is that him?" pointing to Barnabas.

"Nah. He's Security. Loss Prevention is the old lady, wears a nice church hat. Made a complaint, you gave her a Twinkie right off the shelf, without paying."

"I paid for that when she wasn't looking, so she wouldn't be embarrassed. She said she had no money."

"I trained her to say that," "Bob" said proudly.

Leland blew out his cheeks and sank onto where the stool had been.

"I'm afraid I got to let you go, Leland. You might make it in management someday, but . . ." It was clear that he didn't think that day would come. "You'll have to clean out your desk and be out in a half hour. Barnabas'll escort you out. Well, maybe take forty minutes, cause I gotta go pick up some corn pads. Be back in a jiff."

"This Cruise Wear," Leland said when "Bob" got back. "I want to return it but someone must have taken the receipt . . ." His back was killing him.

"No returns without a receipt," "Bob" said, waggling his finger. "But somehow I don't see you in Cruise Wear."

Leland saw dancing red pinwheels in front of his eyes. Eye hemorrhages or something.

"You think I couldn't go on a cruise?" he said, quietly.

"Oh, no, no, not what I meant at all," "Bob" said, backing up behind the counter.

"Matterafact, it's Bert's. He came in on Tuesday and I couldn't take it as a return so I paid him myself in cash, and then was going to return it on Friday but I lost . . ."

"How'd he buy it?"

"Credit card, I think."

"Bob" threw up his hands. "Never, never, *never* give cash back for a credit card purchase. First thing they teach you at AIF in Cleveland. No can do."

He thought a moment. "You should go up there, Leland, learn about the business world, the line management system and all, and I'd get a little something for Introducing a Friend. We'd all be happy." He started to arrange the Cruise Wear in a new window display, putting a teeny halter top on a teen-aged mannequin and laying out some tent-sized shorts and top for a simpering amazon.

Leland grabbed him by the collar and shoved. "Bob" landed on the teenager and lay sprawled there in the window.

Leland got his lunch bucket from behind the counter and left. Gone.

When he drove into his driveway and caught the whiff of slow-cooked sauerkraut and sausage, he knew he was at the one place he wanted to be.

"What're those things?" Bridget asked.

"Extra Large Relaxed Fit Cruise Wear," Leland said. "Plenty for both of us." He put $14.38 on the counter—his wages minus the lady's tea and Twinkie.

"I'll have the pork chops and let's see, maybe some yellow wax beans," Bert Whump told Butch Winkle.

Randy joined him at the counter. "Me, too," he said. He picked all his yellow wax beans off his plate and put them on Bert's.

"All these arithmetic problems in *The Vindicator*," Randy said. "How about we try today's one? But I don't like it when they call the people "A" and "B," not "Bill" and "Jim." They should try to make them more humane."

"It dudn't matter," Bert said.

"Sure it does. How would you like to be called 'A?'"

"So call me 'A.' I'll read it out. Let's just get goin'," Bert said. "I gotta go over to Cairo, see "Bob" Matthews. Take the missus to pick out some linoleum."

"Okay. I'll be what, 'B?'" Randy asked.

"Fine. If it takes a day and a half for two men to suck the water outta their basement ..."

"Whoa," B. said. "Where you gonna get anybody for half a day? They'd charge a full day just for comin' out, and if it was a Saturday, it'd be double time for sure." He squinted at the problem. "Hold on," he said. "If it takes a day and a half for two men to suck the water outta their basement ... *their* basement. These guys living together, or what?"

"No, they ain't living together," A. said. "Or maybe they are, who knows. It dudn't matter."

"Matters to me," B. muttered.

"... how long would it take three men?"

"Three?" B. said. "That's a new one on me. Sick! Wait'll you hear this," B. said to Septus, who had just come in. "These two guys, maybe three, even, living together, spend a day and a half suckin' the water outta their basement ..."

"They want to get theirselves one a them Wet-Vacs," Septus said. "I cleaned out my basement in five-six hours all by myself."

B. looked at Septus. He put his arm on his shoulder. "Looky, Septus. They don't need a Wet-Vac. There ain't any water. It's only a 'rithmetic problem."

"Then how come you're so riled up about them guys living together?" Septus asked.

"Well, hell's bells," B. said. "Jeez."

Chapter 18

Leland

"WANT TO INCREASE YOUR LEVEL OF INTENSITY AND PERSISTENCE?" The magazine ad shouted. Viagra, Leland thought. But no, maybe not. "CAN YOU PREVAIL OVER REJECTION?" Yeah, had to be Viagra. Then, bullet three: "HOW TO USE THE PREGNANT PAUSE EFFECTIVELY!" and bullet four: "HOW TO GET A MASTERY OF PHONETICS!" He scanned the rest: The last one was "DO YOU KNOW YOUR WEASEL WORDS?" Actually, they'd written "weasal."

"This must be for one of those novel-writing courses," he said to Bridget, setting down the magazine after dinner one night. "Probably online, they give a website. I always wanted to write, and now I sure got the time. Not the money, though."

"Isn't it always the way?" Bridget said, trying to restring a Venetian blind. "Let me see that. Well, it says here, 'no-cost training.'"

Now the blinds were all bunched together on one side and hanging fanned out on the other.

"You want to let me do that," Leland said, as they all fell off the string on one side and clattered to the floor. He did some little thing with one of the hickeys, Bridget noticed, and they were back together again. He was a really smart man, Leland, and she hated it that no one had a job for him. Hated it beyond anything.

Leland went over to the kids' computer in the dining room and clicked on the website. He entered his name, zip code and phone number. His phone rang.

"Inbound or outbound?" a voice demanded.

"Come again?" Leland said.

"Are you planning to work in inbound or outbound? Pay's good in either one."

"I wasn't . . ."

"We're telemarketers. We train you. Do you want to take calls or make them? Simple as that."

Leland reflected for a moment.

"Outbound, I suppose," although he sounded a little doubtful.

"Sure? Outbound, you need to be pretty people-orientated, whereas inbound, you gotta be able to answer questions. You sound like you might be good at answering questions."

Leland couldn't imagine what kind of people would *call* telemarketers. "No, I think I'll stick with outbound."

"Well, I see from your zip you're in Hope And Glory. We're operating out of North Vienna, in the old police station. Can you be here at eight tomorrow? We'll give you on-the-job training."

Leland put down the phone and looked at Bridget in amazement. Was it really as easy as that? "I maybe got a job," he said cautiously. Bridget gave his arm a squeeze.

Next morning Leland went over to North Vienna. The new police station looked like a smaller version of the White House. They could afford it now that they were responsible for Hope And Glory. Probably aiming to cover the whole of eastern Ohio, as well. Randy Anderson ought to be impeached, recalled, whatever it took.

As he got closer to old police station, little flags with "One Up Call Center" on them were stuck into the grass on the curb.

"Welcome to One Up, Ohio's answer to India!" the banner over the station door said. The logo was a drawing of a hand, middle finger up. The old foyer had been divided into cubicles, one person in each, ten or twelve cubicles, and more where the Chief's office and mug shot area used to be. Leland walked to the back where three people were crammed into each cell, two working with computers on the flat bed and one standing up with a computer on a plank across the sink.

A guy, thirties, in a red golf shirt with a Finger on it, came running over. "Can't walk around, buddy. Top security. Besides, no space."

Some of the other workers, head-phoned, were standing, smiling, talking, waving their arms, looking into mirrors, silently correcting each other's posture. A confident, cheerful babble filled the room.

"You told me to come in at eight," Leland said.

"Oh, yeah, I forgot. Daryll's the name, a 'y' and two 'lls.' You Leland? Okay, well, we lost a few yesterday so that's great. I'll start you off selling right away, and train you as you go. I trained at the Institute in Cleveland, so I'm on top of this stuff. C'mon, let's go, a minute wasted is a sale lost." He gave Leland the Finger. Everyone who saw him silently joined in, and Leland got about twenty Fingers.

"What are you selling?" Leland asked.

"Every thing you can think of. Some guys selling life insurance, some cell phone packages, some Caribbean vacations, some two-for-one dinner promotions at local restaurants. Some are informing people about discounts at Rickle's Plumbing. You name it."

"So what would I sell?"

"What you *will* sell," Daryll said. "Be positive. Let's try you on the vacations. What you do is call and explain the offer. Simple. You just gotta remember a couple of the basics."

"Which are?"

"Have your primary and secondary goals. Primary is to get people to sign up for the vacations. Secondary is whatever you pick, yourself. Like leaving them with a good feeling, even if they hang up on you. Or being able to answer two questions that they ask. Anything like that, so that you're not Staring Into the Face of Despair. Common problem in this game."

"Okay."

"You want to organize your Special Selling Points. What's special about this vacation? Help people to feel their pain. Say, 'What do you do when you're fed up with our Ohio winter and would kill to get away and put up your feet?'"

"Take a Caribbean vacation?"

"Exactly! You're good! Let them talk a little. Don't interrupt. Listen. Here's a inside tip: Count to two after they talk before you say anything."

"Okay."

"A good time to call businessmen is right before noon. They're happy, thinking about lunch, and their girl has probably left her desk and can't block you getting to him." Daryll looked pensive, then said, "Course, it could be a business *person*, and her assistant *person* has left the desk, and can't block you. Getting to it. Her."

"Okay."

"So now, we'll give it a try. First time, I'm not even gonna listen to the other side of the conversation, just to you. See how you talk, handle yourself. Second time, I'll hear the person on the other end, too. Remember, good posture, wear this headset so you can take notes, stand so you can move around and be natural, smile so it comes through your voice. The tone is friendly, pro-fessional, crisp."

Leland hit the dialer. "Your opening is critical," Daryll whispered. The phone rang five times. "You're not smiling," Daryll snapped. "Here!" He held up a mirror to Leland's face, and then handed it to him. "Check your expression constantly! Move your arms for a more natural voice effect!"

The phone rang another couple of times. "Keep a hand free to take notes," Daryll barked.

Someone answered. Daryll stopped breathing so he could listen in. "Crisp!" he hissed.

"Heh wohhh!" Leland said, beaming.

Daryll's eyes snapped wide open.

"Well, what are you wearing?" Leland asked.

"No," he said, in reply. "I never wear them. What else you got on?"

Daryll flipped a switch and both sides of the conversation could be heard.

"I am sooo sorry," a breathy-voiced woman said. "I just can't help myself." Daryll looked daggers at Leland. "Joshie is just so cute, I love to let him answer the phone. And he's got the sweetest little cowboy outfit on, spurs and all, he loves to tell people all about it when they call."

"He sure sounds cute," Leland said. "How old is he?"

"Two and a half next Friday." Daryll was almost dancing in place.

"What would you do if he said, 'Mama, I want to get out of this snow and play cowboys someplace warm?'"

"Ohh, I'd say, 'So do I sweetie.' I'm fed up with snow up to my . . . I'm dyin' for a day without havin' to shovel the drive. My husband, too."

"How about a Caribbean Vacation, children free . . ." Leland was reading from a brochure. "Pina coladas on your own sun-drenched terrace, 500-thread Egyptian cotton sheets, babysitter . . ."

"I'd love that," the woman squealed.

"I can give you . . ." Leland searched for the price . . . okay, $899."

"A vacation and $899!! Did I win something?" Daryll moved to cut off the call. Leland held his hand.

"So would you like to sign up now?"

"I would! Definitely. But not right now. I'm booked in to have triplets the day after tomorrow, and between them and Josh, I'll be tied up about eighteen years."

"Well, hon, thanks for your time. Tell me where you're living and I'll send the babies a card and Josh a little gift. Not much, just a memento."

"You are sooo sweet. I just wish my husband was as enthusiastic as you are. Well, I got to go now."

Daryll was making whimpery little sounds. "They never covered this in Cleveland," he said. "Parts of your performance were amazing. Parts were surprising. Parts were *terrible*. We don't *have* gifts to send people. And 'Tell me where you're living.' How creepy is that?"

"I'm sending the gift myself," Leland said primly.

"Why?" Daryll was almost weeping. "*Why?* Keep that up, you'd be spending more than you're making, no time flat. And it's not appropriate!"

"That's Kimi Lynn Arbogast, Whump that was. The minute she said triplets, I knew it was Kimi. Bert's daughter. I couldn't not send her a present, any more than fly." He gave Daryll a scolding look.

"Let's try it again," Daryll said. "Not with real people. I'll be the customer. I'll sit right here, on my phone, and you call me, sell me a vacation."

"Okay."

"Call. Smile. Start waving your arms."

"Hello, is this Daryll D'Agostino? Mr. D'Agostino, my name is Leland DeWitt and I'm calling you today from Caribbean Vacations . . ."

"Is this Caribbean Vacations?"

"Yes, sir, and I'm . . ."

"The *real* Caribbean Vacations?"

"The real thing."

"Well, thank heavens for *that*," Daryll said. "I been waiting for you people to call me for weeks."

"Well, here we are now, sir. I want to . . ."

"Oh, no you don't," said Daryll. "Not so fast. I want an explanation. I was supposed to get a free exploratory dinner from you people, sit down with a tour guide and have the whole thing explained to me in a fine dining establishment."

"Well, okay."

"Can you arrange my free dining experience right now? Send me a voucher?"

"Yes, sir."

"Or better yet, the cash? Let's see, I'd have me a couple beers, then maybe some Manichevitz with my dinner, a sirloin steak, medium rare, some mashed potatoes, some French cut green beans, a side of gravy, and a tiramisu for dessert. That'd be about forty bucks, easy. But the hell with it, if it costs more, I'll suck it up. A check for forty bucks would be just fine."

"Yes, sir," Leland said meekly.

"Oh, but wait, there's the wife. So eighty bucks."

"The wife? But I thought . . ."

"You thought wrong," Daryll said with a smug smile. "Lotta people think that."

"Well, sir, now we might get down to thinking about that vacation. Research shows a Caribbean vacation this time of year improves the quality of your life for the whole rest of the year."

"That so?" Daryll asked, interested. "Where's the research on that? I'd like to look it up, study it."

"Well, it's *our* research, but . . . well, it makes sense, don't it, there you are, laughing at the folks at home shoveling snow, and you with your pina colada, lying on the white sands . . ."

"I take offence at that," Daryll said.

"At what?"

"*White* sands. That's racist. My people have put up with enough down through history."

"You sure have," Leland said, "But I thought you were . . ."

"Thought wrong again," Daryll said.

"But, there's an innocent explanation—see, your rocks and your shells in the Caribbean are white, and they make the sand." Then, to get things straight, he asked if Daryll had a problem with snow.

"No, I don't got a problem with snow, as such. With Snow White, yes, but not snow. No, I tell a lie, I hate the shoveling part."

"Me, too."

"But I got a little business, snow shovels with a special spring on the bottom of the blade, helps hoist it when it's full of snow. Also got a battery-operated heated edge, for ease of cutting into the snow. Invented it myself." Daryll preened.

Leland was intrigued enough by the mechanics of this to stop smiling. "Like to see that."

"Well, I can sell you one with a money-back guarantee, you don't like it, just send it back, free."

"Huh."

"You also get a mug and a pair of socks. But wait! There's more: you also get a bag of grass seed and a scented candle. That's a seventy-dollar value for only $19.99!"

"Boy!" Leland said.

"Postage and packing not included."

"How much is the postage and packing?"

"Fifty dollars and two cents."

"Don't want it," Leland said. "That's ridiculous."

"Course you want it. Guy like you, getting older, needs some help in the snow season."

"I'm only twenty-six."

"I thought . . ." Daryll hesitated.

"You thought wrong."

"Anyways, you need this. I'll send it out, charge it to your card, you don't use it, send it back, you get ninety per cent of your money back."

"I just thought you said free."

"That was then. Seventy bucks. Visa or MasterCard?"

"I want to talk to your supervisor."

"Well, you can't. He ain't here."

"*Someone* there is the supervisor," Leland insisted. "Put him on. Or her. It's my right."

"I *am* your supervisor," Daryll shouted.

"Connect me to a supervisor or I'm hanging up."

"Oh, wait a minute." Daryll motioned for another telemarketer to come over. "Guy wants to talk to a supervisor. Too dumb to follow what I'm saying. Pretend to be my supervisor."

"Okay, boss," the guy said. He nodded absently at Leland, and took the phone. "This is Trevor, the Supervisor. I understand you're having a problem understanding the offer?"

"Oh, no, not at all," Leland said. Trevor raised his eyebrows at Daryll.

"I was trying to get him to take my order," Leland said, "but he's not really with it. The economy's pretty bad right now, loads of people looking for work, you don't need to hire sub-standard material."

"I'll take your order myself, sir," the Supervisor said.

"Okay, here's the deal. He takes the Caribbean vacation, no fine dining option, and I take the shovel. I'll come over and get it myself, don't need any shipping. That a deal?"

Daryll held his head in his hands.

Trevor cradled the phone on his shoulder and signaled Daryll, palms up: *What now?* And Daryll, head still down, made a swatting motion: *Whatever.*

"Well, I guess so," Trevor said. "Or wait . . ." He looked
at again at Daryll. "Yes, sir, I suppose that's okay. I'll get
you his card details."

"Bingo," Leland said, smiling, and hung up.

Leland loved the job. He loved Daryll's belief that there
was a science underpinning their work. He loved the idea
of "secondary goals," which were really a form of whis-
tling in the dark, so you didn't get your spirit broken by
rejection, abuse, and insults. Most of all, he loved talking
to people, hearing their stories.

This surprised him; the boiler factory had been pure
noise, of course, but he could've listened to plenty of stories when he was at the Union Dollar. For the first time,
though—for him, not for Bridget—he realized he was
slightly deaf, but that on the phone he could really make
out all the ins and outs of people's situations.

And Daryll, despite their rough start, loved him. At
the beginning, he'd only kept him on because he was
short-staffed. So many locals were taking off for Arizona
or California or even Alaska, thinking that this recession
was just more of Ohio's unique fifty-year-long downturn.

But within a week or so, Daryll discovered that Leland
was unlike anyone else he'd ever met; his sweet, humble
exterior housed a mind furnished with verandas, niches,
balconies, attics, and Tilt-a-Whirls connected by round-
abouts, byways, and jet paths, all of which he could
flip or rotate like a map, seeing things from new, as yet
unexplored, angles. He could also fix almost anything
including, after a few days, computers, cables, headset

malfunctions, etc., perfectly, but in off-the wall ways that instantly cancelled warranties. Why bother with warranties, though, when Leland could invent a substitute? Daryll became Leland's groupie.

Leland loved the idea that calls tapped into a fathomless universe of people and situations.

He left the day the company head, Jamie, gathered a little group of new employees to show how a master handled calls.

The first was from a sad-sounding woman who called to say her husband had passed away. She wanted the insurance department.

"I'm real sorry, Ma'am. How did he go?" Jamie gave a thumbs up. "Remind me to change our protocol. Limited sympathy works great."

"Heart."

"And how are you doing?" Leland asked.

She began to cry. "Well, I'm on my way to the cemetery now. I'm calling to find out when his life insurance payments start. I want him in a nice plot that I can visit."

"Of course you do. What's his name and policy number?"

"Ralph Little." She read off the number. "We . . . I . . . live in New Middletown. I'm sorry to be crying on the phone . . ." Leland found the number and was about to reassure her when Jamie grabbed the phone.

"That policy has lapsed!" he said.

"It can't have . . . I sent this month's check last week. We've been paying for years."

"Lapsed."

The woman began sobbing.

"We can't talk to you any more without a court order."
Jamie hung up.

Leland stared at him.

"That company often cuts them off right before they're
entitled to get a full payment. They toss the check."

"I *know* that woman," Leland shouted. "I knew
Ralphie. What kind of company does that?"

"A prudent one?" Jamie laughed.

"Hope *you* got insurance," Daryll called as he poured
something into Jamie's computer.

"Whew! What's that stuff?" Leland asked.

"Nail polish remover. It's okay, I got plenty more." He
followed Leland out.

Chapter 19

Leland

"I'll kill you before I let you go," she snarled, waving the gun in her manicured hand.

"You seen today's paper yet, Leland?" Bert asked on the phone.

He hadn't; he was fixated on the TV soap opera. Which one it was, he didn't know: the characters on all of them were named Vance or Vanessa, far as he could tell, and a lot of them were on life support machines. Today, Vance and Vanessa were being taken off the machines. And this Kirk, here, running around behind Megan's back, boy, was he in for it.

Suddenly a news flash scrolled across the screen: "RUNAWAY TRAIN TEARS THROUGH OHIO." Leland switched to the news channel. Just then, a guy stopped the train: he hauled himself up on it as it whizzed past, and stopped it. Wow! A guy about his age, no chicken.

Man oh man, thought Leland. What would it be like to be an ordinary guy, going about your business one minute and wham! The next minute, your life is changed. You get to *do* something. He could imagine the guy walking in for supper that night, his wife and kids so excited, and all the neighbors, too, and him just pretending it was nothing, insouciant, like it's what he'd been doing for the last thirty years. Leland got up and swung off the banister, trying to imitate the guy's moves. It was okay, but of course the banister wasn't going nowhere.

"Leland?" Bert knocked at the screen door.

"There's a guy on TV just caught a train," Leland said.

"Haven't done that in years. Train used to come right in to East Federal Street, I'd ride up to Cleveland maybe once a month. All the tracks tore up now, though. Listen, Leland, turn off the TV, would you, I need to talk to you. Your *Vindicator* come yet?"

Leland turned down the sound but he really wanted to see that guy when he came on, see his face. He bet he'd be an ordinary guy like him. He tried to pretend what it would feel like to be him now, what he would say and all. He looked out front, scanning the front yard for the paper while trying not to miss anything on the TV.

The newspaper was in the wet petunias below the porch. Bridget liked to read the Births and Deaths when she got home, and look at it, all soggy.

"Hold on," he said to Bert, hanging the pages across the porch railing.

The headline said:

DEWITT NAMED CHIEF OF POLICE

"This headline's a good one. My ma had one made up for my dad when he was sick, 'Buck DeWitt Arrested for Bank Heist.' He really liked it." It was nice of Bert to think of him, cheer him up like that. Typical of the guy.

"It ain't a joke. Randy's been going on and on about needing a police force for months. Thinks Earl Arbogast's been setting out to humiliate Hope And Glory for a while now. I woulda told you last night but we thought we better get ourselves over to the jail in North Vienna first and tell Randy. He's there for that potty mouth conviction, happened on Groundhog Day, remember? He's fought the case for months, as you know. And they had him mopping floors, *our* mayor. At first, he suggested 'Bob' Matthews for the police job, but when we said the chief would also have to maintain the city vehicles, including the snow plow, it was a real joy to see Randy's face. 'Leland!' he shouted. It was like a cross was lifted from his shoulders.

Anyhow, we promised to move him back here when our jail opens. Wants to serve the balance of his sentence near his loved ones."

Leland held up a hand as the train guy came back on.

"The pay's not too bad, neither," Bert said. "But we ain't got a uniform. Maybe Bridget could run you up something."

They showed the guy catching the train again, over and over in slow motion. He clicked the volume up again but instead he got Vanessa or whoever saying goodbye to her loved ones. He scanned the paper.

THE HOPE AND GLORY VINDICATOR

Volume 234 Issue 5   Hope And Glory, Ohio

DeWitt Named Chief of Police

In an edifying development, Deputy Mayor Ronnie Zweig, acting for the incarcerated Mayor Randy Anderson, (see below) has appointed Mr. Leland DeWitt as Hope And Glory's Chief of Police, with special responsibility for snowplow maintenance.

The appointment came after Bert Whump pointed out that the Council can afford only one salary, and DeWitt was the sole person in town with the mechanical ability, brains and temperament to tackle all aspects of the job.

Hope And Glory's police station will re-open for business as soon as a committee of local ladies is recruited to get it cleaned up.

Mayor Jailed for Potty Mouth

Mayor Randy Anderson was sentenced to 30 days or 30 dollars last night by Judge Quinn for cussing in the presence of a lady a couple months ago at the Groundhog Day celebrations. The mayor didn't have his wallet on him, so he said he'd take the thirty days. In speech from the court steps, he said he was going to jail on behalf of all the American people and everyone whose God-given rights were being wiped out. Only last month, he said, the Chief of Police over in North Vienna, Earl Arbogast, had suggested he resign, charging that the mayor had uttered "an ethnic slur" when he accused Chief Arbogast of letting last year's Party-Pak burglars go "Scot"-free.

Mr. Anderson can be visited in the North Vienna jail until ours is spic and span.

Local Notes:

Prior to his incarceration, Mayor Randy Anderson, and his new bride, the former Mrs. Septus McCardle, took in the sights of Perth Amboy, New Jersey, after their recent nuptials. They went on all the rides in Marshall Park and had a swell time. The Mayor said Perth Amboy was a real get-up-and-go place, and he had made some useful contacts in the sanitation world. When he had his God-given freedom again, he would be calling a Council meeting to discuss some garbage ideas.

Mrs. Randy Anderson, back from her honeymoon at Patel's Motel in Perth Amboy, New Jersey, told a reporter that Mr. Anderson was a swell fellow but a stranger in paradise when it came to snowplows.

Septic Tank Shocker!
Chief Earl Arbogast of North Vienna, who has been holding on to the body of Zeke Anderson, says he wants to hold on to some parts because he might have an idea.

Algebra Antics!
Here's a fun problem our younger readers will get a real kick out of.

If A is filling a bathtub at the rate of two gallons a minute and B is emptying it at the rate of a quart a minute, how long will it take before the bathtub has twenty gallons?

INSIDE THIS ISSUE

2 Cooking Wieners! Fast Tips

2 Making knick knacks from glue and bread

3 Mayor Anderson wants rest of Dad back

4 Dry Cleaning Disaster: Persia Pelted with moth balls

Other current news on page 3
Where is Chief Grey Wolf?!!

TWI-LITE MOTEL: $22 A NITE

CASINO NITE: FIN 'N FUR KENNELS AND BIBLE SCHOOL. EVERYTHING MUST GO.

PERSONAL MAKEOVERS. CALL LAURINDA "S" AT 330-0186. ALSO GENDER EMPOWERMENT.

DRAINS, YARD WORK, ANYTHING CONSIDERED. BILL McG. 330-6020

YARD WORK. McCARDLE 330-9554

LIGHT HAULING. ANGELO 330-9435

ELECTRICAL WORK. CALL REV. DWIGHT WAYMAN. 330-6666.

"Leland? What about it?"

Chief of Police. Snowplow mechanic, too. It was like some kind of goofy dream: trains drifting by, your name in the headlines, poor Bret here, sobbing at Vanessa's bedside. He switched back.

"You needed what, good marksmanship, be able to fix stuff, maybe direct traffic, fill out forms," Bert said. "Lead parades and such."

Leland would die rather than lead a parade.

"Leland?"

Well, he *was* a good shot, matterafact he had been the Western Ohio junior champion once, and also came first in archery. He'd fixed a lot worse than that snowplow. He knew chaos theory backward and forward, he read everything about it he could get his hands on, and that was all you needed for your basic traffic management. And he had a pretty good vocabulary now from doing so good in his correspondence course, so he'd be okay on reports.

Anyhow, did the train guy sit around wondering if he could do it or not? He'd been getting himself ready for that one chance all his life.

"I'll give it a shot," said Leland. "But I won't be in any parades, okay?"

"Fair enough."

Wait till he told Bridget. Chief of Police. Okay, he'd be the only policeman, but still, unemployed one day and Chief of Police the next! Incogitable. He read the paper again, smoothing out the sheet; he had to hand it to Bert and to Ronnie Zweig at that Council meeting. Him and

Ronnie had always been close, even when Ronnie got on the City Council. The two of them bullied so much by Randy's fool stepbrother in school every day, well, it made them close. Wrought an inextricable bond. Ronnie really stuck it to Randy over that snowplow. So did Laurinda, give her credit. He'd need to get another copy to save. He wished his dad was here.

He needed to make some plans. One thing, he wasn't going to carry a gun. Nosir. To his mind, guns had no place in police work. Did the British bobby need a gun? Weren't your British the most civilized people on earth? Negotiation, reasoning, maybe jujitsu if there was a call for it, but guns were out. Most of your criminals were young boys who just needed some fatherly direction. If his dad hadn't been such a good father, why, he himself could have gone to the bad. Second, he was going to go in for rehabilitation and humane conditions for the poor bastards that never had a chance. Before his carburetor went, he used to run down to Everton to see Mickey McCardle once in a while, and it was pitiful to treat humans like that. Especially over somebody like Squint Sheehan.

But first he had to do something about that snowplow. It was criminal; Randy Anderson shouldn't be allowed near motor transport. That guy in the diaper helping Randy to push the snowplow out of the Twi-Lite Motel room; he never saw a picture like that in his life. And Randy's Chevy, humping along the road like a little car in the cartoons. Every tire at a different pressure; had to be nearly 60 in one, maybe 25 in another, 38 or 40 in a third. People used to stop just to watch Randy at the gas station: never once in thirty years was he known to pull up to the pump and get the tank on the right side. Then he'd go around to the other side of the pump and could never figure out why he was still on the wrong side.

It would be a little awkward at the beginning, Randy being the only prisoner in the jail and all. He might try to teach Randy how to put air in tires and pull up to a pump. If rehabilitation worked on Randy, it'd work on anyone.

He'd also try to figure out what had happened to Zeke Anderson, all that hubbub. Earl Arbogast would have to hand over those body parts.

Leland sat back and watched the guy catch the train again. Now he knew what it felt like. Even if the new job didn't come to anything in the end, he just wanted to remember this minute, hold it for a little bit.

Chapter 20

Laurinda

"It was a major epiphany," Laurinda would tell people in later years, when acolytes and groupies surrounded her at conferences and retreats, begging to hear the story again.

She could go out again since she heard a good cure for agoraphobia was to double your distance from home every day. Maybe you were supposed to walk, but she drove, starting at half a mile, and in no time flat she was part way to Cincinnati. When the next stop was Winnipeg, she was better. She met all kinds on the trips, interesting people, fascinated by her story. But now, at home, the house was just a cold empty lifeless shell, a hollow mockery, what with Randy in jail the last two days.

Today she was sitting in Winkle's, reading up on her anthropology course. But it was hard to study in here with all the racket. She'd suggested the idea of a Library Corner to Glenora Winkle but Glenora said the only place she had was beside the live bait tank and people would be splattered head to toe. So Laurinda was in a regular booth. Catty-corner, a woman with half-moon painted eyebrows was explaining to another woman that a satanic cult over in Cairo was after someone named Edwin.

"A person just can't keep irritating people," she said. "You know yourself, Nadine, what those cults are like. Do you remember the last time Edwin got in trouble, that man and the wart remover, nothing but trouble for weeks. The first time he got a brick through the windshield, he shoulda known."

Nadine asked the woman with the eyebrows why the satanic cult was after Edwin.

"Well, you know how he gets people's backs up. He won't cut his grass; he says he likes the meadow effect. And anyhow, those satanic cults, they sure don't care for gay people."

"I don't think Edwin's gay," Nadine said.

"Nothing wrong with being gay."

"I didn't say there was, Anthea. I was just surprised to hear he was gay all of a sudden, at age sixty-two."

"It can strike at any time," Anthea said, "just like anything else. Look at you, you got hay fever now, never had it as a kid."

Laurinda turned around, introduced herself and welcomed them to Hope And Glory. "You know, your homosexuals have it tough in a lot of places, I know that from my anthropology class. Wait, I'm telling a lie; the Etoro of New Guinea, they actually *make* people do it, even your normal people."

The women shifted a little. Laurinda said she supposed this Edwin wasn't from New Guinea, by any chance? She sure would like to meet someone from there. That hair! And those oh-so-fierce faces, but you knew underneath they had to be sweethearts. "But could I ask you ladies for a teeny favor? Can you keep it down because I have to study?" The women looked surprised, and after some Jell-O and ice cream, they left.

Right now what Laurinda was trying to read about was trial by ordeal. It seems in some cultures, they didn't have judges and lawyers, they decided whether a person was guilty of something, say stealing a mango or suchlike, by sticking their hand into a pot of boiling water. If their hand blistered, they were guilty. This seemed more sensible to Laurinda than the system Judge Quinn used, which seemed to depend on whether he was constipated or not. Some of these cultures, they poisoned a chicken, instead. Easy enough, thought Laurinda, remembering her experience with that peep, but anyhow, what they did was, they poisoned the chicken and said, "If So-and-So is guilty, let this chicken die." But wait. These people weren't dummies. They had crosschecks. They poisoned another chicken and said, "If So-and-So is guilty, let this chicken live." It was pretty close to modern science.

She needed to know all this by Friday night for her anthropology test. Her teacher looked like a gorilla. She wondered if this held for all the subjects. She knew for a fact people looked like their cars, so it might be true for the subjects, as well. The botany professor sure looked as close to celery as made no difference. Anyway, she was doing okay for the test until she happened to see a picture in her book: "A Tuareg man. Tuareg men wear veils and Tuareg women do not."

"That was one of your Ah Ha Moments," Laurinda told people later. "I started to think about those women, and the men, all veiled, and I thought, 'Why not?'"

Not only that, she had the backing of science behind her. Men's beards and ladies' breasts were both secondary sex characteristics. The primary ones were your privates, and Laurinda agreed they should be covered up, all right, neither kind was much to look at. But how come women had to hide their secondary characteristics, things that were actually useful if you went in for breast-feeding, which Laurinda never did, while men got to parade around in their beards? What good was a beard? Well, of course if you had a weak chin, but the only person she could think of who had a weak chin was Mrs. Bert Whump, and she didn't think Bert would be all that happy if she had any more of a beard than she already had.

She decided then and there to do something about it. Randy had his garbage, but what did she have? You needed a higher purpose in life. Make a Difference. That's how The Movement began. B.I.B.—Beards in Bags. And to think it all came from Zeke firing her, and then the factory closing. Would she have gone to college, otherwise? Would she know a secondary sex characteristic from squat?

Still, he was an evil old cuss. Deserved what he got.

"Says here we're all gonna be taller in the future," Bert announced, poking his finger at the newspaper.

"Huh," Randy said. "I think I'm as tall as I want to be. I had them suits made when I was elected, and it set me back a bundle. I'm not lookin' to buy any more for a while."

"No, it says people are going to be taller in the future," said Bert.

"*I'm* people," Randy said, kinda hurt.

"People in the *future* are going to be taller," Bert went on, "because of evolution. Survival of the fittest, and all."

"Ah," said Randy.

"Now that's a thing I never understood," said Bert. "Survival of the fittest. How does that work, exactly?"

"Beats me," said Randy.

213

Laurinda came in. She really liked Bert. What was it about him? "What're you boys talking about?" she asked, giving Randy a little peck on the cheek. It was so nice to have him back from jail. Leland had made it his first act as chief.

"Survival of the fittest," Randy said, kinda bored.

"Well, don't that beat all," said Laurinda. "I just been reading about evolution in my physical anthropology class. See," she said, wiggling her backside firmly onto the stool, "in life, the aim is to have a lotta descendants; the more descendants you have, the better chance your genes will live on into future generations. Bert," she poked at him playfully, "you better get busy."

Bert shifted on his stool and looked unhappy. "Well," he said, "what about this survival of the fittest thing?"

"Well, a lotta people think it means the strong and beautiful and smart are the ones who survive. Not at all." She looked at Randy.

"What's that look supposed to mean?" asked Randy.

"Oh, honey, I was only looking in your direction, not at you. Now," she said, getting warmed up. "Here's how it works. Let's say you got two guys who are good shots and one guy who's a bad shot, and they're fightin' over something."

"What're they fightin' over?" Randy asked.

"It don't matter," Laurinda said. "Maybe they're fightin' over a woman. Yeah, they're fightin' over a woman."

"Wouldn't you know," Randy said. "It's always a woman."

"Ain't it the truth," said Bert.

"So here's the story. If you was one of the guys who was a good shot, who would you shoot at first?"

Randy perked up. "Well, stands to reason, the b . . ."

"Nope," said Laurinda. "Think about it. You'd shoot the other good shot first, because otherwise, he could shoot you. Same for the other good shot, he's going to fire at you, first. And being good shots and all, one of you kills the other, but the bad shot has time to pick off the winner. So he's the one left; he's the fittest."

"Well, I'll be," Bert said. "You're going to be a real professor one of these days, Laurinda." Laurinda admired her nails.

"Well, that sure explains how come there's so many bad shots over at the Rifle Club," Randy said.

They picked at their pissaladiere. "You know, more folks are killed by anchovies than you think," said Laurinda.

Chapter 21

Leland

Later, of course, every Joe Blow in the country claimed he came up with the idea of running the jails through French. Leland didn't actually care who got the credit as long as it worked.

As soon as the Hope And Glory jail re-opened, he had way too many prisoners. Some were sent back home from the jail in North Vienna, and some were new folks, even a few outsiders who had been passing through. Judge Quinn didn't like sending local fellows outta town, he saw how Septus and Laurinda missed Mickey, so he'd shorten their sentence to make sure they could do it in the Hope And Glory jail. Anything above six months, they got sent away. But the ones that stayed here, he made sure they did the whole six, none of this stuff about good behavior. They could practice good behavior on their own time outside. So between one thing and another, the place was booked out.

There was still the mystery of Zeke Anderson's death. Everybody in town had a theory, and everybody had seen somebody else going over to see Zeke that night. Most claimed they went to complain about that smell coming out of his septic tank; Zeke never had much of a nose, working in garbage all his life. Most thought somebody had knocked him over the head with a hammer or such. Bert had been due to retire as police chief a few days after it happened, but he'd left some notes and a brief autopsy report. "Death by drowning," it said. But the case had gone to Chief Arbogast in North Vienna, and he could care less.

That sure was a wicked bruise Zeke had on the back of his head in the photos. Seemed like that could have killed him, easy. And the trouble was almost everyone who turned up at Zeke's place that night had been carrying something heavy: Septus, a tire jack he'd borrowed; Juanetta, her go-everywhere Lee Enfield rifle; Laurinda, a mincemeat grinder so Susie could make some Swedish meatballs for the Church breakfast next day. Randy arrived with a cast iron turkey roaster. Even old Idora had turned up with a steam iron.

At least Randy was out of jail now; Laurinda paid the thirty dollars after Randy spent two nights there. Randy had wanted to stick it out in the name of suffering humanity, little kids without gloves and what all, but Laurinda said she needed her downspout hosed out, and he was to come on home. Randy wrote up a jail journal, and he was talking about getting it published.

Anyhow, here was Leland, prisoners coming out his ears, it was all he could do to keep them entertained. Bridget left the Party-Pak and she and Idora worked full-time for the city now, cooking for the jail. Bridget did the entree and Mrs. Z. did the dessert. One day Bridget gathered the prisoners up and said she didn't want to hear any more whining, this one didn't care that much for tuna, that one got queasy over tapioca, she was fed up, they were all just to tell her the day before what they wanted and she would cook it. Sylene printed out little menu request forms on the computer, and people could also check off vegetarian, kosher and the like. All this opened up a new world of cooking for Bridget: crepes, osso bucco, zesty honey-orange pork chops, finger sandwiches, pierogies. She had to go over to Tommy Brown's ma to get her angel food cake recipe, Tommy wouldn't touch Bridget's. Soon the prisoners were asking Bridget to bring in a cookbook, so they could pick and choose more dishes for her to try.

The jail had no TV; someone stole it before the prisoners ever got moved in. Poltroons. So in the evenings, Leland showed home movies or got them to give him a hand with some project or other; he was rebuilding the engine in the pickup right now. Other times, he might give them an archery lesson with his old bow, or take them out in the yard when the stars were out and explain the principles of navigation. A guy from Quebec on a bad check charge taught some French. They all caught on pretty quick, but Leland decided the only way to go was total immersion, so in the third week of the course, nobody was allowed to speak English any more, except to Bridget and Idora, who had no time to be learning French.

Even so, all this didn't fill the day, some people were kind of listless, nice as pie to Leland's face but he had heard through the grapevine a few were saying they weren't reaching their full potential. Then he started hearing some of the City Council members were worried now the jail was costing more than they thought, they liked the glory and all but they had forgotten a jail was so expensive. He couldn't think how he could cut costs more than he had. The guy from Quebec was even doing ironing for the nuns at Our Lady of Perpetual Sorrow; his ma used to do it for some fancy French order up there in Canada. He was bringing in about thirty dollars a week.

He decided to worry about that later, and concentrate right now on rehabilitation. He started doing remedial calculus with some of them, and Tommy Brown's mother taught decoupage. Sylene raised money for a used computer and after Skip Anderson blocked all the porn sites for her, she asked would anyone like to learn how to use it.

"*Moi*," Troy Winkle said. And Billy Matthews, who was having a lot of trouble with his verbs, real fed up, looked interested, too. "*Moi, aussi*," he said.

They also started building furniture, simple things at first, like birdhouses. Some of them were all thumbs and the jail rang with shouts of "*Merde*!" but they soon learned, and worked their way up to fancier things, veneered TV consoles, whatnots, étegères, and even an antique birthing chair. Some sold real well, and soon they were making library tables and desks for the school.

Some of the fellows didn't care for furniture- making, said it didn't pique their interest much, and they concentrated on the computer. Pretty soon a few of them were real pros, on the Internet at all hours, doing their taxes, publishing a jailhouse newsletter. Sylene came in to do her homework on the computer, and a couple guys would check it. Lonnie Arbogast, one of Kimi Lynn's twins, was in awhile for his specialty, bad checks. He was a whiz with numbers, not surprising since Bert was his granddad, but he always got caught because he couldn't really read or write. He made it his business to sort out the horse problem with Sylene. She read it to him, and he went and put a hole through the bottom of an old metal garbage can, tied a knot inside to hold it there, and hooked the whole lot up to an outside corner of the jail. Sylene said it didn't look much like a horse so he welded a watering can on one end for the head. Lonnie moved the horse around on its rope, and Sylene saw instantly. She was pretty annoyed no one had done that before, but she did say it was cruel to keep a horse tied up that way.

If the armoire hadn't got stuck in the front door frame, nothing more might have happened. But four or five guys had made this 17th century armoire, carvings and inlays up the whatsit, a beautiful piece, and they were sending it over to Yoder's Antiques and Collectibles when they discovered it wouldn't fit through the front door, or any door, for that matter. They were cutting through the door, Tommy Brown saying "*Coupez un peu plus ici*" when Leland came along and yelled "*Saperlipopette!*" and stopped them; it wouldn't look good, prisoners hacking at the jail door. It was bound to rile some of the folks on the Council.

So it sat for weeks in the reception area of the jail, sticking out like a sore thumb because some of the guys had decoupaged the walls in a kind of tropical theme, and the combination just made the whole thing look cheap. Each was fine in its own way, but not together. "*Quelle horreur,*" some said.

Laurinda came in to ask had Leland had heard anything about Randy being followed? He was getting into the garbage business real big now and he wondered had he maybe crossed somebody. Might be there was a contract out on him. Leland said he hadn't heard a thing, but he'd look into it for her.

Laurinda agreed it was a shame about the decor. "Furniture is a big investment," she said. "You take a sofa from Sears, a good one can be real dear, and you get it home and it don't go with your other things, or it does and you're stuck with that style for years. You get your Colonial, you're stuck with that, even if you see a real cute French Provincial coffee table, which would look plain stupid with it. I got my eye on a Early American credenza right now, but my whole living room suit is

Mediterranean, and I just know in the end, I'll have to get all new."

Leland hadn't thought much about furniture before. He hated it like anything when Bridget moved theirs around, and he never did like a night table with pointy corners, you could blind yourself, accidentally, while you were sleeping. He and Laurinda chatted about this awhile, and then she said she had to be getting on home. Anybody following Randy, she was to let him know. No one in his right mind would want to follow Randy, Leland thought. He perked up. Maybe it was a maniac, homicidal. Nah.

But Laurinda had started him thinking. Why should folks have to buy all new, just because they saw a sofa or coffee table that didn't match what they had? Half the stuff they had was only for decoration, anyhow, the side tables, the piano, the pictures, and such.

That's when it hit him. Changeable furniture. No, Faux Furniture, that's what he'd call it. Faux Furniture, Inc. All the guys were trained on the computer now, it would be a cinch.

L'ESPOIRE ET LE GLOIRE VINDICATOR

Volume 234 Issue 29   Hope And Glory, Ohio

Garbage Heats UP

In a surprising development in the ongoing local garbage saga, Police Chief Leland DeWitt announced a new speed limit of 15 miles per hour in Hope And Glory.

This has arisen, according to the chief, in an attempt to control the 50,000 garbage trucks expected to pass through Hope And Glory in the next year. The garbage initiative is part of Mayor Randy Anderson's plan to address the economic woes of the town.

To date, only four trucks have actually deposited in the Hope And Glory facility. Hundreds of others have been stopped and fined for brakes, falsified logbooks, and leakages.

Mayor Anderson blames Chief DeWitt for the fact that the trucks are moving through to North Cairo without stopping. He also objects to the chief deputizing jail inmates to enforce the limit.

The chief had no further comment. The jail and its inhabitants are currently under a strict no-English policy, as part of the chief's rehabilitation. Hundreds, incuding people from as far away as East Lisbon and Cairo, marched last week to protst the smell from the facility.

Chief Announces Fine Furniture Factory

Chief of Police Leland DeWitt released a press statement today which, when translated, announced that the Hope And Glory Jail is to be the site of a major computerized production venture. He hopes this will produce revenue and provide prisoners with useful skills.

The furniture will be produced in hologram form, which Chief DeWitt says is the big thing these days for those of us with tight budgets but a yearning for a different davenport. He has no time for 3D-printing, which could be used to make escape tools, masks and house keys.

"Most people don't think of that."

Fancy Do at the Facility

Mrs. Laurinda McCardle Anderson, who goes by her maiden name, held a Summer Bloom dance at the Hope And Glory Waste Management facility.

Her mother, Juanetta Wilcox, opened the facilities with a show of marksmanship at an impromptu range featuring garbage can targets.

Cute party favors in the shape of tiny garbage cans graced the festive tables. Waiters served bread rolls from recycling bins decoupaged with little waste vehicles. Mrs. McCardle Anderson said all the talk about smell was plain silly.

INSIDE THIS ISSUE

Inside This Issue

2 Pastry pointers from the poky!

2 Slimming in the slammer

3 Crocheting classes at H&G jail

4 Hologram toilets: surprise your guests

5 Forensics for beginners

WHILE THE REV'S IN JAIL AGAIN— ELECTRICAL WORK, CALL MURPH 330-6450

LIGHT HAULING, ANGELO 330-9435, DAY OR NIGHT

FIN'N FUR KENNELS AND BIBLE SCHOOL, ANY OFFERS

Readers please note:
The Vindicator's printing and feature writing contracts have been won by *Compositors with Conviction*

Chapter 22

Leland

L eland looked at his notes.

√ One rotted jackrabbit

√ One broken whiskey
   bottle

√ A booklet, "A Guide to
   Your Bio-Waste," moldy

√ Footprints all over the
   place

√ All kinds of blunt
   instruments

Well, he thought, maybe that little French guy on TV could figure this out, but this was his first time as a detective, and he didn't know where to start: meat grinders, turkey roasters and the like all over the place. He'd never had a chance to see a waste system like this before. It was a real beaut, and the smell wasn't that bad considering it hadn't been looked after for months. Susie had returned home when she heard about Zeke, but after the funeral she went to live with her widowed sister in Nirvana.

Okay, some of the pages in the booklet weren't rotted, and he could read them. Real nice pictures, too. The sludge sitting at the bottom, naturally, and oxygen pumping through the system to keep the particulate matter breaking down. Particulate, that was a new one. What was that? Oh, yeah.

But why was the Wet-Vac in the tank? Had Zeke electrocuted himself? Leland got a heavy snow shovel from the garage and levered it up until he could grab ahold of the cord. Didn't look like anything was wrong with it. He dumped it out to look at it better. Well, well.

√ One rotted jackrabbit

√ One broken whiskey
   bottle

√ A booklet, "A Guide to
   Your Bio-Waste," moldy,
   some pages ruined

√ Footprints all over the
   place

√ All kinds of blunt
   instruments

√ One Wet-Vac, submerged

                  *

√ One wedding ring

He called Susie.

Chapter 23

Randy

"Three men check into a hotel rooms and each pays ten dollars . . ." Bert read out the puzzle in *The Vindicator* as he ate his Sloppy Joe in Winkle's.

"Damn! I don't believe it," Randy said, discarding the veal and kidneys from his Veal and Kidney Stew. "Is that the same three guys was suckin' water outta their basement? What do they need a hotel room for? Wait, don't tell me, I don't want to know."

Bert wrote down some figures.

"Some of them things in *The Vindicator* are so unnatural. Some fool filling up a bathtub while some other fool is emptying it. A and B racing in opposite directions. And this here tongue twister. They're trying to get you to say 'Why why wee ree . . . wry why ree ry . . . .'"

Bert looked at where Randy was pointing in the paper. "Ripe white wheat reapers reap ripe white wheat right." "Now who in hell would ever need to say that? Or not often, anyhow," said Randy. "And this one, 'Ships slits shits.'"

"What?" Bert asked.

"'She sits in her slip and sips Schlitz'," Randy read slowly, his finger on each word. "All I can say is boy, some kinda lady, drinkin' beer in her slip." Randy couldn't keep his mind on artificial problems now; he had too many real ones.

Things weren't working out the way he planned, unless he liked to pretend he planned to have every thug in the area speaking French and dining like kings. Making Japanese flowers out of polygraph paper. All he wanted was a little police presence, and someone running the snowmobile, and a good flow of garbage, and lookit the mess he had.

Laurinda came in and joined them. She really did like Bert, there was something about him . . . no, it was hard to put your finger on. He had a lot to put up with, too. Not so long ago, she had mentioned to Mrs. Bert that she was taking Rollo, her new dachshund, to have his you-know-whats cut off. Mrs. Bert was a real lady, even if she did have a little chin hair, so Laurinda was trying to be delicate. "What are 'whats'?" Mrs. Bert asked. "Testicles," Laurinda said, shortly. "You know, *balls*. Poor little thing, his balls are so big they bang on the steps when he goes up and down."

"That's the same exact thing happens to my Bert," Mrs. Bert said. Laurinda was a bit surprised. Obviously, Mrs. B. was getting awful deaf.

Anyhow, she was glad to see him, and said she thought she'd have a couple pancakes.

"Them prisoners are down there right now in the jail printing newspapers and ironing wimples," Randy told them.

"What's a wimple?" Laurinda asked.

"That hard white starched thing nuns wear, sorta like a bib," said Randy. He was surprised at Laurinda, her being so obsessed with the Catholics, that she didn't know what a wimple was. Anyhow all the more reason any kids they have shouldn't be brought up Catholics. He himself didn't know what it was until Leland DeWitt told him, but then he wasn't much of a theologian.

Bert said he had to get on home, put up some railings, it was getting harder to get up and down his steps.

Randy studied Laurinda. Did she know she was probably going to be wearing black, soon, a widow at her age? But right now, she was wearing a sheep costume. Since she was able to go out again, she wanted to keep herself occupied, get some job experience until she could be a professor. Loving dogs and all, she decided to become a trainer. "Canine educator" was what they called it these days, apparently, but she was just starting out, so "trainer" was good enough for now.

"Well," she said, to get Randy's mind off his problems. "That's one more dog won't scare any sheep." She mopped some maple syrup off her woolly front.

"How's that work, anyhow?" Randy asked.

"Well," Laurinda said, "you know how some dogs got a taste for chasin' sheep. Farmer'll shoot them if he catches them. Mary Lou Pusser's dog was like that, and Bill Pusser said one more time and 'Blam!' So what I do is, I make them scared of sheep. I go out there in this outfit, and when the dog comes running, I rear up in my capacity as a sheep and get him in a half Nelson, or make scary noises, or whatever. I'm taking this off the minute I get home, it's itchy as hell. My next job today's teaching old Idora's dog to dial 911 if Idora falls down. I dress up like Idora, you can't expect an old lady to keep falling down just to oblige her dog. Tomorrow, I go over to North Vienna, to Mamie Arbogast's. She wants a dog that won't eat her parrot, and I got one trained specially."

"Or you could train the parrot to yell, 'Sit!'" Randy said. Laurinda loved the goofy ideas Randy came up with.

Randy wondered how come Laurinda could make such a go of scaring dogs. When he announced his moose-scaring plan on the radio that time, he never heard the end of it. And then those cartoons in the *The Vindicator*, him in a diaper on a moose, just plain cruel. And inaccurate, but that's what you pay for a free press.

Randy wanted to show an interest in his wife's career, encourage her, especially if she was going to be a widow before she knew what hit her, because if things kept up that's exactly what was going to happen. Randy was in real trouble; someone must have put a contract out on him. One of the Big Boys. Someday soon he was going to be ambushed behind the Dairy Isle and blown to kingdom come when he switched on his ignition; he wouldn't be the first.

Truth was, the garbage business was not working out so good. It started out fine; he sent in a good high bid to the Garbage King. He sent in a low one after Laurinda mentioned it worked the other way around: Randy wasn't buying the garbage, he was being paid to process it. He built a beautiful facility; the town borrowed some money, and to be fair, the revenue the prisoners were generating didn't hurt. Things were finally working out. The mayor of North Vienna, Gilbert T. Arbogast, the chief's brother, was spitting, he was so jealous. Randy hadn't lorded it over him too much; some people were just born without giddyup, no point in hurting their feelings.

But what happened was the Garbage King took forever to get back to him. Randy called him five, six times a day, and only got a message saying, "Ace Waste Management and Collectibles. Rocco can't come to the phone right now. Please leave a message and he'll get back to you as soon as possible. Have a good day."

After hearing this twenty-thirty times, Randy thought he could nearly say it himself. Rocco could hardly still be laid up with liposuction. One night, around ten, Randy figured out how to put the number in memory and set up "redial;" boy, you nearly needed a Ph.D. for that, but a little while later, he was pretty proud of himself when someone answered right away.

"That Rocco?" Randy asked.

"Noo," said a cautious Voice. "Who's this?"

"This here's Randy Anderson, callin' from Hope And Glory, I need to talk to Rocco."

"There's no Rocco here," said The Voice. The phone got dropped. He could hear muffled noises in the background, grunts and curses, like, and Randy knew damned well he was there. Talk about sinister; the guy sounded gruff, maybe even doped a little. Randy wasn't going to be scared off; too much was at stake. The Voice seemed to have some kinda accent, Irish, maybe.

"Listen," Randy said, bristling. "I'm in real trouble here, and I been worried sick waiting for him to call me back. I need to talk to Rocco, and *now*." He liked that; it sounded steely.

"Why don't you just forget about Rocco, there's a good lad? Your health is the most precious gift you have. Get some sleep." The Voice hung up.

Randy was hopping. Sleep? It was only nine p.m. He called a few minutes later. The Voice actually got kinda snotty and even tried to pretend to Randy he had the wrong number, no Rocco there. Randy kept calling and letting it ring. Finally, The Voice answered again and snapped, "Listen, boyo, I was asleep, what do you want?"

"I'm waitin' on a shipment of five hundred loads of garbage this week. I'm already three weeks behind in my garbage."

"Oh, God," The Voice said, wearily. "What garbage would that be, now?"

"The garbage Rocco's supposed to send me. Rocco,
the Garbage King," Randy said, a little sarcastic. This
was intolerable.

"Ah, *that* garbage," The Voice said soothingly. "Well,
as you said yourself, Rocco handles that." He paused; he
was obviously trying to think up a cover. "Rocco's indis-
posed. He got eight to ten, out in six with good behavior,
I'd say. Of course, you know how Rocco is in the behavior
department."

"In jail?" Randy yelped. He could empathize with that.
The desolation, the heartbreak. Poor Rocco. "Well, who
are you, then?" asked Randy.

"Paddy McPhillips, at your service." That was more
like it. "Listen, could you ever call me in the morning?"

"Whatever you say, Paddy, but I sure hope we can
do business. I was real close to Rocco. I need garbage,
now." Randy was almost pleading. He hated himself
when his voice went up like that. "I got this quality
facility, idle, I got people waitin', everyone depending on
me. I'm the mayor of this town. The newspaper here, I
don't want any more diaper pictures, or moose pictures
either, Rocco, he'd understand how delicate it is when
you're at the top . . ."

"Okay, okay," Paddy said soothingly. "I'll send you
some first thing in the morning. No need to get into a
state. But please stop tormenting me with these feckin'
phone calls at all hours. You got Goretti and myself cru-
cified here."

"Who's Goretti?" asked Randy.

"My daughter," Paddy said. This sounded like a one-horse operation to Randy. He wished he had checked this all out more thoroughly, but oh, no, not him. Old Randy Anderson, he thought, always wading in where fools feared to tread. Would he ever learn? But right now, he was going to follow through, come what may.

Sure enough, a truckload of garbage arrived within two days, and Randy flagged it down and waved it into the landfill. The guy said another one was coming in the afternoon, and Randy got a few City Council members out on the road with him to mark the occasion. He called Paddy to thank him.

The next two days, more trucks came but they whizzed right through Hope And Glory. Only two more stopped, and only after he directed them in himself. The drivers seemed nice enough, happy to stop and take a load off for a while. But he couldn't be out on the road every day.

Randy called Paddy McPhillips again.

"*Ni Bearla agam!*" Paddy snapped when he heard Randy's voice.

"What the hell is that, Paddy?" Randy asked, recognizing the voice.

"The Irish language," Paddy said. "For your information, it means 'I don't speak English.' Is there no getting rid of you? Now what's the problem? Didn't you thank me yourself for sending you some garbage?"

"I need five hundred loads a *week*. Where's the rest?"

"Well, now," said Paddy, obviously trapped. "That would be telling."

Suddenly it all became clear to Randy. People thought
he was dumb, but he wasn't all that dumb. The trucks
passing through Hope And Glory, going on down the
road. Damn! "I know what's going on," he said to
Paddy. "I'm on to your little game. You and the mayor
of North Vienna."

"What North Vienna would that be?" asked Paddy.
"Austria?"

"You make me sick," said Randy. "I bid fifty dollars
a ton for that garbage, and I happen to know Gilbert T.
Arbogast bid fifty-five. I won. I want that garbage."

"Merciful Hour," said Paddy. "Sure, how would we
live on fifty or fifty-five dollars a ton? That's not the way
business works, Mayor. Goretti here is doing a course
in homeopathy, part time, and I have a lot of expenses,
myself. Only yesterday I had to put a flea in the bank
manager's ear when he tried to call in my little loan for
the new shed."

Randy wasn't going to be put off by implied threats,
no matter how grisly. But Paddy was right; he was a babe
in the woods in regard to this kind of thing. Gilbert T.
Arbogast must be giving him some kind of sweetener. "All
right, *all* right," he said, in a world-weary voice. What're
you paying him? Forty-eight? What's he kicking back?"

"Forty-eight!" Paddy hooted.

"Forty-five," said Randy, "and two dollars a load on
the side. That's my last offer."

"Done," said Paddy. "I'm after spitting on my hand.
Our custom here, when we make a deal."

Randy didn't like the sound of that, and there was a sound, all right, but people would be laughing outta the other sides of their faces at 50,000 loads a year.

"Make the extra out directly to my account in the Ulster Bank, Dublin, Ireland, Gerry Rafferty, Manager."

"You keep your money offshore? I heard you big guys do that."

Right now, Randy could keep his own money in a gum wrapper, he was so broke from subsidizing this garbage enterprise. And he would have to scrape together more money after this to cover his new loss.

But one thing, the trucks were stopping in Hope And Glory now. Some of the local ladies set up a kind of free soup kitchen, them coming from so far with no decent cooking, and the poor guys were real grateful. Joked that that was the only reason they stopped. Randy let them have their fun, and the ladies their glory; he had the satisfaction of knowing it was all his work that had achieved this, and pretty soon Hope And Glory would be turned around. Right now, five fellows were working over there, and soon, who knew how many.

It wasn't all roses, not by a long shot. One of the trucks turned over on Route 123, and held up traffic for nearly a day. Randy lived on 123 himself, and the Twi-Lite Motel was there, too, and the smell lingered for days. Pretty soon, the quality facility smelled, too, a combination of rotting raw chicken and open sewer. His own late stepfather was so particular about his Bio-Waste, and here was Randy with cones of Kleenex stuck up his nose.

And on top of it all, whatever had gotten into Leland DeWitt, he was stopping every garbage truck coming through town. Citing them for being overweight, bad brake systems, leakage, false logbooks, you name it, and fining them. When he didn't have anything else on them, he fined them for speeding, because he had lowered the speed limit to eighteen miles an hour. Then fifteen, thirteen and now traffic was nearly going backwards.

Worst part, he was using the prisoners to do the policing, said he could hardly do it all himself. Randy was irate. "Them prisoners could escape," he said. "Plenty more where they came from," Leland said, and told Randy to concentrate on running the facility. He asked Randy to go over with him to Zeke's old house so's he could look at the toilet. He was only trying to humiliate him, playing the big shot. Even put a "Police" tape around the toilet.

Trouble was, the people in the town were behind DeWitt, because of the smell from the facility. And the trucks were leaving, going on to somewheres, maybe North Vienna, or else back to New Jersey.

Randy called Paddy. "*Cen chaoi a bhfuil tu?*' asked Paddy. "How are you?"

"What kinda garbage you sendin' me?" Randy asked. "Half of it ain't sealed, the trucks are leakin', the facility smells like I don't know what."

"You should be able to eat your dinner off a good facility," Paddy said. "You must have a very poor class of a dump there."

"I got an almost state of the art process here. And people are startin' to kick up, protests and all. The police chief is fining the drivers right and left. I have to pay my people time and a half just to go near it. I'm broke."

"You're committed, mayor. I went to a lot of trouble on behalf of your good self. The mayor of North Vienna is gunning for me, says I'm a marked man, *le do thoill*, would you believe it. Fifty thousand loads a year: you're committed. No backing out, now. If you want to play with the big boys, you'd better shape up. I send, you take. No questions asked."

"Can I ask a question?" Randy asked.

"Shoot."

"How come the Mafia is speakin' Irish?"

"You got to move with the times."

So, here was Randy, the public screaming, garbage on the roads, huge paydays to meet, getting pitiful money now from Ace Waste Management, none actually, yet. He tried to be positive, but it was getting real hard. Zeke had warned him many times that his little habit of looking on the bright side would turn around some day and bite him on the behind. Whatever you thought about him, Zeke did have some deep insights. And on top of everything else, a big ugly guy was followin' him all the time now. He didn't know who the guy was, but he looked like he was carryin'.

Randy wanted out.

"Well, me bold bucko," said Paddy McPhillips when Randy called and begged to be released from the contract.

"Top o' the morning," said Randy. "Sorry I don't know any other words in Irish."

"That's not Irish. Do you know the word smithereens?' Do you know the word 'galore?' Or 'slew?' All three are words borrowed from Irish. As in 'You are in trouble galore. A slew of people are after your head, and smithereens is what you'll be if you don't pay up. Stop playing the fool. That's my last word."

Randy was shaking when Laurinda came home and asked, "Who's that creep out front?" She checked the messages. Most were about her campaign. But one was for Randy. Who's Rocco?" she asked, as she wrote it down. "Says he's better now and wants to talk to you."

That night, Randy dreamed he was color-blind, stuck in a prickly shrub with bad breath. He woke up. It was that wolfhound of Laurinda's, Pixie, it had got into the bed with them. His eyes were fine: Pixie was black and white.

He fell asleep again. Now he could see himself hanging in Winkle's freezer, and then being processed in his own quality facility. He woke up again, shaking. Okay, well now he knew he could dream in color, or red, leastways.

Chapter 24

Leland

Thud! Leland could almost picture the blow and hear the sound, like a melon being thumped. Could happen to anyone; happened to him once. His eyes watered a little when he thought about it. But the blow didn't kill Zeke; everything Susie had told him on the phone made sense. That only expanded the pool of suspects.

Leland trekked over to Zeke's old place again, this time with a fresh booklet from the Bio-Waste manufacturer, so he could read the pages that had been ruined by mold. He'd love to see this baby in action, so he got the electricity company to turn the power back on. If it was as good as it sounded, he might splurge and get him one himself. Bridget would be in seventh heaven.

Okay. So now the juice was on and he took off the
cover. Nothing. Leland poked around some. Who wired
this thing, anyhow? According to the booklet, the alarm
system should warn you when things go wrong. He went
over to the house and clambered through a cellar window.
No alarm system that he could see.

Back out again. The booklet showed the wires were
all underground, snug. But knowing about Reverend
Wayman's electrical fiascos, he poked around in the leaves
and mud, and found them trailing here and there on top.
And *there*, well, there it was, clear as day.

He looked at the booklet again. Well, no wonder. He'd
go back to the office and call the manufacturers.

When he got there, the phone was ringing. "*La Prison
de L'Espoir et de la Gloire*," Leland said.

"Mother of Mercy," Paddy McPhillips said. "I thought
I was ringing the USA. *Excusez-moi. Parle Anglais?*"

"Acourse," said Leland. "I 'pologize."

"Not at all," said Paddy. "*Je m'appelle Paddy McPhillips*.
Well, listen till I tell you. I got your number from Directory
Inquiries here in Ireland. This character from your town,
I don't know how he got my name, but he's ringing me
up every hour of the night. Doesn't seem to understand
that the earth rotates. He has me demented. And now
he's sent some money to my bank. Eight dollars, before
it was converted."

"Who is it?" asked Leland.

"He says he's the mayor, if you don't mind. Thinks I'm
connected to someone named Rocco. I played along for a

while, I thought the poor devil was missing a gear or two but now he's ringing all night long, crying and begging. A grown man, mind you. I humor him by pretending to send him a bit of garbage now and then, scraps from my paper shredder. Maybe I took it too far. Poor devil, I don't think he's the full shilling, and I don't want to send him over the edge. And telling me he's the mayor! Some poor eejit, more like it."

"Nope," said Leland. "He's both."

"Get away!" Paddy said. "And tell me this, how would a fellow like that get elected? Although God knows it happens here, too. And you speak French in the jail? I suppose you're following the Napoleonic code?"

"Nah, you got your Napoleonic Code down in Louisiana," Leland said. "Here we got the Common Law system, same as you." He settled in for a nice long chat. After a fairly brief history of your U.S. unwritten legal system versus your civil codes, Leland asked, "How's things over your way these days? Suppose you're dodging bullets, regular?"

"Not at all. Very quiet here. You're thinking of the North in the old days. Nothing ever happens here in Killeenaran. Randy Anderson was the most interesting thing ever happened here. I'll be sorry to lose him."

That Randy sure was a pistol, Leland thought. Imagine trying to get garbage from Ireland. And he seemed to be having a bad effect on Laurinda, too. A few weeks ago he saw both of them in Winkle's, Laurinda dressed up like a sheep. Never saw anything like it.

"Well, I don't want to run your phone up," said Leland, "but it sure has been nice speakin' with you. I never spoke to anyone further than Cleveland." He told Paddy not to worry about Randy, and not to be a stranger, to drop by any time he was in the area. He should avoid Route 123, it had a temporary bottleneck. Paddy said he'd love to come; he had never been out foreign. He was a widower himself but his daughter Goretti was still at home and was dying to visit the States. Randy had her nerves destroyed, waking her up at night. Paddy had changed his telephone number. "And if you know anything about the Irish telephone system, all I can say is that it would have been faster to climb Kilimanjaro backwards."

"Well, you're welcome here any time. We're dead flat."

"À *bientôt*," Paddy said.

Leland decided to keep nabbing the trucks as they passed through to North Vienna. But Mayor Gilbert T. Arbogast made an official complaint against Randy, saying he had been hijacking Gilbert T.'s garbage that he had bid fair and square for.

"I've had Mrs. Ramsey's boy Bobby tailing Randy," said Gilbert T., "and I have evidence. By the way, Bobby's a big boy and he's not all there, so we want to be sure he gets his meals. If you see him around, Leland, will you tell him to get on home now?"

The fines on the trucks had been a good earner; a couple more weeks and there'd be enough to patch the school roof. It gave the prisoners an interest, too, because they got to talk to fellows from out of state, learn a little about long-distance hauling. Leland himself was shocked at the condition of some of the trucks, and was giving PowerPoint presentations to the prisoners in the evenings. Tonight he was doing one on worn air lines. And the hologram furniture, well, who would have thought it! It caught on just like wildfire. Filled a real hole in the market. People were ordering brocade chaise longues, flying geese, grandfather clocks, paintings of the Last Supper, china closets full of fine crockery and such. Each item was supplied with three in-built styles, Early American, French Provincial, and Minimalist, and people could change in a minute, giving their home a whole new look at affordable prices. You could project a new veneer on your old kitchen cabinets. The kitchen people, Sears and them, were hopping, but their prices had come down quite a bit since.

The prisoners were real computer whizzes now, and they tried cuspidors, a nice antique touch, but people who ordered them soon wanted their money back, said it wasn't a bit funny when folks took them for real. And one man had put his shoulder out on a hologram door, hit the wall instead, but other than that, very few problems. In fact, it was the real furniture that was causing the trouble, people smashing cups down through plate glass tables, kidding around and whacking real chandeliers, and that guy who was showing off, thinking he was walking on a hologram swimming pool, well, what could you do? Some people became real nervous and gingerly, feeling their way around their furniture, but most were completely satisfied. A few thought the plaid items were ugly, but Leland never was much on colors.

He wished his dad knew about all this. He was thinking about him a lot lately. So was somebody else, it seemed. On the first Sunday of every month, fresh flowers appeared on Buck's grave. Black tulips. Leland thought his ma was putting them on until she told him what a nice thought it was, him and Bridget going to all that expense. Bridget wasn't doing it, and Sylene had no money. Ryan wouldn't know a flower from a cow plop.

Leland began to wonder if Buck had another side to him. A secret lady friend? Yeah, he supposed he'd be disappointed, but God knows, his dad never had much. Would he begrudge his dad a fling in his waning years? Or his ma, now that his dad was gone, although he laughed at the idea of his ma ever having an affair in her life. Never even had a boyfriend before his dad. She was so proper. But she was a good-looking woman, people always used to say she was a real beauty when she was younger. He'd heard Bert was sweet on her once. He'd have to make a little joke about it to Bert in the Party-Pak sometime. Or maybe not, wasn't very respectful. Anyway, these flowers on his dad's grave were a mystery. The only old lady he could think of was old Idora, and that didn't seem too likely.

He headed over to Winkle's Party Pak. Bridget was visiting her ma and the kids were at the game. Butch Winkle was serving Raw Beef Salad with Capers on Toast Points; Leland got an almost painful flashback to a baloney sandwich Bridget used to put in his lunch bucket. Boy, he'd pay good money for that sandwich right now.

Winkle's
Party-Pak
and Live Bait

"Bum bandits," said Mrs. Bert.

While they were waiting on the meatloaf plate at Winkle's, she and Bert were each working through a pile of his mail. Ever since he signed up for all those mailing lists, it took them ages every morning.

"What?"

"'All you randy bum bandits out there,' this here booklet says. Has a lotta ads for videos and such."

"Gimme that, for cryin' out loud," Bert said. "How come they're sendin' me that stuff?" He snatched it.

"Been comin' for months," Mrs. Bert said.

"How come I ain't seen it?" Bert asked.

"Well, some I threw out. Some I kept in my good drawer, with my hankies and such."

"That stuff ain't for ladies," Bert cried.

"Been a lady all my life," Mrs. B. said.

251

"Acourse you have," Bert said, patting her hand. "Nobody more."

"Well, no need for a person to be a lady twenty-four hours a day."

Bert was still studying her when Randy came in, looking a bit drawn, and sat down with them. "There's fifty socks in a drawer, ten each of black, white, plaid, red and brown," Randy read from *The Vindicator*. "Now what they want to know is, if these fifty are all mixed up, and it's dark, say early in the morning, what is the lowest number of socks you have to pull out to get at least two socks the same color? How come he don't keep them together in pairs?" Randy asked. He handed Bert the paper.

Bert squinted at it. "It don't say," he said.

"Laurinda keeps mine rolled up in pairs."

"I thought Laurinda was a feminist."

"She is. Nothing in their platform about socks. It's bras and beards. Her bras is in the drawer under my socks."

"Okay, okay. If these fifty are all mixed up," Bert said.

"Was me, I'd get me a night light. Listen, that guy that don't vote, the one that likes sherry, you say he don't like fast cars or women?"

"Nah," said Bert. "Likes fellows, though." Who woulda guessed it, thought Randy. The Lone Ranger, of all people. Randy had always been too gullible, he guessed, too ready to follow his star, no matter how hopeless, no matter how far. And now lookit. Well, he was awful disillusioned.

Chapter 25

Laurinda and Friends

"They always say your average housewife could run the Russian Army, but where's she supposed to get the time?" Laurinda asked Juanetta. She had about twenty minutes each day before Randy got home from work. No army's going to sit around all day until 4:40 P.M. She pinned a crocheted fancy piece to her ironing board so it would dry straight.

She needed to strategize the Beards in Bags Movement, get all her ducks in place, but she had her hands full, what with helping Randy, crafting his vision statements, paying his bail and living up to the public's image of The Mayor's Wife. And now here was Juanetta, gabbling on about something.

"All this fuss over them deadbeats in the jail being able to speak French is nonsense," she said. "Anyone can do it. I have, all my life. just dropped the final sound of most words." For example, "petite" became "pettee." Her friend Genevieve McGowan became "Genavee." Robo, vichyswah. Simple.

Laurinda had already had enough of this French stuff when she was a teenager. "You should read more French authors," Juanetta had said to her when she was about fourteen. "Daffeen Da Meer, she's one of the best." Laurinda had gone down to the library and asked a really cute man librarian, a guy from out of town, for some of her works. Okay, maybe she pranced a little, trying to impress him with how cosmopolitan she was. It all backfired when he handed her Daphne Du Maurier's *Rebecca*, and kind of sniggered.

What Juanetta had really come over about was why the people in the vet's office had given her such a look when she brought her parakee in. They asked her was Laurinda her daughter and started laughing.

"So what's up?" Juanetta asked Laurinda.

Could she continue to withstand this kind of relentless public scrutiny that came with power, Laurinda wondered? This example started when her wolfhound Pixie had two litters of the sorriest looking things you ever saw, half spaniel or something. Her feminist side didn't want Pixie spayed, but her carpet owner side won out: a big dog like that, she had to wear a diaper when she went into heat and Randy about blew a gasket when he saw her, thought Laurinda and Pixie were mocking him. But the minute Laurinda made the vet's appointment, she began to worry.

"I'm worried about doing this in case she might be pregnant," Laurinda said to the vet's assistant when she got there.

"Oh, that's okay," one of them said, kinda airy.

"Well," said Laurinda, "I know it's different with dogs, but I sure wouldn't do this if I was pregnant."

"Really?" asked the girl. "What would you do?"

"I don't know," said Laurinda. "Wait, I guess. Have it, first."

"Huh," said the girl, who was looking at her highlights in a hand mirror.

"No, I mean, I'm not strict right-to-life or anything, but after all. And what happens to the puppies? Do they just fall out, or what?"

The girl didn't answer. She stretched her chin up, trying to see a little whisker. Of course, these girls, they don't like to face up to things like that, but they'd have to, soon enough. "Would you like to talk to the doctor, Mrs. Anderson?" the girl finally asked. "He'll be in pretty soon. He'd probably be really interested in talking to you."

Laurinda let the 'Mrs. Anderson' pass. No point in debating feminist issues with a girl as insensitive as this one. She left with strict instructions for them to call and let her know how things were going. It wasn't that she thought of animals as children, oh, no. Not like those women in New Guinea she read about in her anthropology books who breastfed their pigs.

About noon, no one had called Laurinda, so she phoned to ask how Pixie was doing. "She's just fine," said the girl. "Beautiful."

"Is she still groggy?" Laurinda asked. "Is she alert?"

"Um, I think maybe you should talk to the doctor," said the girl. "I'll put him on."

"Laurinda," the doctor said. "I'm Doctor Prendiville." Typical, Laurinda thought. He doesn't know me from Adam and I'm "Laurinda" and he's "Doctor." Wait till she got that Ph.D.

"You seem to be distressed," he said. "I'm told you had a lot of questions."

"Matterafact, I do," Laurinda said. "That girl, she couldn't care less whether Pixie was pregnant or what happened to the puppies. I asked was she groggy and she didn't even bother to give me an answer."

"Bathing doesn't usually hurt the puppies," the doctor said soothingly. "And we don't put a dog under for a shampoo."

"Who said anything about shampoos? I'm talking about spaying."

"It says here you sent the dog in to be bathed."

"I sent the dog in to be spayed. S-P-A-Y-E-D."

"Tsk, tsk. No need to spell, Laurinda. Well, that explains things. A bit."

Laurinda was so irritated, she had Randy go get Pixie. In fact, she thought, this was the kind of thing that happened to Randy, not her. Maybe it was catching. Next thing, she'd send Pixie over to be de-fleaed and she'd come back with her ears cropped.

When Randy came back, he said, "Those people over there, I know they're voters and all, but boy are they nibbynoses. I guess when you're a public servant, your life has to be an open book. Above reproach." He looked at Laurinda sorta reproachfully.

Later that night when they were relaxing together in the tub, candles and wine and all, Randy asked, "Is it true you never took a bath when you were pregnant?"

Okay, now Juanetta had gone down to the jail. Leland wanted to interview her some more about Zeke's death or Juanetta wanted to interview Leland in French, Laurinda didn't know which. She doubted that Juanetta was the one who killed Zeke, but she sure had enough armaments to do it.

Anyhow, it gave her a few moments' peace to think about the Movement, that was the important thing. It was one of those ideas that when it comes to you, you want to hit yourself over the head with a brick for not thinking about it before. She was getting calls from all over the world about Beards in Bags (B.I.B): Norway, Ireland, Denver, France. A group of women from an ethnic group called the Hairy Ainu in Northern Japan sent a message saying it wasn't a minute too soon. A woman wrote her from Sweden saying she supported her in principle, but Swedish women liked to go topless a lot, and if they demanded their men wore their beards in bags, it could all backfire.

People were signing up like mad, and she had cadres of local women now, sewing little beard bags and sending them out with the literature. The literature had pictures showing your primary and secondary sexual characteristics, men and women, and were in great demand, especially in schools, because she had a good outreach program to elementary schools. Most of the bags were muslin, but some were designer models, denim, crochet, even raffia. A reporter came from *The New York Times* to talk to her about it; he said the *Times* was thinking of having a correspondent in the area to save him the trips. Lyle Stivanski was the name; he used to be on WHAG before he went back to New York. Funny, Hope And Glory was the hub of a lot of things right now: prisoner rehabilitation, holograms, the B.I.B movement, and he had heard something about the Mafia, too. Odd how little seemed to happen while he was living there.

Some men were being real good about it, the gender sensitive ones, like Randy. Right now, Randy was only wearing his beard bag around the house, symbolically like, since he didn't have a beard, but he said he would soon be taking the message to the public. Maybe in his next State of the City speech. On the other hand, some real ignorant guys said they weren't wearing them, and it was fine by them if women didn't have to wear anything on their breasts; they'd pay good money to see that, in fact they already were. She had developed a more intensive outreach program for the bags, and Mickey said he would give it a shot on some of the fellows up in the prison in Everton, anything for his ma.

It was all falling together now. Sharing the mayoralty spotlight had given her a graceful touch with her public, her brain sparkled with anthropological ideas, and thanks to agoraphobia, she was widely traveled. She was Making a Difference. Now there was just Mickey, still in jail.

B ert and Mrs. Bert were having Succulent Morsels of Veal with Celeriac and Raisins in Rum. "I don't know how to bring this up," said Bert. "A while back you said you didn't care to be a lady twenty-four hours a day. Which hours was you thinking of, exactly?"

"The night hours," said Mrs. Bert, scooting the celeriac onto her coffee saucer.

"How come you never said this before?"

"You never asked," she said. "You always treat me like some kind of plaster saint."

"Well, but," said Bert. "Before we was married, you never let me . . ."

"Certainly, *before* we was married. Afterwards is a different story. How come you think I married you, anyways?"

"Well, I guess I don't know," said Bert.

"All those girls, before we was married, all I ever heard was what a Romeo Bert was, a real Casanova, the Great Lover. Bert, Bert, Bert, that's all they could talk about. I was kind of looking forward to it. Of course," she said, sitting up straighter, "I don't want you to think that was the only reason I married you."

"You knew about all those girls?"

"Every little thing."

They saw Randy and Laurinda coming in. "Nice girl," said Mrs. Bert, "but she seems to think I'm deaf, for some reason. And she got no sense of humor to speak of."

Randy and Laurinda sat down in the booth with them. They ordered BLTs on rye toast, no mayo.

"Okay, here's one," said Laurinda said, flattening the newspaper. She shouted a little for Mrs. Bert's sake. That last episode, talking about Bert's balls and all, she didn't want any more of that kind of talk. "You and I both have some paper clips. I say to you, give me a dozen so I can have twice as many as you will end up with. But you say, you don't really need all the paper clips you already have. Give me a dozen, so we can both end up with the same number. How many paper clips do you have and how many do I have?"

"Well, that's not nice," said Randy. "We should have the same. Anyhow, this state has community property."

"Yeah, but how many do you have and how many do I have, it wants to know?"

"I don't believe I ever seen you with a paper clip," said Randy. It was amazing the way you could be married to a person and not notice a thing like that. It was part of the magic, he guessed. "Now, in my line of work, you'd be surprised at the paper clips I go through, maybe twenty or so a day. They nearly fly outta the box."

"You work too hard, honey," said Laurinda. "You oughtta take it easier."

Bert stood up and got Mrs. Bert's coat. "We gotta go, kids. Alberta and me got to catch up on some things."

Chapter 26

Randy, Juanetta

"Nauseating," Septus said to Juanetta as they sat on her front porch glider, snacking on grape Jell-O with marshmallows. He'd been down to the jail to be interviewed some more by Leland.

"All I could remember was the awful stench over there, sickening, and even when I lit a match, I could barely make out Zeke with that bottle. Was me, I woulda installed some lights out there, but Zeke, he was always so cheap."

Today was Juanetta's Rifle Tots day with a brand new class at the Precious Lambs, so she'd had to step out of the way pretty smartish a couple times. Septus always calmed her down: he'd been a good son-in-law to her, he was a quiet, intelligent man, and the last thing in the world you'd think was he lived on the same planet as Laurinda,

Reenie, Teeny or Mickey, much less was related to them. Something had gone wrong, somewhere.

Of course she wondered where she'd gone wrong herself; two of her daughters had married Randy Anderson, which was nearly like saying two of her daughters had married a pot plant. Her grandchildren could fill a book; matterafact, someone from Cleveland was writing a book on Mickey alone.

Randy pulled into Juanetta's drive. Her car was there. Good. No matter who was after him, they wouldn't mess with Juanetta, 1) because she was crazy, and B) because she was big. Armed, too, usually. He could see Septus was there as well. A bit booky for a man, Randy always felt, but sensible.

He got out, fell to a crouched position and ran up the steps to the porch.

"I'm leaving town for a while," Randy told them, straightening up behind the honeysuckle trellis. He kept rolling Juanetta's side awning up and down.

"Stop fooling with that. Where you goin'?" she asked. "Is Laurinda goin', too?"

"No," said Randy. "It's kind of a rush thing. I'm going to, ah, Akron. Or Canton, maybe. See the sights. Maybe take in the holiday decorations." He didn't like to mention the Mafia. "Howdy do, Septus."

The phone rang. Juanetta went inside. Randy motioned through the front door screen. "I'm not here," he mouthed.

It was Laurinda. She'd landed a temporary job as a wiener demonstrator over at the supermarket and was going over there right now. This was her first full-time paid job since she left the factory, and she was real pleased, she said. A small step for a woman, but a giant step for . . . anyhow, a package for Randy had been left at the front door.

"A package?" Randy twittered. "Okay, tell her to see what's in it. No, way mint, tell her don't go near it, don't . . ." But Laurinda had set the phone down to go see what was in it.

"Holy Smoke," Randy said, covering his ears. "I knew it. I knew it." He squinched his eyes shut.

Juanetta just looked out through the screen at him.

"Oh, sure," Randy said, eyeing her. He put on a snotty female voice. "'Here's old Randy, makin' a fool of himself again.' Well, not this time. Nosir. That," he shrilled, pointing to the phone, "that was a *bomb*."

"Nah," said Septus. "That's Teeny's old Princess phone. I give it to Juanetta when the nine went bust on hers."

"I don't mean the phone," Randy shouted. Laurinda came back on the line, and Randy went in to talk to her. "It was your *Readers' Digest Classics*, Randy. I'm leaving them on the coffee table. See you after work."

Randy came out on the porch and slumped into a wicker chair. He always tried to look on the bright side, but his nerves were shot. "I'll tell you something, my nerves are shot. Remember that speech I give on Lincoln's birthday?"

"Was that the one about the government should free those little silver men out in New Mexico?"

"Nah, that was Groundhog Day. This was the one where I said the Coast Guard was in cahoots with the Mafia to sabotage the garbage plan." No point explaining all this to them; Randy could see they weren't keeping up with civic affairs. Probably not even aware that as mayor he had called the Coast Guard in to form a *cordon sanitary* to let the garbage trucks come through when Leland was stopping them.

"Wait," said Juanetta. "What's the Coast Guard got to do with anything? We're landlocked here."

"Well, who was I supposed to call? The sheriff was out sick, and I could hardly call Leland DeWitt. All I know is, some high-up big mucky muck musta got sore over that speech."

"But it wasn't a bomb. It was them books. Laurinda said so."

"Dudn't matter. Once they set their sights on you, you're a goner. They send thirteen white roses one day, then twelve, and so on, and on the last day, they hotwire your car and blow you to kingdom come."

"Funny way for the Coast Guard to be carryin' on," Septus said. "Always glad I did my time in the Marines."

"The Mafia, not the Coast Guard." Randy was more disappointed than angry, really; your ordinary voter was pretty uninformed. "Anyhow, it ain't just the bomb that's got me worried. I get up this morning, my pickup's gone. A hearse is sitting there, instead. And before that, my car was making a weird noise, kind of a low whistle, real eerie." He wiggled his fingers in the air.

"Leland DeWitt had that problem, too."

"No kidding," Randy said, interested. Maybe this was a major Mafia war against the establishment.

"Yeah, damn near had to disassemble the car to find it. It's goin' okay now, though."

"Well," Randy said, peering into his wallet, "I can't go back over to the house. Juanetta, I need you to lend me a few dollars . . . eleven." Not much to do in Akron, if that's where he decided to go. Might need a little more for Canton; he could go to the Baseball Hall of Fame, except he would probably have to stay in hiding. Assume a identity. That big creepy guy, probably one of Rocco's boys, was on his tail 24–7, it seemed like.

"Randy, have sense. Go over home, get some clothes if you want, pick up Laurinda, and come over here a couple days," said Juanetta. "I'll come over with you."

Septus looked nervous. "Nah, Juanetta, don't you bother. I was just gonna go anyway, do a little fishin', so I'll ride over with Randy, instead." Juanetta looked put out. "If we need the heavy artillery," said Septus, "we'll give you a call from his place."

Randy put up an argument, but in the end he and Septus went off in Randy's Chevy. When they passed the DeWitts' house, Arthur Leroy was moping around in the front yard, so they stopped and hoisted him in. Randy felt a little better. Dogs were good at criminal work. Their nose was one hundred times better than your human nose, and they could find a bomb or whatever, just like that. Then Randy remembered he had lost a teeny bit of pot somewheres when he was college age, not *in* college, actually, and he wondered if your spaniel breeds were more into drugs than bombs, say, than your Golden Truders.

But it was hard to tell anything about Arthur Leroy, he always just sat looking depressed. Your Golden Truders looked more like Gerald Ford.

The driveway was empty over at Randy's, no hearse, no pickup, nothing. Randy bucked up. "You never been over to the house since Laurinda and I . . . " Randy realized this might be a little touchy . . . . "Well, come on in. I'll show you my Noto-Republic stamp. I can witness your legal papers, if you got any on you." Randy stopped dead. The frame was ripped off the front door. Laurinda was still at work, and Skip, well, he hoped he was out with some of the guys but he was probably over at Sylene's. Although whenever he called there, Leland would say he wasn't. It was real childish, Randy thought. The older generation should put their feuds behind them. Look where bad blood got you. And what was Leland doing about Zeke's death? Asking people where they were that night. Well, for that matter, where was *Leland* on that night? And where was he now, when you could use the police?

"Why don't we let Arthur Leroy go in first? Dogs like to get to know a place on their own." He gave Arthur Leroy a shove. Septus tried to go in, too, but Randy was leaning across the door frame, pointing out which walls were support and which were nothing but your cheap wallboard. After a while, Arthur Leroy wandered out again with cornflakes on his chin.

"Well," said Randy, "there's no point in us standing out here all day." He shooed Septus in and sat him down on the davenport. Septus was never a one for interior decor, but he perked up as he looked around. A velvet day-glo picture of the Lone Ranger leaned against a broken card table, and for chairs, there was a lady's vanity stool and part of an exercise bicycle. A huge mantel clock with fairies or something, dancing, sat on the floor beside a large fish tank filled with different colors of sand, arranged in levels. There were some fat dolls and a life-size statue of a saint.

Randy collapsed in the recliner. It occurred to him that Septus being Catholic, maybe he could tell Randy who the saint was. In fact, Randy might take this chance to get straightened out on Catholics: for example, he knew they used a thermometer for sex, but how in hell did that work? What did you put it *in*? Randy was really happy with Laurinda, and if that's what she liked, he'd do it. Trouble was, he couldn't even read a thermometer, much less use it for sex. The red part kept disappearing just when he thought he had it. Of course, Septus being her ex-husband and all made that a touchy subject, too. He'd work his way around to it, subtle. No point in hurting his feelings.

Randy sat down on the back seat of a car.

"Nice place you got here," said Septus.

"Oh, this furniture's not *mine*, except for the picture of the Lone Ranger and the Beanie Babies," said Randy. "I'm minding it for Rodney Romdey. You remember Rodney. Always had good taste."

"Yeah, he's in jail now, right?"

"Nah, he's out now. Did five years and got out on good behavior."

"What's he doing now? Why don't he come get his furniture?"

"Mormon missionary. He got the call. On the road all the time now."

They sat for a while.

"Question," said Septus. "Where's your pickup?"

"That's *right*, said Randy, trying to snap his fingers. "Damn it, I nearly forgot. I'll give Harley a call over at the sheriff's office." He was *not* involving Leland in this. He traced a cord under the piles of furniture, into the dining room, and came back talking on the phone.

"Roger, Harley," he said when the sheriff answered. "One count of grand auto theft, plain and simple. A Six-Oh-Two. Correct. Roger. Where did I see it last? Ah . . . Harl, let me get back to you on this one."

"Well, where *did* you see it last?" asked Septus.

Randy was deflated. "Yesterday, about three, going toward the Ohio turnpike. A hitchhiker stopped by the Twi-Lite, and I tried to unload that van of Rodney's on him. Rodney asked me to try to see could I sell it."

"That red thing with the ice-cream truck front and the ambulance back? 'Roamer' in big gold letters on the side?" Septus asked.

"Yeah, Rodney Romdey's red Roamer. Real weird rear wheels. Anyhow, it was too expensive for this guy, said he didn't need an RV, anyhow, and he made me a good offer for my pickup, two hundred dollars, twenty on the nail and the rest in time payments. Name of Zrbgj. I'm so riled up with these death threats I don't know what end's up. I'm not ashamed to say that hearse spooked me. Those big boys, they play rough."

"Zrbgj?" asked Septus. "What kinda name is that, exactly?"

"Don't believe he said. Said it was pronounced the way it's spelled."

"Where's the Roamer?" asked Septus.

"Donated it to the police department," said Randy. "Leland said he could fit a snowplow on the front. Has himself a nice all-purpose police vehicle now."

Septus and Randy sat for a while and had some cold macaroni and a couple beers. They were watching a little TV when Laurinda came in.

"Have I got something tattooed on my head that says 'Tell me all about your bowel movements?'" she asked. Both men looked at her. Randy hated these kind of trick questions. "Don't believe so," said Septus, finally. "Not that I can see, anyhow," Randy said, looking a little closer.

"Well tell that to all those old bats at the supermarket. Nothin's too personal for them to tell a stranger. Hi, Septus, honey, hi Randy, I am *pooped*. This wiener demonstratin' ain't for me. People are too picky. Some wants their wiener dipped in mustard, some won't touch mustard, oh, no, they gotta have ketchup or barbecue sauce, some wants ketchup and mustard together and they mess the little dishes up and I got to. . . ."

Randy felt Laurinda was a swell woman but she had a tendency to go on. "Listen, wait till I tell you . . ."

"Don't interrupt me," said Laurinda. "In my gender class, they showed a video on how women get interrupted about a hundred times more often than men."

"Well, I was just wonderin' about supper," said Randy. "All this talk about wieners."

"I got some in the car. I'll heat them up in a jiff. This stuff," she said, sweeping her arm across the room, "gotta be outta here by tomorrow, no two ways. I got a big Early American credenza goin' out and a nice leatherette living room suit, cash and carry, comin' in here. They was supposed to come first thing this morning. I talked Rudy over at the funeral parlor into bringing them; they're too big for my car, and of course dufus here sold the pickup yesterday, did he tell you that? Rudy couldn't get them through the front door, so I started takin' the frame off so's he can bring them back tomorrow. Septus, think you could get the rest of that frame off for me?"

Chapter 27

Juanetta and Idora

uanetta thought about it the next day when she and Idora were having some Duck with Fresh Figs and Port in Winkle's. Septus had told her very little, but she had the gist of it. Maybe a pot plant was putting it too high.

Idora had had her hair done real nice for her interview with Leland about Zeke's death. All she could remember about that night was the rotten smell, and how cold it was, and Zeke, with that jagged bottle. Now she was showing Juanetta some new pictures of her grandchildren. They were so cute. Among Juanetta's grandkids, only Skip and Don had anything going for them. Skip and that nice Sylene, maybe they'd kick-start the family line back into normality. Randy was always going on about having a big family, lots of grandkids.

"Don't think so," said Idora when Juanetta mentioned it. "Sylene is adorable, but I never thought that was such a good idea, her and Skip running around together. This duck is exquisite."

"How come?" asked Juanetta.

"Well, being cousins and all. You know. Same grandfather. I guess they're just half-cousins, so maybe it's okay. But cousins can have some funny kids. You look at Prince Charles."

Juanetta put a suspicious-looking part of the duck down on her salad plate. "What same grandfather? What in hell are you talking about, Idora?"

Idora paused for quite a while. "Well, Juanetta, I'm real sorry. I guess I spoke outta turn. You know, I always thought you *knew*."

"Who?"

"Why, Bert Whump, of course," said Idora, faintly. She looked sick.

Juanetta pushed the rest of the duck aside. "Tell me."

"Oh, God. Well, don't you remember Bert and Nora were really gone on each other that summer before Bert joined the Navy? He was going with Susie right before that, he sure did get around." Idora picked at Juanetta's saucer of duck liver. "You know, I always thought Buck DeWitt was a very decent guy. When he saw the trouble Nora was in, he asked her straight out to marry him. Bert out there in the Navy, he didn't even know. Buck was crazy about her, anyhow; you couldn't meet a nicer girl, everyone always said that. Still do."

"I'll be damned," said Juanetta. "How come Bert didn't know?"

"Well, I can't remember too good, it was pretty confused as I recall. Something about her letter going to Berlin over in Pennsylvania instead of Berlin, Germany. Bert was stationed there for a few weeks. Happens a lot, there are way too many Berlins and Cairos and Londons in this country, I always thought. The U.S. could declare war on the Middle East and the declaration might end up in Lebanon, Pennsylvania. We're just laying ourselves open for trouble. Anyhow, after a while, Nora got pretty nervous. Poor Susie couldn't reach Bert, either."

"Susie, too?" asked Juanetta, astonished.

"Yes, of course Zeke probably didn't know anything about it when he married Susie, he thought Randy was her late husband's kid.

"Maybe, as Randy got older, he might have figured it out. Zeke was awful brutal to Randy sometimes, so maybe he did."

Juanetta let this sink in. Yes. Randy and Bert Whump, she could picture them sitting in Winkle's, there was definitely a resemblance across the shoulders, kinda round. Leland, too. For sure, Leland got Bert's brains, as well. Well, heavens. How come she never noticed?

"How'd you know this?" asked Juanetta. "And how come I didn't?"

"Why Bert told me. I suppose I was the homely girl
fellas always came to for advice. Zeke once told me I was
the homeliest girl in Hope And Glory. For years after
that, I didn't really look in a mirror more than I had to.
Those other girls, though, always looking at themselves in
Woolworth's window, most of them thought their behinds
weighed a ton."

"Idora! That don't even sound like you."

"Well, I don't care, they did. I guess you weren't all that
homely, Juanetta, but somehow, I thought you knew, too.
Bert was in Germany no time at all, so he didn't write,
he planned to surprise Nora when he got back. I guess
he just thought of Susie as a friend."

"Huh! A 'friend?'"

"That's what I say. Anyhow, when he got back, they
were both married. He was all broke up. I felt real sorry
for all of them, not Zeke, of course, but it worked out fine
for Nora in the end, Buck was a great dad and Leland
thought he walked on water. Didn't work out too good
for poor Susie, though."

"Whaddya know," Juanetta said.

"Well, I see now I never shoulda never mentioned
it," Idora said. "But I know you can keep it to yourself,
Juanetta. Anyhow, I thought you knew what Bert Whump
was like. A real Casanova in his time."

Oh, yes, Juanetta knew what Bert was like. *And* she
could keep her mouth shut. Kept it shut all these years,
didn't she? Always the good sport, Bert said. Good thing
Randy had Skip with her daughter Sherry and not her

older girl, Laurinda. It was almost funny to see him wiggling out of being a witness at Randy's and Laurinda's wedding. Should she tell Laurinda? Nah, she was through The Change, no need.

She forked up a fig.

THE HOPE AND GLORY VINDICATOR

Volume 234 Issue 45   Hope And Glory, Ohio

Whump In!

In an expected development, Bert Whump unseated Randy
Anderson in Tuesday's election by a vote of 1986 to 43. Former
Mayor Anderson said he would not ask for a recount, that he
knew the election supervisor, his old teacher Miss Mildred
Pettipaw, could count real good.

Mayor Whump said he was honored to step into the shoes
of Mr. Anderson, who had presided over such fraught times in
Hope And Glory. Mr.Anderson said he was real pleased to hear
that because he had voted for Mr. Whump.

Jail to close; private peniteniary to bring new employment?

Mayor Bert Whump and Police Chief Lelan DeWitt held a joint
press conference to announce the closing of the Hope And Glory
jail. Mayor Whump said that the jail's rehabilitation programs
were being copied widely, and that Chief DeWitt had been as
good as a father to the inmates. He was real proud of the chief,
and wanted to wish him the best of luck in his new business,
which was catching on like all get-out.

Chief DeWitt, speaking in English, said don't mention it, it
had been a real pleasure. He presented a 17th century armoire to
the outgoing lady mayoress, Mrs. Laurinda McCardle Anderson,
who goes by her maiden name. The armoire had to be hoisted
through a skylight in the jail's roof.

Mayor Whump announced that he was in negotiations with
FedCop, a corporation that runs private penitentiaries. "I'm
looking to get one of them for Hope And Glory," he said. "We
could show them a thing or two, and it would bring in a little
money." Ex-chief DeWitt has agreed to serve as advisor."

Rev. Wayman sentenced

Rev. Dwight Wayman was charged last night with causing
grievous bodily harm to Mrs. Juanetta Wilcox, mother of the
ex-lady mayoress, who received second degree burns when
using Rev. Wayman's new electric toilet at Muddy Branch
Church. The idea of the toilet, according to Rev. Wayman,

was that not only would the seat be heated, the church being so cold and all,

(con'td p. 2).

Chief Grey Wolf fails to get casino
Chief Grey Wolf, head of the Native American tribe living behind the Precious Lamb Daycare Center and Rifle Range, has failed in his attempt to set up a legal tribal-associated casino in Hope And Glory. Lyle Stivanski, formerly of radio station WHAG here, and now a reporter in New York, says that the Chief is a former Mafioso, currently participating in a Witness Protection Program, here, as are the other tribe members. Chief Grey Wolf apologized for any inconvenience.

INSIDE THIS ISSUE

Inside This Issue

2 Gumdrop and sauerkraut Jell-O! Try it!

2 Answers to all those riddles (p. 2)

3 William F. Buckley in town

4 Knit for Norway! Perky potholders

5 Composting old lamps

Chapter 28

Laurinda!

Philadelphia! When Laurinda gave a paper a few months ago on the cultural handling of breasts and beards at B.I.B.'s national conference, she made a real impression on a guy in the audience. Turned out he was Professor Goodenough from the University of Philadelphia, a nice man, clean-shaven, and he invited her to apply there, said she had gone as far as she could at Jim Bob Bagby Community College. She needed to be stretched. She didn't think he meant anything funny, he seemed like a real gentleman.

Randy, the sweetheart, he said why not, and right away he started planning. He thought he would go into motivational speaking up there, and it was true, he would be wonderful at it, always looking on the bright side. He could do it in between terms as mayor, because he was sure he would get back in next time.

"That last election, honey, that was just a fluke, William F. Buckley coming down to campaign for Bert Whump, Bert being a Democrat and all," she'd said to Randy. But it sure got him elected. Leland DeWitt had told her he was stunned to see Mr. Buckley. She saw him following him around like a puppy, writing everything he said down in a notebook. He probably had no idea who William F. was, before that. Randy sure didn't until Mr. Buckley sat him down in Winkle's one day and filled him in. Said no hard feelings, it was just the Republican Party could take only so much. It was so noble, Randy said, and he sure was proud to be in the same party as Mr. Buckley. And Mr. Buckley was such a good sport about all that jail stuff. Another real gentleman.

Of course, Randy was a teeny bit hurt when B.I.B. endorsed Bert instead of him, who wouldn't be, but Laurinda wasn't one bit sorry she had gone over to Bert's and suggested that he run in the first place. Bert hadn't been crazy about the idea, but he agreed Randy was awful agitated lately and needed a break; he had given his all to Hope And Glory and wore himself to a nubbin. She told Randy she would vote for him next time, but right now he needed to take a deep breath and get in touch with his female side so's he could feed his inner child.

And that Rocco! So precious, and he was so grateful to her and Randy for keeping up with him all those long lonely months after the liposuction turned on him. He was out of circulation so long he lost a lotta his so-called friends. Lost most of his backside, too, Randy said; Rocco was too much of a gentleman to discuss it with Laurinda. Randy wanted Rocco to sue, but Rocco said he didn't really have a leg to stand on.

Laurinda thought it was great Rocco was helping Randy set up his new business in Philadelphia. He was already marketing Randy as "The Giddyup Guy," and had him booked into your Rotary clubs and such, and even one college. Randy was thrilled. You couldn't meet a nicer man than Rocco. She could never understand how Randy was so scared of him during the garbage thing. Or how Randy had him figured as Irish. Or, for that matter, why Randy really did make 118 calls to Ireland, which they'd be paying off for the next couple years.

The only real problem in all this excitement was she would be further away from her boy Mickey, but of course Mickey might be out in a while, depending on the new parole board. Laurinda had been saying for *years* it had been an accident, but would anyone listen? Well, now Bert was the mayor and he was really working on it. In the meantime, Mickey had a movement going on about beards in the prison. That was one thing Laurinda had done right: her boy was real gender sensitive, and if this movement swept through the prison system, them hard cases, it would be a real breakthrough. She had briefed him thoroughly. He wasn't too smart, Mickey, but once he got the facts clear in his head, he was a real dynamo. Odd, her girls Teeny and Reenie weren't one bit interested in The Movement.

It would have broken her heart if none of her kids had carried on her legacy. Of course with Don, she was counting on him to give the family a professional tone. Now that he had finished his crop dusting exams, he was going to pass over as often as possible. He even buzzed the house here, once; she was wiping up for a week, after. But she didn't mind, because Don was so nice; he was going to do a special birthday present for Randy, some skywriting! Bert had set it all up with Don, to make up to Randy for the election.

Laurinda wasn't the only one going off to college. "I'm so proud of you and Skip," she'd said to Sylene. Her teachers said Sylene was a real whiz at math now. It had all snapped into place for her one day, according to Sylene; something about the Shipskys and Randy and Arthur Leroy and a watering can, Laurinda didn't know what all. She was also talking about maybe doing some of her college in Ireland, some new friend of Leland's was over there, but Laurinda hoped she wouldn't go. Sadly, she could see now Sylene and Skip were really only friends. She blamed Juanetta for that; lately she'd been trying to fix them up with other people.

But who was going to run B.I.B while she was gone? "Maybe you might do it after you're able to sit down right again, Ma," she'd said to Juanetta one day when they were going over some old photos. Trouble was, it seems Juanetta had always had a weakness for a beard: one picture showed Bert, right before he went into the Navy all those years ago, with a kind of Ernest Hemingway beard. Beardette, really. And there was a young Juanetta, simpering at him. Come to think of it, Laurinda realized it was the only picture she had of Juanetta unarmed. That one of her breastfeeding Laurinda's little sister Sherry, boy, that was one for the books. Anyhow, Laurinda thought maybe Juanetta might have been a little sweet on Bert one time.

But it was funny, she didn't seem to be Bert's biggest fan these days. Laurinda noticed a lot of these old people just took notions, no reason. She hoped she and Randy wouldn't take notions as they moved into their golden years.

Laurinda was half asleep when she got to bed that night; reminiscing often wore her out. She was usually way too busy to dream, but the next day, a faint memory drifted to the top: a monster, was it? Randy in a beard? No, it was Pixie in a gent's suit. Laurinda thought dreams were more trouble than they were worth, pickles on bicycles and suchlike. She read somewhere some famous professor had a "well-furnished mind." Well, she wanted a well-furnished mind, too, and she didn't want it cluttered up with stuff like pickles while she was lying there, helpless.

Chapter 29

Laurinda

"We got bills coming out the wazoo here," Laurinda said, as she and Randy packed for Philadelphia. "118 calls to Ireland? These gotta be someone else's. I made four, five, max, to this girl Goretti, she'd called me here, all incoherent, said she hadn't slept right in weeks, some nuisance caller bothering her and her dad. She had the wrong number, but we got to talking and now she's setting up an Irish branch of B.I.B. And here's florist bills that's not ours, unless you got a girlfriend somewheres. I'm not payin' these, I'm callin' them right now."

"Phone calls to Ireland? Yeah, that's wrong. I sure don't know anybody in Ireland. Goretti, though, that name rings a bell. Nope, gone again. But the flowers, well, that's me." Laurinda gave him a look, "No, it ain't a girlfriend. It's a long story."

"Well, let's hear it," Laurinda said, sharpish.

"Fact is," said Randy, "I put them on old Buck DeWitt's grave."

"Way mint," Laurinda said. "I thought your family hated the DeWitts. I never could understand any of that. Although I was a little annoyed with Leland that he didn't interview me as a suspect in Zeke's death."

She'd taken the trouble to go over to Zeke's with a meat grinder, as good a weapon as any. She remembered the terrible smell at that septic tank, and the dark, and Zeke roaring and banging around with a broken bottle. He got what he deserved. She slammed her suitcase shut on Randy's finger.

Laurinda was a swell woman, Randy thought, sucking his finger. Different from Sherry, but swell. But she was wound a little tight. Jabberin', brain always going a mile a minute. And a smidge violent.

"I never hated *any* of the DeWitts," he said. "I know Leland didn't do me any favors with them garbage trucks, and he's driving me crazy with his toilet experiments. But he was real good to me in jail. I can fill a tire with my eyes shut now. Nope, all that bad blood with the DeWitts, that was my old man. Funny, you know in a way I respected Zeke. He was real smart. A monster, but smart. I still ask myself ten times a day, 'What would Dad do?'"

"Well, I hope you have the sense to do the opposite, then," Laurinda snapped.

"But he didn't do right by Buck DeWitt." Randy could see he was going to lose that nail. Maybe even the top of his finger. "Never saw a man with so many grudges. He messed Buck up real good a few times, bought that land beside his house so's he could set up a scrap yard. Coulda bought land somewhere else, easy. Blocked a promotion at the boiler factory. There was a few more things like that. I didn't know what he had against Buck. I thought maybe Buck got the girl he wanted; I heard Nora had a lot of admirers when she was a girl."

Laurinda opened the suitcase again and stuffed in a cute top. She was getting kind of busty, and you could get away with that in a place like Philadelphia.

"Anyhow, one night, Buck and Leland came over to the house to tell Dad one of my stepbrothers was a bully. And boy, he was. Beating up Buck's kid Ralph, nearly ten years younger than him."

"He was a psychopath," Laurinda said. She never actually knew that until she went to college. A real psychopath.

"I never heard anything like what my dad said to Buck that time. No call for it at all. 'You're nothing and you'll always be nothing.' I can remember Buck's face. He was outta work in those days, got hurt at the factory. People's feelings can get hurt awful bad, you know," said Randy, kind of misting up.

"And after they left, I tried to make a joke about it, calm him down, and he said some things to me, too, as bad as you could hear." Randy could still hear them, though: "You're no son of mine," Zeke had said, "and your mother's a no-good slut. And so's that Nora, Buck DeWitt's wife, with her bastard, everyone thinks he's so smart."

Laurinda put in some shorts, shortish, but not too much for a party town like Philadelphia. Now that Randy wasn't mayor, she didn't have to uphold her position. She bet the poor Queen wished she could take off that crown sometimes and slip on some cute shorts.

"Everybody got a blast that night," Randy said. A tear teetered on the corner of his eye.

He sat down on the bed. It was as clear as yesterday. He'd tried to kinda laugh and smooth it over but there was no stopping Zeke; he said maybe DeWitt was fooled but he wasn't, nosir. And that Randy was not only dumb, he was . . . well, it changed everything. Maybe Zeke hated Buck because he musta figured he was a stupid sap that got tricked, same as he did. Maybe that's why he was so hard on Randy; he was a reminder.

For a while after that, Randy even wondered was Buck his father, the way Zeke was always going on about him. Randy would have liked that, Buck was awful good to his kids. But no, when Zeke figured out what he was thinking, he laughed at him, took a lot of pleasure in telling him straight out who his father was. The guy was Leland's, too.

The Tomb of the Honorary Veteran, Randy felt putting up that had more than repaid Zeke for keeping him. But he still wished Zeke woulda treated him more like his own kids, the way Buck treated Leland. Zeke was vicious; he made fun of every little thing Randy did. He remembered his first date with Kimi Lynn Whump, before he knew. He didn't have his license yet and was really surprised Zeke offered to drive him over to Bert's house to pick her up. He made a big point of coming up to the door to say hello to Bert. Pure nastiness, Randy knew now. All that pining he did over Kimi Lynn, and Zeke egging him on. Kimi Lynn ended up with Earl Arbogast, nearly broke Randy's heart.

"The thing about Bert," Randy said to Laurinda, "was he was too big a man for Zeke. Everybody liked Bert, things rolled off him, he had a little money. Zeke probably couldn't figure out a way to really get at him." Randy never got a chance to know Bert, him working so much over in Cairo, it was only in recent years they had done much more than say hello.

"Anyways," Randy said, putting his shirts in plastic bags and blowing them up the way Laurinda had shown him, no wrinkles that way, "I tried to make it up to Buck when I got older, paid for the siren a few times when he had to go to the hospital at the end. I told the ambulance boys it was on me, the louder the better. Little stuff. Buck didn't know. I figured if anybody was a good guy around here, it was Buck. I remember I was out on the sidewalk one day, just a little kid, crying real hard, and my ma crying, too, and a man in black got me a Klondike ice cream bar and took us to my grandma's. I wanted to think it was the Lone Ranger. Buck always wore black. I think he even wore a mask for me."

"What were you all crying about?" Laurinda asked.

"Don't know," said Randy. "It's only just lately I remembered that much. Anyhow, I don't know what I'm supposed to do with all these blown-up bags now. They're takin' up too much room in the suitcase."

Laurinda remembered Buck's funeral. It was as big a crowd as she could remember. And the flowers. "All those black tulips at the funeral home?"

"Yeah," said Randy said. "Everybody was outta work at the time, but even more people woulda sent them in a minute if they'd had the money. Plenty did, anyway. You could see they all thought a lot of Buck. He was an odd old coot in some ways, but he was real good to kids, to everybody, matterafact."

"Well, talk about your epiphanies," Laurinda said later to Juanetta at Winkle's counter. "The minute he told me about the flowers I knew that I would be with that man for the rest of my life. And brave! He hurt his finger bad somehow and never a word, just a teensy tear in his eye."

"In fact," she said, "we're gonna renew our vows. I know you meant well, and all, Ma, but we didn't have much of a wedding first time around."

Juanetta looked a little put out.

"And Bert! Who would have thought?" Laurinda said. Although she herself had always had a soft spot for Bert; something about him. Juanetta said she ought to be pushing on, couldn't sit in Winkle's all day.

R andy was having the Frank and Bean Bake at the counter in Winkle's. Bert came in, said he'd try the Sautéed Radicchio Noisettes.

Randy was still riled up over the guy in the newspaper, the one who liked sherry and would vote for Juanetta but not for him. Now it appears he liked coffee but he didn't like tea. Not a Mormon, anyhow. He couldn't picture a Mormon Lone Ranger.

"Listen," he said to Bert, "this guy, the one that likes fellows, you seem to know everything about him. Sounds like you could answer anything I ask about him, his likes and dislikes and all."

"Yep," said Bert.

"He's not really a guy at all, is he?" asked Randy.

"You got it," said Bert, thumping the counter. "I knew you would. See, Randy, the principle is . . ."

Septus walked over. He had just got a part-time job designing some of the jail's hologram furniture programs. It sure was a lot better than running gutter. First thing he did, he threw out the plaid recliners.

"Here's a good one for you," he said, reading out of *The Vindicator*. "While walking through the school's parking lot one morning, George noticed all but three of the cars in the lot were made by General Motors, all but three of the cars in the lot were made by Ford, all but three of the cars in the lot were made by Chrysler, and all but three of the cars in the lot were made by Toyota. What is the minimum number of cars parked in the parking lot?"

"Hmm," said Randy. "This here is one of the major problems voters face today. Why, I had to run out to Home Depot the other day to pick up some gutter, and I couldn't get a parking space. Had to go to K-Mart."

"K-Mart don't sell gutter," Bert said.

"Exactly," Randy said.

"Okay, here's a different one, Randy," Bert said. "When you get back into office, you hold a meeting over at the Town Hall, and some voters come. All but three of them are Republicans. All but three are Democrats. All but three are Independents. All but three are Reform Party. What is the minimum number of voters in the hall?"

"Four," said Randy instantly. "And that new Reform Party, that's not goin' nowheres. You heard it here first."

Bert studied Randy awhile. "Gimme some of that Pep-O-Mint cake," he said to Butch Winkle.

Chapter 30

Leland

Magical, like Camelot, that's what it had been. It was over now but Leland had a lot more going for him than he did a couple years ago. When he thought of that Christmas Eve, the time he was going to run away to the Croatian Club with Arthur Leroy and six dollars in his pocket, he could hardly believe the change in his life. Unfathomable, that's what it had been.

After the election, everyone could see what they had was a vanity jail, the way some of your Third World countries have vanity airlines. They couldn't afford to keep it up. Sure, the prisoners were bringing in money, but the operation wasn't big enough to withstand the skill losses as the fellas were released. The good ones went over to *The Vindicator*; in fact, *The Vindicator* was probably the only all ex-con run paper in the country now. Well, probably those papers you see in the supermarket, sure, but he was talking about your quality papers. And Chief Earl Arbogast over in North Vienna, he had taken a few lessons from the Hope And Glory jail, and he had the money from the garbage to keep his place going.

Leland was now a part-time consultant to the state of Ohio, showing how to teach fellas in jail some useful skills. He had even run into Mickey, down there in Everton. Mickey had some kind of movement going, Leland didn't have time to stop and hear about it, but Mickey was into it, real big. "M.I.B." he called it, something about beards. All those McCardles, nice people, but except for Septus, they mostly had a screw loose.

But consulting wasn't how Leland made his living. Nosir. When the jail closed, he bought the computers and moved them and six of the ex-prisoners and Septus into his garage. He had one of the first bilingual Hologram Garages. They put in some dry wall and skylights and a little mood lighting, and they were off, making hologram furniture like there was no tomorrow. A reporter came from *The New York Times,* Lyle Stivanski, he used to be at WHAG, and there was another guy came from the *Catholic Exponent.* They were branching into hologram landscaping now, and had just finished a Japanese maple. They had a hologram ad in the air behind Winkle's, and now some pretty big companies wanted them. Sure, it could be over in a flash, that was the way with holograms, but he knew now he had the confidence to start over. He didn't know that a year ago. He might even sell the whole thing as an app.

If he had to pick one highlight of his life, he'd have to say the night he arrested William F. Buckley. Bill. Leland knew it was all nonsense, and Juanetta kept saying nobody had tried to rape her. She was caught short while she was showing a Mr. Buckley around the Civil War church, so she ran to the toilet. She was sitting, peaceable, when sparks flew from the seat and burned her backside medium rare. Mr. Buckley raced in and pulled her up but her drawers didn't come with her. That idiot Wyman, and his seat-warming ideas.

Idora did a citizen's arrest on Buckley.

Leland arrested Reverend Wayman, he was a real danger to the public until they could get him off to trade school, get him some sort of electricity certificate. It wasn't religious bias, nosir, nothing to do with Leland being Catholic. In fact, Leland had half a mind to charge one of them nuns for cheating that poor guy from Quebec out of a week's ironing money. The nun said he'd scorched her wimple, when Leland could see it was old coffee.

Anyhow, he and Bill had had a chance to have a real nice chat; he wasn't condescending or anything, a real nice guy. Okay, he was Republican, but so what. Leland thought he was the smartest man he'd ever met, after his dad.

He wished his dad could see all the good things that had happened, though. He would have loved computers, and the Internet, and all. The Internet as a library, but none of that chat stuff or naked ladies.

Kids today were whizzes at everything to do with computers. His own son was on his way to becoming CEO of Faux Furniture in a couple years. He had changed his name back again from Ryan, he said John Paul II had better public recognition quality. If he didn't make an initial public offering before he was twenty, Leland would eat his hat. JP II had his own little business now, helping stressed-out computer hotline people, his own domain name, too, JohnPaulthe2.co.

And Sylene. Leland was still annoyed that Randy and even Randy's mother-in-law Juanetta had been so eager to break Sylene and Skip up. The idea that Sylene wasn't good enough was ludicrous; lookit her now, going to college same as anybody else. Better, because she was going to be an astrophysicist. It was a proud day for him, the day she made the breakthrough on her horse problem. If you just love your kids and let them flower, they'd be fine. He never did know what that peach chiffon thing on the WHAG Swap Shop radio program was all about, never heard another word.

It was all for the best. Skip was a real nice kid, but he and Sylene were too much alike. You needed complementarity. Sylene was writing often to some other guy now, he didn't know who, and she had gone out a couple times with that Kimi Arbogast's boy, Lonnie, nothing serious, thank God. An illiterate check forger: she surely could do better than that. As long as she stayed in school, that was the thing.

Leland didn't know what came over him, he must be getting soft in the head, but he almost felt sorry for Randy

when he lost the election; Leland voted for Bert, of course.
So did everyone else; when William F. Buckley supports a
Democrat, you have to sit up and pay attention. He was
surprised at William F. He thought in his speeches he'd
be using big words a mile a minute, but he spoke very
plainly except when he got all worked up about the local
Republican Party being in danger of self-immolation.
And he wasn't much to use French, either, but of course
he must be a whiz at it. *Un polyglotte.*

Still, it was kind of sad to see Randy's face the day the
Democrats put Bert up against him. When he lost, he was
a complete sport, bounded straight across the platform
and shook Bert's hand, and you could see he truly wished
him all the luck in the world. But the smirk was not really
a smirk, more a look of pain. He guessed Randy couldn't
help his face. Leland himself was no oil painting.

Randy was not a bad man. It wasn't his fault his old
man was so cruel. And give him his due, he was a good
father, and a good husband, too. Treated Laurinda like
a queen.

Maybe if Randy'd had a dad like Leland's, who knows?
Maybe he woulda been more . . . what? Secure, maybe. He
supposed the saddest part was the poor bugger wasn't too
quick on the trigger and was just smart enough to know
it. It really bothered Randy when people laughed at him.

Leland never thought much about that before. People
didn't laugh at him. Then he remembered those morn-
ings at the El Dorado, when he thought the guys were
snickering behind his back, with him out of work, maybe

Bridget having an affair. He wondered now how could he have ever thought that about Bridget? Anyhow, it hurt, thinking they were making fun of him. A lifetime of that would get to you, all right.

What he *did* think about, sometimes in the middle of the night, was people in the *future* laughing at us.

"Like the way we pitied people in the nineteenth century when they invented the tin can in 1810 but didn't invent the tin can opener until 1850," Leland said to Randy one day when they both ended up at the counter in Winkle's.

"So that was like what, forty years of beans piling up?" Randy asked.

"Say around 4000 AD, will they look at our cars and snigger? Will they pity us for still not being able to cure baldness, or for the way telemarketers are allowed to disrupt our dinners, or that we can't open our own medicine bottles?"

"Laurinda opens my bottles," Randy said. "You gotta have the knack."

Leland decided when he had a little free time, he'd think about maybe making a time capsule. He would put pictures of computers and lawnmowers and the electric grid of Hope And Glory, and maybe something about cancer research and a piece of paper saying WE ARE DOING THE BEST WE CAN. *And* he was going to put one of those aspirin bottles in, without any instructions.

Actually, the more he thought about it, the more he saw why Randy felt bad when people laughed at him.

Well, his time was up. He couldn't put his last task off any longer; he had to go over to Bert's and get this Zeke mess all sorted out, his last official act, so to speak.

"You lied about the cause of death, didn't you?" he asked Bert. "Zeke didn't drown." Leland didn't think he should call him into the station, a man his age and all, but he was uncomfortable sitting in Mrs. Bert's living room with a heavy, old-fashioned toilet seat in his lap. "You must have thought Susie whacked him over the head from behind and killed him, so you recorded that he'd drowned."

"Susie. Well, I must have. Yeah, well I couldn't stand to see that woman in court, not after a lifetime's suffering with that bastard. Why she coulda put him through a blender, for all I cared. Not that I like to see a mockery made of the law. Drowning seemed as good a way as any to go."

"Fine way for a police chief to carry on," said Leland. "Anyhow, the autopsy shows he had nothing in his lungs. Hard to make a case for drowning."

"That's why I secretly figured someone, Susie, killed him. A bang on the head, a fall into the tank, nothing in the lungs. Acourse," he said, after a while, "it coulda been any one of the folks that turned up there that night to complain. I wasn't going to send any of them up, either." He eyed Leland sideways.

"If they did it, they gotta face up. But no matter, I been studying the photographs, and I figure he must have got that whack before he ever went near that tank. What do you think?"

"Well . . . how do you figure that?" asked Bert, real interested.

"Lookit this seat," Leland said. Both of them looked nervously toward the kitchen, where Mrs. Bert was making some lunchmeat sandwiches for them. He held the toilet seat behind his head, like a halo, with the hinged part on top. "Exhibit A."

"Ah huh," said Bert, even more nervous now.

"Lookit this wedding ring. Exhibit B. Now lookit C, this photograph of the back of Zeke's head after he died."

"Took that myself," said Bert. "That's when it dawned on me that Susie whacked him. I thought I threw that picture out."

"You wrote some baseball scores on the back and stuck them on the station refrigerator. Same with the autopsy, but it was bowling scores," Leland said. "Anyhow, if you had talked to Susie, you woulda known Zeke got mad that day and threw her wedding ring down the toilet. After a few drinks, he was sorry; he didn't *say* he was sorry, naturally, but he did decide to fish it out. He was poking around with a snake when the toilet seat fell down and hit him real good on the head, a hell of a whack."

Mrs. Bert came in with a choice of salami or baloney. Bert whooshed her out again.

"Zeke went out to the septic tank, Bio-Waste, whatever. Beautiful machine he had there," said Leland wistfully. "Told Susie if he could get it out with the Wet-Vac, okay, but he sure as hell wasn't paying for somebody to come and pump it out. So he started sucking it out, and the wet-Vac must have fell in."

"And he electrocuted himself?" said Bert.

"Bingo," said Leland.

"Leland, you ain't just a pretty face," Mrs. Bert yelled from the kitchen. Leland blushed.

"I got to be pushin' on," he said. "I got gutters waitin' for me at home."

Toilet seat, my eye, Leland thought as he pulled out of Bert's driveway. He's too smart to fall for that, but he'll grasp at any straw, he's covering for someone.

That night, Leland dreamed his dad came back. "I thought you were dead," Leland said. "No," said Buck. "That was all a mistake." In the dream, Leland was younger, a little kid, and he and his dad were walking along with Randy Anderson between them. Buck was holding Randy's hand and Leland was trying to give him a Klondike ice cream bar. Randy was crying hard. "Don't you cry, son," Buck said to Randy. "You're a real good boy. And smart. We'll take you and your ma to your grandma's. You'll be fine." Leland woke up. The nightstand was damned near putting his eye out again. That was one thing you could say for virtual furniture: your eyes were safe. Anyhow, that dream about Randy; did that happen? Was Buck really wearing a mask?

Chapter 31

Bert and Leland and Randy

"Do you remember," Bert said to Leland DeWitt and Randy Anderson, "the time the fella came to paint the sign at the Hope And Glory train station? He was so worried about runnin' outta space that he bunched the letters all together."

"Don't believe I recall that," Randy said. It was his birthday and Butch Winkle had just sung to him. Funny, it was never as exciting after Randy learned someone had actually *written* the words to "Happy Birthday." It was almost as bad as when he found out there was no Santa Claus, when he was a kid, or nearly.

"Well you were both too young, maybe. Anyhow, another fella came along, and what do you think he said to the painter?"

Leland forked up some coleslaw. "I bet he said, 'You didn't leave enough space between 'Hope' and 'and' and 'and' and 'Glory,'" Bert laughed. "The five 'ands' in a row.

"Well, what's your point?" Randy said. "Train station's not even there, any more."

They were sitting in a corner booth at Winkle's, eating Aromatic Turkey Mole, and a tian of Mediterranean vegetables. Randy was only having the *Poussins en cocotte*.

"You know," Randy said, "I been blocked up ever since Butch started this new cookin'."

"Same here," Leland said. "I woke up with a cramp the other night would gut a horse." He pushed a large cardboard box he'd brought in with him further under the table.

"Butch don't do it right," said Bert. "For one thing, he uses way too much cornstarch. That stuff solidifies, you're finished. Two teaspoons in them *poussins* is plenty. And he goes way overboard on the eggplant. Eggplant is the shoe soles of the vegetable kingdom."

They both looked at Bert. What would they do when he was gone?

Right now they each had a little business to transact with him. Randy was handing over some files from the mayor's office. He had gotten really fond of Bert, and he admired him, but he didn't know how a man of close to eighty was going to take to the rigors of the office. Lord knows it had nearly finished Randy off.

Things were different for Randy now. He was starting afresh, setting up the new business in Philadelphia with

Rocco, his mentor. Rocco had explained things in plain English after that Irish sidekick had disappeared. And not only was Randy going to be in a college classroom, *he* was the one going to he doing the talking. Him, the "Giddyup Guy." His eyes got kinda damp. He was going to give motivational talks but he was also going to say a little about how it was bad to hurt people's feelings. Not nearly enough was said about that.

Leland was handing over the keys to the jail and the snowplow-Roamer to Bert. "It's so big, I left it over at the jail," Leland said. "Needs some gas, little air, maybe. I had to drop Bridget at Idora's and I didn't get a chance."

"Leave it to me," said Randy. "I'll fill it up, get some air and then drop it off at Bert's." Bert and Leland looked at each other. Leland shrugged. "Thanks," he said.

"Welp," Bert said, "Gotta be pushin' off. My basement's flooded." Heads jerked up at all the neighboring tables. Over by the bait tank, a lady put down her BLT and gave a little moan. A flooded basement was the worst, even more than clogged gutters or roots in the drain.

"I got a Wet-Vac," both Randy and Leland said at the same time. They paused a minute. "Hell," said Leland, "why don't we go over and help him clean it up? You know the answer to the old problem, 'If it takes one man a day and a half . . .'"

"Sure, sure," Randy said, hurriedly. "Anyhow, let's try it with three. I'll fill the Roamer and scoot over home and get the Wet-Vac. You two hold on here, and we'll go pick up Leland's on the way to Bert's place." Randy went up to the counter.

"Couple things before we go," Leland said to Bert. "One, I got that Roamer set up so's anybody can drive it when a snowplow's attached. Anybody," he said, glancing over his shoulder at the counter.

"And two?" asked Bert.

Leland hauled the cardboard box up from under the table.

"What you got there?"

"You remember Exhibits A, B and C?" asked Leland.

"Yeah, let's see, the toilet seat, the wedding ring and the autopsy picture of Zeke's head?"

"Yes. Well, this here's Exhibits D, E, and F. You and I both knew all along that A, B and C weren't the answer." Leland pulled out a cracked coffee pot, a length of electric cord, a frozen rat in a plastic bag, and a cast-iron frying pan.

"Uh oh," said Bert, eyeing the frying pan. "Where'd you get that?"

"Found it under the seat of the old snowplow today, before I sent it away for scrap," said Leland. "Knew the minute I saw it this was probably what hit Zeke. Not that it matters, but I wish you'd been straight with me."

"I *told* Randy to throw that out," Bert said, peevishly.

"How come you didn't come clean with me last week? You knew darned well Zeke didn't get that whack from a toilet seat. You told me yourself that you went over his house with a fine-tooth comb. So you must have known he had one of them soft padded toilet seats, not that wood one I showed you."

"Well . . ."

"And a woman couldn't have hit Zeke with this pan. I pretty near put my shoulder out trying to swing it."

"No," Bert said. "Juanetta, maybe, but she wouldn't use a frying pan. Not her weapon of choice."

"So. It wasn't Susie you were protecting."

"That was all *your* idea. Susie would never hit Zeke. She was scared of him, and anyway, beats me, she didn't love him, but she was loyal to him. I tried to help her fifty different times over the years to get away from him, set up in another town, maybe. She wouldn't."

This was all new to Leland.

"Anyhow," said Bert, "it was *my* frying pan. Or Alberta's, I mean, Alberta asked me to take it over to Susie, Susie wanted to make some giant-sized omelets or such at the church breakfast next morning. But when I got there, no one was in the house, so I left it on the back porch."

"And you never saw Zeke at all?"

"Nope. Randy called me later that night, all upset, and told me the whole story, how he'd found Susie crying. You know, Zeke hadn't beat her up for a few years. Randy told him once he'd kill him if he ever did it again, but this time she was crying because Zeke threw her ring down the toilet. Randy didn't know that. He just took Susie over to his house and stormed back to find Zeke. He must have seen the frying pan on the porch and grabbed it."

"And when he found Zeke, he whacked him in the head from behind with it," said Leland. "I can see he might have been upset, sneaking up on his old man with a thing like that."

"Yeah," Bert said, "although he didn't mean to sneak up, he couldn't see anything and somewhere, Zeke was yelling to watch out, he had a broken bottle. But when he gave Zeke a good swipe with it, Zeke started shouting some pretty awful stuff about a frying pan being a woman's weapon and all. That really bothered Randy; he didn't even realize he had it in his hand. A baseball bat, or a fist, even maybe a crowbar, now that'd be different story."

"Sure would," said Leland. He couldn't imagine hitting someone with a frying pan, nearly as bad as a handbag.

"Zeke talked about pantywaists and such. Said he was too dumb to even kill somebody right. That really cut Randy up," sighed Bert. "The fact was he hadn't *intended* to kill him, just scare him enough to stop hitting Susie. And by midnight, when he called me, he'd found out that Zeke hadn't beat Susie after all, not that time, anyhow."

"Well, it don't matter," said Leland. "Randy didn't kill him."

"*Randy* thinks he did," said Bert. "He turned himself in I don't know how many times. One of the reasons I was glad I retired. Anyhow, I didn't think he killed him. I figured the most he did was concuss him. To tell you the truth, the blow didn't look that bad. But I knew Zeke didn't drown, so what did kill him? Alcohol? He had a lot, I got it tested, but not enough to kill him. He coulda had hypothermia, but it wasn't cold enough. So I figured whoever'd hit him would get blamed, if not by law by word of mouth, you know this town, and I didn't think that'd be fair."

Leland looked at him sourly.

"Let me in on it," Bert said. "You got it all figured out, I know you, Leland. First of all, how does the coffee pot figure? You got me interested. You're getting like a real detective," he said, smiling, punching him on the shoulder. He took some of the grape tomatoes out of his salad and starting arranging them in a pattern.

"Forget about the coffee pot," Leland snapped. "Bridget lent it to the jail, I'm bringing' it back home."

Bert looked disappointed. "And the rat don't mean anything, either?"

"Would I be carryin' a frozen rat around if it didn't mean anything?" Leland asked, sharpish.

He pulled out his notes.

√ One rotted jackrabbit

√ One Wet-Vac, submerged

√ One broken whiskey
   bottle

√ A booklet, "A Guide to
   Your Bio-Waste," moldy

√ Footprints all over the
   place

√ All kinds of blunt
   instruments

√ One wedding ring

√ One electric wire, chewed
   through

√ One dead rat

"Okay, I'll tell you. Remember a lotta people showed up that night, and stumbled down in the dark toward Zeke? Most of them complained about the awful smell."

"All of them did, far as I recall," said Bert.

"Yep, but a Bio-Waste don't smell. As long as oxygen is pumped in, the whole thing works like a dream."

"Right!" said Bert, slamming his fist down on one of the tomatoes. He wondered would he get a Bio-Waste himself. Alberta, she'd be over the moon.

"But no oxygen was going in. The pump was off. Supposed to be an alarm that goes off if the electricity supply fails. Zeke was too cheap to install the alarm, told Dwight Wayman to forget it. Anyhow, the way Wayman wired it, it was lucky to be working at all. He didn't put in a separate electricity supply, wired the whole thing up to the outdoor lights. Rats ate them."

"And?" asked Bert.

"When Zeke went to fish out the wedding ring, he saw the tank wasn't working, traipsed back into the house, called the Bio-Waste people and told them to get their asses out there. Then he back went out to wait."

"Yeah?" said Bert, starting in on a new tomato pattern.

"The system had been off for days," Leland said. "Those fumes would have killed a horse. Everybody who turned up there that night went home with a headache, but they expected that, talking to Zeke. Zeke was there for a couple hours, chasing them off, fooling with the Wet-Vac, waiting for the expert to come, having a snort or two every little while."

"So he was asphyxiated by the fumes?" asked Bert.

"*Voila.*"

Bert sat there, all misted over, surrounded by tomatoes. He could hardly talk. "You got a certain kind of mind, Leland, that most people don't have," he said, at last. "My dad had it, too, but it skipped me."

"You know, I don't think I ever met your dad. Never had the pleasure."

"He was long gone before you were born. Now, your dad," said Bert, pausing for a minute. "Your dad, he woulda been real proud of you, I know that. And he had a soft spot for Randy, felt awful sorry for him. He woulda been glad to see things come out right."

Leland picked up a tomato and ate it.

At the counter, Randy glanced back at them while he was paying the bill. Both had round shoulders, like bears. Like him. Real big brains. Oh, well. And he sure would miss these debates in Winkle's with Bert. He was going to keep in touch with him.

Funny about Leland, though, smart as he was, the things he never noticed. He guessed brains wasn't the be-all and end-all. Thank heaven Sylene and Skip finally were *really* just good friends, not "friends." Sylene was supposed to be sweet on some guy she was writing to, according to Leland, and she had somebody else in the wings, too, didn't know who. But whoever, it was a relief, Sylene was just the nicest girl he knew, deserved all the happiness in the world. God knows what kinda kids she and Skip woulda had: you hear about them folks in the hills marrying their cousins and the next thing you know, they got kids that look like E.T. And don't forget your royal houses of Europe. Randy shuddered.

But old Juanetta still wasn't satisfied, all het up as usual, still sticking her nose in Sylene's affairs, never knew when to stop. To tell you the truth, Randy was getting just a little tired of Juanetta.

Right then, Juanetta came hobbling in on Laurinda's arm, still pretty bad from the accident over at Muddy Branch church. They sat down with Bert and Leland. Randy went outside. A plane was skywriting; Randy hadn't seen that in a long time. What was he writing? It said PPY BITHDAY, whatever that meant. Anyway, it was nice to see, on such a clear, beautiful day.

Damn it, wouldn't you know, a tire on the Roamer was flat. It was no joke, changing a tire on that puppy. He got down on all fours to get a better look. Well, one thing, at least no more could happen. Acourse he wasn't going to say that, cause the minute you did . . .

"Give you a hand?" a deep voice asked. Randy looked up to see a bunch of kids: Kimi Lynn Arbogast's twins, Lonnie 'n Jonnie, and their sister, Danielle, who called herself 'Dee Dee' now. Bert's three grandkids. Well, his five grandkids, matterafact, cause Skip and Sylene were there, too.

Lonnie had his arm around Sylene's shoulder, and looked like he had died and gone to heaven. Oh boy. Randy guessed he was the one in the wings, not the one she was corresponding with. Far as he could tell, Lonnie couldn't write. Or read, one or the other. Well, Randy would just have to have a fatherly chat with Sylene, get her off to college and out of town as soon as possible. She was wrecking his nerves.

"Sure," Randy said, and got under the car; Lonnie joined him. "What're we doin', mayor?" he asked, which touched Randy.

"You don't want to change a tire from underneath if you can help it," said another deep voice. "I *know* that," Lonnie snapped, "but now is as good a time as any to rotate the tires, if I was just left to it. And this Roamer needs a trip to HubCap City, give it a bit of pizzazz."

Randy peered up at this latest voice, banging his head off the exhaust. Stars everywhere. In the sky, it said RTHDAY! And now here was a guy with a suitcase and a big fluffy beard. Sure didn't see many of those around Hope And Glory these days, thanks to Laurinda. Dee Dee was squealing and wrapping herself around the new guy, kissing him,

looking into his eyes, jumping up and down. Randy looked
up into his eyes, too. Laurinda's son, out of Everton?

"Mickey?" he asked.

"My ma don't know I'm comin'," Mickey said shyly.
Day Release. I sure hope she'll be surprised. When I was
writin' to Dee Dee, I told her not to say. I got this M.I.B.
movement goin' real good, this Men in Beards thing. Place
looks like a forest up there in Everton. About time my ma
had a chance to be proud of me."

"Mickey and me's thinking of getting engaged," said
Dee Dee shyly. "We could have a double wedding with
you and Sylene, Lonnie. What do you think, Mickey?"

"Whatever you say, sweetie. You're the boss," said Mickey.

"You ain't marrying any sister of mine," Lonnie yelled
up at Mickey.

"You little snot," said Dee Dee. "Do you see me trying
to stop you marrying Sylene?"

"That's different," said Lonnie. "I ain't a convicted
murderer. Just a couple bad checks."

"Well, la-di-da," said Dee Dee. "Don't *we* think we're
something special!"

"*And,*" Lonnie said, "soon's Sylene forgets this college
idea of hers, we're getting hitched. I'm getting' a lease on
that old converted gas station over in Two Corners, and
Sylene could fix it up real nice, a few curtains and stuff.
Real homey."

"But . . ." Sylene said, pointing up in the air. OVE
U SYLENE, it said. Randy was moaning. She squatted
down to see him better.

Something in Randy had just snapped. He didn't mean it to, but Sylene setting up housekeeping in an old gas station was the last straw. He wanted to give her such a shaking; he reached out and managed to grab her shoulder. Later, when he was explaining it to the *New York Times* reporter, he told him something had just snapped. Maybe his brains were damaged when he hit his head on the exhaust.

"You are not marryin' Lonnie," he shouted.

"How come?" Dee Dee asked, poking her tongue through her bubble gum.

"*Or* Jonnie *or* Skip *or* . . ." He looked up around him.

"Hmph!" Lonnie said. "S'pose now you're going to say all three of us is gay . . ."

"Not *all* three," said Dee Dee.

"Shush!" hissed Sylene. "Not in front of his father!" She let Randy shake her a little; otherwise he was going to put his shoulder out, his angle was all wrong under there.

". . . as a coot," Lonnie was muttering under the Roamer. "Came out in sixth grade."

Skip stood on Lonnie's hand.

"Always hidin' behind Sylene," Lonnie muttered, holding some bolts in his teeth.

The skywriter was doing a fresh message: ITS DOUBLE LETTERS, it said.

"What's that supposed to mean?" Mickey asked.

"It's a stupid puzzle in *The Vindicator*," Lonnie said, peeking out. "This guy, he only likes things that have double letters in the words. Beer, grass, football—football's a good one, two sets of double letters. I got it in five minutes."

Randy stared at Lonnie, who was watching a mean-looking mob advancing on them. No, that bang on his head was blurring his sight a little; it was just Laurinda and them, strolling out of Winkle's, waving at Randy. What a swell woman Laurinda was. She had Juanetta leaning on her arm. Bert was trotting after them with Juanetta's ring for sitting on, and Leland was carrying Juanetta's groceries and her umbrella, no, wait, her rifle. It was her day for the Rifle Tots. Lonnie had a tire iron in his free hand and was glaring at Mickey from under the bumper. He was yelling something at the plane, now, too, which was starting another I LOVE U again.

What the hell was this? Leland could see a crowd over there, Randy and some kids. He couldn't make very good time, lumbered down with Juanetta's rifle and her groceries, but it looked like Sylene was one of them, and Randy was what, under the Roamer, grabbing her shoulder and yelling at her? Skip was pulling her away. I get it, thought Leland. Randy thinks she's going out with Skip again, doesn't know she's been writing to Laurinda's Don, up in crop dusting school, not that it means anything, Sylene's in love with physics. But Randy, he still thinks she's not good enough for Skip. How could that Bert have wasted so much effort "covering" for a fool like Randy? I'll kill him, just let me get my hands on him, shaking my girl silly like that.

And lookit up there in the sky! Over and over, I LOVE U SYLENE.

So do I, Leland said to himself, and she's going to college. Indubitably.

Laurinda was well intentioned and dedicated, Juanetta thought, as she limped along. Trouble was, a lot of your well-intentioned and dedicated people had absolutely no sense of humor. Like, if you told someone you were speaking French or Japanese or whatever, when all the time you were just speaking English kinda funny, most people would have enough sense to take it as a joke. Not Laurinda. So earnest. She could get Laurinda going from nothing to sixty in three seconds flat by pretending to speak Navajo. Funny, Juanetta thought she herself had a good sense of humor. So did Bert, matterafact. Genetics, phooey. Phoooeau.

Boy, Juanetta wished Leland wouldn't carry her rifle that way. Liable to shoot someone accidental, just like Mickey did. Sooner they brought back the draft and taught men how to bear arms, the better for everybody. Speaking of Mickey, surely that couldn't be him over there, looking kinda distinguished? It was! It was! She'd know those roundy bear shoulders anywhere, same as Bert's, Leland's, Randy's. Laurinda's, too. Well, glory be. And what was that he had on him, a monkey? No, wait, now she had her glasses on, she could see it was that silly Dee Dee Arbogast. She was hanging on him like—oh, *no.* Impossible! Her nerves was already shot steering Sylene away from Skip and now Lonnie and Don. Pretty soon she'd need to keep a family tree on her.

Well, wouldn't you know, Leland had shot Mrs. Herman "Bob's" cat, accidental, but nonetheless. Okay, that was it, she'd had enough. She was an old woman, she deserved some peace at her time of life. Wait 'til I get that rifle.

Huh! Laurinda thought. It just shows you can't be any too vigilant. Over there by Randy was a guy in a big beard, a real patriarch type, some little slip of a thing under his arm. He looked real boorish. She wondered was it a good idea to entrust B.I.B. to Juanetta while she was gone. Was she up to it? Well, she'd watch to see how she handled this creep who was standing there with Randy. It might give her something to do; at the moment, she was driving Laurinda crazy. She had taken up Spanish. The thing with Spanish, according to Juanetta, was you just didn't say "x" or "v" or "j." So, "pahamas," and "three, four, figh." It was *so* irritating. She took a deep breath. If you wanted to Make a Difference, you had to let little things wash over you.

But another thing. She might as well come out with it right now; no time like the present. She'd failed her physical anthropology exam last week because she wrote that two blue-eyed parents couldn't produce a brown-eyed child. Only under very unusual circumstances, but she'd forgotten to write that. She was brown-eyed, and her dad, Harlan, and Juanetta were blue. Were their circumstances unusual, or what?

"Ma," she said, "I been meaning to ask you a couple things."

Bert had made a decision. Here was Randy, leaving town, just when he was beginning to know him. He'd hated running against him for mayor, but he could see that otherwise Randy was going to end up in jail/bankrupt/

rubbed out/mental, you name it. Still, he was going to miss him, and he decided he would have a little talk with Mrs. Bert, she wasn't as standoffish as he'd always thought, and if she didn't throw him out they would work together to get to know his grandkids, all of them. They were his legacy. God knows, Kimi Lynn's three were nice kids, but they were kinda slowish. He was missing out on the others, and anyhow, their official grandpas were all dead now, God rest them, well maybe not Zeke, he'd told Bert early on he'd beat Randy black and blue if Bert ever came near him. Now maybe he could at least teach them what he had learned. He always wanted to be a teacher, pass something on.

Once the kids all got used to him, they'd be real glad he was taking an interest. Grandpa Whump. Skip and Sylene knew each other, sure, but the rest, why after they got acquainted, they might even become friends, same age and all. He was really proud of Don, so good at the skywriting, even though it wasn't his profession, only a hobby. What was he writing there now, something about Sylene? But hold on . . .

Well, even though it wasn't a mob coming toward them, Randy saw that some of them were looking pretty agitated, and over here the five kids and Mickey were all in an uproar. Everybody fighting, cursing, hitting each other with rubber rings, tire irons, suitcases, rifle butts. And lookit that cat.

Okay, Randy reminded himself, he was "The Giddyup Guy." Look on the bright side. All his life, he wanted a big family. He probably wasn't going to get it from Skip. He'd heard Sylene; that explained a couple things. Well, it seemed to be good enough for the Lone Ranger. Maybe he'd got his wish anyhow: there they all were, his dad, his son, his step-brother, his nieces, his nephews, his mother-in-law. His lovely wife and her kids. He hoped there weren't any more surprises. Seeing Laurinda's shoulders from this angle, kinda rounded . . . Just be grateful. It's a family.

Laurinda was screaming something at Juanetta and Bert, he really couldn't hear it over the racket, the plane, the shots. She was whacking Bert and pointing at her stomach and over at Randy. Well, whatever it was, thought Randy, it couldn't be much. She'd tell him later.

Maybe the best thing to do would be to get back under the Roamer for a while. Might as well start rotating as long as he was down there. He hummed the Lone Ranger song.

THE HOPE AND GLORY VINDICATOR

Volume 234 Issue 49   Hope And Glory, Ohio

Terrible fracas outside Winkle's Party-Pak

In a startling development, Earl Arbogast, Chief of Police in North Vienna, was called on late yesterday afternoon to quell a disturbance near Winkle's Party Pak in which shots were fired and epithets hurled. A man sustained some damage to his beard from an attack with a dog clipper, but he said forget it, it was nothing.

Former Police Chief Leland DeWitt, who was involved in the fray, said the situation was reprehensible and dastardly. He didn't want to say anymore, but its tentacles were labyrinthine, and even Chief Arbogast's family was involved. Warming to his theme, he said that he wanted to personally thank former Mayor Randy Anderson for the concern and vigilance he had shown over the years to the tender young folks caught up in the debacle. Former Mayor Randy Anderson, in a prepared speech, said it was his pleasure. The whole thing was a good instance of why Hope And Glory needed its own police force again, people from North Vienna had no understanding of the cultural milieu of Hope And Glory. He also called upon folks to let bygones be bygones and to look on the bright side.

The former Mayor invited former Chief DeWitt to lead the parade to the Tomb of the Honorary Veteran next Sunday, where Zeke Anderson will finally be put to rest in piece.

Mayor Bert Whump, speaking from his hospital bed, said he truly regretted every (con't on page 6)

Baby shower held

Mr. And Mrs. Randy Anderson are packing up these days, getting all set to move to Philadelphia, where Mrs. Anderson will be studying anthrocites. Mrs. Anderson was surprised last week by her friends and family, who gave her a nice baby shower. The little stranger is expected in about four months, and Mr. and Mrs. Anderson are already planning the décor of their nursery in Philly.

After the stork visits, Mrs. Anderson will pursue her studies of the bug kingdom and Mr. Anderson will combine baby care with his new career as a motivational speaker. He said the news had hit him like a brick in the head, and he would be tickled pink, whatever it was.

Engagement announced

Earl and Kimi Lynn Arbogast are pleased to announce the engagement of their daughter, Dee Dee, to Abdullahi Osman Al-Rashidi, son of Mr. And Mrs. Al-Rashidi of Jeddah, Saudi Arabia.

Mr. Al-Rashidi, a student at Jim Bob Community College, said it was love at first sight. Ms. Arbogast said it was kind of a process of elimination. The couple is hoping to live over in Two Corners, close to the college, where Mr. Al is studying genealogy.

INSIDE THIS ISSUE

2 Kute krafts from roofing felt

3 Hate fish gutting! Try the fun way!

4 Canada re-surfaces

5 Whither the brown booby?

Judge Dick Quinn, in a heated statement, said he was sending Rev. Wayman to the Correctional Trade School in West Geneva to learn electricity once and for all. However, he was not accepting Rev. Wayman's plea of murdering Zeke Anderson, since Mr. Anderson had been gassed, not electrocuted, although no thanks to Rev. Wayman.

Judge Quinn told Mr. Buckley that it had been a pleasure to meet him, and that he looked fatter on TV.

ALL-PURPOSE POLICE VEHICLE. (RED). CALL B. WHUMP

FURNITURE CLEARANCE, DE WITT, 362-1358.

FAMILY RECONCILIATION THERAPY. REV. DWIGHT WAYMAN, 365-6666. ALSO, ELECTRICAL TOOLS GOING CHEAP.

LEASE ON TWO CORNERS GAS STATION FOR SALE. MAKE A COMFY LITTLE HOME. CALL LONNIE, 965-1886.

SO WHAT'S THE STORY WITH TONTO, THE NEW SMASH HIT BOOK BY RANDY ANDERSON, NOW OUT AT $6.95!

BIG FAMILY REUNION. ALL WELCOME NEXT SUNDAY. TICKETS WHILE THEY LAST. CALL MRS. BERT WHUMP, 822-7273

Correction: Local Woman to Study Savages in Philadelphia
Mrs. Randy Anderson, the B.I.B. pioneer, is packing for Philadelphia, where she will be continuing the *anthropology* classes she started here at Jim Bob Bagby Community College. Mr. Randy Anderson will be going along, too.

New Mayor to Campaign for Release of Local Man
The plight of Mickey McCardle was just pitiful, Mayor Whump said. One of his first orders of business would be to speak to the Governor. Everybody knew it was an accident—Mickey was just cleaning his gun when he shot Mr. Sheehan, a bridegroom. When he was in the army, Mayor Whump himself got shot in the foot by a fool during a training program—it happened every day. Truth was, it wasn't even Mickey's gun, it was his grandma Juanetta Wilcox's assault rifle. Mickey didn't know the bottom of a gun from the top, and the wonder was that he didn't blow his own head off, which would have been a shame, Mickey was such a nice fellow. The Mayor and his Missus are going down to Everton to visit with the warden soon.

Brainy Local Teens!
Skip Anderson, son of former mayor Randy Anderson, and Sylene DeWitt, daughter of Leland and Bridget DeWitt, each won college scholarships. Skip will be going to New Jersey State College to do a double major in waste management and interior design, and Sylene will be going to the Massachusetts Institute of Technology, to study physics. Dare we say that the Vindy's **Algebra Antics!** and **Brain Teasers** might have helped a teeny bit? Good luck, kids!

And speaking of **Algebra Antics!** and **Brain Teasers**, here's what you've all been waiting for—the answers to some of those pesky riddles that have been driving folks crazy!

11

342

Yes, because of course oil is thicker than water

Six men and/or a horse

The sunny side of the street

It all depends on what you mean by a "quart"

James Fennimore Cooper

Four linear feet, or five cubic

Congratulations to our winners, and to Ryan DeWitt, who answered all questions correctly!!!

Chief Grey Wolf heads new tribe

Chief Alfred Grey Wolf, living in Hope And Glory as part of a Witness Protection Program for ex-Mafioso and others in need of shelter, has been permitted to form an "Associated" Native American tribe.

"An 'associated' tribe, is not, as some say, a ragtag group of odds and ends of misfits but a collection of patriots who recognize the contribution Native Americans have made to this country," Chief Grey Wolf said.

Wolfhound for sale. Mrs. McCardle-Anderson 330-9344

Driveway blacktopping. Septus McCardle, 330-5785

"At last, we will be able to establish a badly-needed casino in Hope And Glory. Maybe it will save our lovely town."

It is not clear if any of the new tribe are Native Americans.

Other current news on page 3

HOW OUR OPENING DIAGRAM
SHOULD HAVE LOOKED

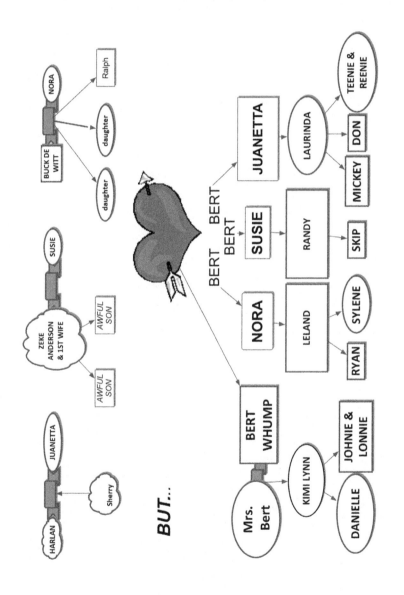

Acknowledgments

Thanks to my husband, Paud Murphy, who has been reading the manuscript for what seems to him like years. He's not in the book; Dr. Lelia Doolan and Patrice Price are, and they offered helpful comments, as did Liadain O'Donovan.

At 1106, many thanks to a team of superb professionals for their patience and the great work they did in designing and preparing the manuscript.

For the Hope and Glory website, which will appear in 2022, I am indebted to designer Noreen Scully, and for some of the character's voices, John West and Patrice Price. Elke Wagner-Murphy and Fionn Murphy helped with photo technicalities.

About the Author

*E*ileen Kane *is the author of eight academic books and computer tools, many of them in the area of applied anthropology. She has also been a consultant to most of the major international development agencies, and focuses on getting more girls into primary and secondary schools in developing countries, particularly in Africa. She says:*

"I grew up in the area of northeastern Ohio that's the inspiration for the fictional little town of Hope And Glory. After reading the book my sister said, 'I saw my whole life flash in front of me.' What a tribute! The fire station wedding, the dog pound stories, the Schnauzer trims, the horse problem and others are hers. Randy's 'Rodney Romdey's Weird Roamer' belonged to a brother. Leland was modelled on my father, and 'Chicken Shit' was a

beloved uncle. I appear, myself, from time to time:
I always have a bed rope. In other words, the book
wrote itself. My mother doesn't figure much because
she was a major character in my book *Trickster: An
Anthropological Memoir*, about the Paiute Indians
of Nevada, despite not being a Paiute.

"Roughly a quarter of the characters are fictional, such as Mickey and Susie; as are many
situations: for example, the French-speaking jail,
the B.I.B. Campaign and the hologram furniture. I
do hope these ideas will be adopted in a nice town,
somewhere.

"Over the generations, I, and many members
of my family, worked for the late, badly missed
Youngstown Vindicator, which closed in 2019 after
150 years. It shared little with *The Hope And Glory
Vindicator* except a fondness for the word "yeggs"
and the mysterious headline, 'Man Found Dead of
Bullets in Cell.'

"I live and work in Ireland, but not in an attempt
to escape my relatives."

Made in the USA
Las Vegas, NV
08 July 2021

26120842R00204